Sky Song

Also by Abi Elphinstone

The Dreamsnatcher
The Shadow Keeper
The Night Spinner

Sky Song

ABI ELPHINSTONE

SIMON & SCHUSTER

First published in Great Britain in 2018 by Simon and Schuster UK Ltd
A CBS COMPANY

Copyright © 2018 Abi Elphinstone

7 9 10 8 6

Simon & Schuster UK Ltd
1st Floor,
222 Gray's Inn Road
London WC1X 8HB

www.simonandschuster.co.uk

Simon & Schuster Australia, Sydney
Simon & Schuster India, New Delhi

A CIP catalogue record for this book
is available from the British Library.

PB ISBN 978-1-4711-4607-7
eBook ISBN 978-1-4711-4608-4

Typeset in Goudy by M Rules
Printed and bound by CPI Group (UK) Ltd, Croydon, CR0 4YY

MIX
Paper from
responsible sources
FSC® C020471

Simon & Schuster UK Ltd are committed to sourcing paper
that is made from wood grown in sustainable forests and support the Forest
Stewardship Council, the leading international forest certification organisation.
Our books displaying the FSC logo are printed on FSC certified paper.

For Logie,
who knew from the very beginning
that he was part of our tribe

Prologue

Beyond the footsteps of the greatest explorers and up past the reach of the trustiest maps there lies a kingdom called Erkenwald.

Here, the sun still shines at midnight in the summer, glinting off the icebergs in the north and slipping between the snow-capped Never Cliffs in the west. But it does not rise at all in the long, cold winters. Then, the nights bleed on and on and the darkness is so thick you cannot see your hands in front of your face.

This far north, even the stars do not behave as you might expect. And that is probably just as well because without Ursa Minor breaking a few rules we would not have a story at all . . .

The Little Bear, some call this constellation, but if astronomers knew the truth – if they could see into the heart of things and out the other side – perhaps they would have used a different name. For these seven stars are in fact Sky Gods, mighty giants carved from stardust, and the brightest of them all, the North Star, was the one who first breathed life into Erkenwald.

Such was his power that he only needed to blow the legendary Frost Horn once and the empty stretches of ice many miles below began to change. Mountains, forests and glaciers appeared. Then animals arrived: polar bears to roam the tundra, whales to glide through the oceans and wolves to stalk between the trees. Finally, the music of the Frost Horn conjured people: men and women of different shapes, sizes and colours scattered throughout the land.

As the years passed, these men and women formed three tribes: the Fur Tribe built tipis from caribou hides in a forest to the south of the kingdom; the Feather Tribe settled inside caves in the Never Cliffs to the west; and the Tusk Tribe built igloos along the cliff tops on the northern coast. Each tribe had their own customs and beliefs, but they lived in harmony with one another, sharing food whenever they passed and offering shelter when the weather closed in.

Because magic often lingers long after it has been used, the power of the Frost Horn hovered over Erkenwald, and as time went by the people learnt how to use it. They spun hammocks from moonlight which granted wonderful dreams; they trapped sunbeams in lanterns which burned through the winter months; they stored wind inside gemstones which granted their boats safe passage through stormy seas. And the people knew all was well in their kingdom whenever they saw the northern lights. For these rippling colours were a sign that the Sky Gods were dancing – and that meant the world was as it should be.

But darkness can come to any kingdom, and so it came to Erkenwald.

The smallest Sky God grew jealous of the North Star's power and, seeking to rule Erkenwald herself, she pulled away from the constellation one winter night and plunged towards Earth. The North Star acted swiftly and trapped her in a glacier before she could spread her evil across the land. But the Sky Gods stopped dancing then because they knew that it was only a matter of time before someone heard the whispers of the fallen star calling out behind the ice.

And, before long, someone did.

One night, Slither, the shaman for the Tusk Tribe, was drawn to the glacier and he listened as the voice within promised him dark powers if he killed his chief and made it look like a plot brewed by the Fur and Feather Tribes using Erkenwald's trusted magic.

Although the words were only whispers, they plucked at Slither's heart and, believing all they said, the shaman slew the Tusk Chief while he slept with an enchanted knife. In the weeks that followed, distrust between the tribes gave way to hatred and faith in Erkenwald's magic died. And it was then that Slither climbed back into his skin-boat and paddled beneath the cliffs towards the glacier.

The voice was still there, only it was louder now – as if the hatred between the tribes had given it fresh force – and this time Slither could make out the body of a woman behind the ice. She was tall and slim, with skin as white as marble and lips a cold pale blue. Her eyelashes were crusted with frost, her silver hair twisted through a crown of snowflakes and in her hand she held a staff of glittering black ice. Slither raised a palm towards the Ice Queen and, because this was a palm that had done a terrible thing, it melted the frozen wall before him and the woman stepped out from the glacier and into the skin-boat.

She held up her staff and thunder rumbled across the sky as every man, woman and child in the Tusk Tribe, now locked under the Ice Queen's hold, stepped out of their igloos. They watched in silence as she pointed her staff towards the glacier she had been trapped inside. An enormous chunk of ice broke free from its tip and slid into the sea, but it did not drift away. The Ice Queen waved her staff and a bridge snaked out between the cliff and the iceberg, tethering it in place. Then domes, turrets and towers formed, shooting out of the iceberg with ear-splitting cracks until, finally, there stood a shimmering fortress carved entirely from ice.

Winterfang Palace was born; the reign of the Ice Queen had began. And to reward his loyalty, the Ice Queen gave Slither command of the Tusk Tribe and taught him how to wield the very darkest magic.

Spring came, then slipped into summer and, from afar, the Fur and Feather Tribes watched as the Tusks left their igloos every morning and walked across the bridge into Winterfang Palace. A battle was brewing – the Fur and Feather Tribes could hear the sharpening of spears and hammering of shields – and, fearing that the Ice Queen meant to drag all the tribes under her command, they launched an attack on Winterfang.

But to fight for something you believe in requires trust as well as courage – and there was not enough trust between the Fur and Feather Tribes that day. There was no faith in Erkenwald's magic either and the weapons of even the most skilled fighters were nothing against Slither's Tusk warriors. They fought with black ice javelins and shadow-shields and soon every man and woman from the Fur and Feather Tribes was imprisoned in the palace towers. Slither's warriors seized a child, too – the only one who had been granted a place in the battle – because this was a child marked out by the Sky Gods, a child that the Ice Queen had been looking for ever since she fell from the sky.

The other children remained beyond the Ice Queen's grasp and, though Slither's warriors scoured the kingdom all through the summer and on into the winter, they found no trace of them. Erkenwald became a land shrunk to whispers, but, because a fallen star can only survive one midnight sun on Earth before its magic fades, the Ice Queen set about finding a way to gain immortality.

Voices, she discovered, were the key, and if she could swallow the voice of every man, woman and child in Erkenwald before the next midnight sun rose she would possess the eternal life she craved. By midwinter, a new sound rang out from Winterfang: an anthem played on an organ made of icicles, accompanied by a choir of voices that once belonged to the Ice Queen's prisoners.

The anthem called some children out of hiding, so desperate were they to be reunited with their parents whose voices they could hear above the music, but most knew better than that. They realised that the stolen voices were a trap and they vowed to lie low until they could form a plan to defeat the Ice Queen and rescue their parents.

But some people are not very good at lying low. They have wandering limbs and fierce hearts and more often than not they have heads full of wild ideas. Our story follows two such children – an unlikely pair, some would say, but you cannot pick and choose who adventures happen to. They pounce when you are least expecting them, then they hurtle forward with surprising speed. In fact, once an adventure digs its claws in, there is not an awful lot you can do about it.

Especially when magic is involved . . .

Chapter One
Eska

E ska sat, knees tucked under her chin and head bowed, on the pedestal inside the music box. Its glass dome curved around her, fixed tight to the silver base, and with her flimsy dress and bare feet she might easily have passed for a mechanical ballerina. But Eska was no clockwork figure. She was a twelve-year-old girl with darting eyes and a pulse that trembled every time the Ice Queen drew near.

Eska closed her eyes and tried to wiggle her toes. They didn't move. She made to arch her back and then stretch her neck. Again, nothing moved. Even her hair – a tumble of red so full of knots it seemed to grow in circles – lay absolutely still down her back. But it was a ritual she attempted every morning in case, by some miracle, the Ice Queen's hold over her limbs had weakened. It never did though. Not for a second. The music box had been Eska's prison for months and she could only blink wide blue eyes at the horrors that unfolded in Winterfang's vaulted hall.

She looked beyond the dome, through the ice arches

in front of her which faced out over Erkenwald. The first sunrise in six months spilled across the horizon. Frozen rivers shimmered, the snow on the tundra sparkled and the sea was a dazzling jigsaw of ice and meltwater. It was mid-March then, Eska thought. That was when the light returned to the kingdom – she'd heard the Tusk guards talking.

Her chest tightened as she thought back to the day she'd awoken in the music box, her body locked under the Ice Queen's spell. The midnight sun had been burning and she had watched it for two whole months before the dark stole in. Eska swallowed. With the light returning now, she knew she had to have been the Ice Queen's prisoner for nine months, but even more frightening was the knowledge that she didn't have a single memory of her life before Winterfang. There must have been something else once – a home, a family, friends perhaps – since the spell the Ice Queen uttered every morning spoke of her as *the stolen child*. But stolen from where? From whom? It was all a terrible blank. Because the Ice Queen didn't only steal people and voices: she stole memories, too, if it suited her.

At the sound of footsteps, Eska snapped out of her thoughts, and from the corner of her eye she watched a familiar scene unravel. The Ice Queen sat, very still, before an organ made of icicles in the middle of the hall, then she raised her hands to the keys. Eska waited. She knew what came next because it was the same every morning.

Chords drifted through the palace – up and down the

snow-strewn staircases, into the towers surrounding the palace domes, across the bridge connecting the iceberg to the mainland and then out over the miles of frozen tundra beyond. The chords were solemn, like the groaning of a faraway glacier, and as they swelled and throbbed Eska winced. The Ice Queen was getting ready to feed on her stolen voices.

A melody rippled out from the silver trees lining the hall. Their roots sprawled over the ice floor and from their bony branches hundreds of glass baubles hung, each one filled with a golden glow. *This* was where the melody was coming from because inside each bauble was a voice. And as the chords grew louder the baubles shimmered and the voices of the Fur and Feather men and women singing a wordless anthem joined with the organ's steady pulse.

Eska watched as the golden glow from one of the baubles drifted towards the Ice Queen's mouth and slipped down her cold white throat. The organ grew louder as the Ice Queen swallowed, then she threw back her head and laughed.

'Another voice closer to immortality!'

She raked her nails across the keys. The chords clashed, the voices stopped and the baubles dimmed. Then the Ice Queen snatched up her staff and strode towards the arches, her sequinned gown swishing behind her.

Eska's insides churned as the woman knelt before the music box and slipped a key into the base. Then she uttered her spell and her voice came hard and pointed, as if full of unpleasant corners:

9

'Three turns to the left then half a turn right
With a key cut black as the deepest night.
The magic awakes, then limbs unfold
As the stolen child comes under my hold.'

The Ice Queen turned the key and, as it wound three turns to the left then half a turn right, music began. It was different from the melody that came from the trees; this was a gentle, almost magical tinkling, like tiny bells chiming or dozens of stars falling to Earth.

And, at the sound, Eska felt her body stir. First her head lifted, then her hands pushed down and her legs extended until she was standing on the pedestal. She tried to hold the curse at bay, to take control of her body, but she was up on the balls of her feet now and her arms were outstretched. The Ice Queen breathed a crystal mist over the glass dome, making it disappear from sight, and, as the pedestal turned, round and round, Eska danced on trembling feet.

Unscrewing the orb from the top of her staff, the Ice Queen held it before Eska. 'Your voice is cursed by the Sky Gods, child. But I can relieve you of it.' She moved the orb nearer Eska's mouth. 'Speak now – let your words slip into my orb – and you will no longer have to bear such a burden.'

Eska's frail arms rose and fell and her body stooped and arched, but she said nothing. Minutes passed, the only sound in the room the fluttering of Eska's dress as she turned, then the music ground to a halt, the pedestal stilled and Eska stopped mid-pirouette before folding herself up into a ball again.

The Ice Queen twisted the orb back on to her staff, then she seized Eska's wrist. 'I am not asking to hear your voice because I value your opinion. I am not asking to hear your voice because I care about your feelings. I am asking to hear your voice *because I own you.*' Her eyes darkened. 'You bear the mark of the Sky Gods, Eska, the very Gods who used terrible magic to stir up hatred between the people of Erkenwald. But I will use your voice to tear the Sky Gods down and rid this kingdom of their evil for ever.'

Eska's mind whirled. The Ice Queen often spoke like this – about cursed marks and dreadful Gods – but, even though Eska could recall nothing from her past about either, some deep-rooted things couldn't be erased, like knowing right from wrong and sensing truth from lies. Something about the Ice Queen's words smelled of lies, as if she was spinning a story that just happened to suit her, and for this reason Eska kept her voice a secret inside her.

The Ice Queen loosened her grip. 'You will remain locked inside this music box until I hear you speak.' She paused. 'And you will go without the dome tonight; perhaps a little cold is exactly what is needed to shock you into behaving.'

Eska stayed silent, huddled on her pedestal, then there was a cough from somewhere nearby and the Ice Queen spun round.

A bald man dressed in sealskins and a walrus-tusk necklace

stood before them. He was small and fat, with an oily smile, and as he dipped his head Eska glimpsed the edge of the tattoo of a large black eye stamped on to the back of his skull.

'Forgive my intrusion, Your Majesty.'

The Ice Queen nodded. 'Come, Slither. It seems I am still not getting through to the girl. My magic holds her body under its spell, but it cannot draw out her voice. She is mute – and perhaps she has always been that way – but somewhere inside her there must be a voice, even if she has never used it.'

'I have some news that may interest you.' Slither smirked. 'The contraption I have been working on these last few months is almost finished.'

The Ice Queen paced back and forth beside the music box, a smile forming on her blue lips. 'You're quite sure it will work?'

Slither ran a hand over his bald head. 'I am the most powerful shaman in Erkenwald. It will work.'

'We cannot delay any longer. I must have Eska's voice in the next few days.'

'There are still adjustments to make. I need at least a week before—'

The Ice Queen tilted her head and the sunlight flashed off her crown of snowflakes. 'Work through the night, Slither. Get it done. To achieve immortality, I must steal every single voice in the kingdom before the midnight sun rises in two weeks' time.' She paused. 'Even your fiercest warriors have not been able to find the Fur and Feather children, but if I have Eska's voice I can use it to summon the tribes to Winterfang.

Then I will tear the Sky Gods down from the heavens and all will surrender to me.'

Slither bowed and then scurried from the hall. The Ice Queen followed slowly, but, when she reached the shadows, she glanced over her shoulder at Eska.

'I *will* take your voice,' she snarled. 'I get everything I want. In the end.'

Eska stayed with her head bent over her knees until the last of the Ice Queen's footsteps faded away. Then her eyes flicked open and fixed on the key. Distracted by Slither, the Ice Queen had left it in the lock. Eska remembered how the woman had turned it the wrong way by mistake one day and it had undone the spell over her body for a moment. If only she could reach it now . . .

But Eska's limbs were frozen; there was no chance of escaping and she could only gaze through the arches at the world beyond, wondering who she really was. A child cursed by the Sky Gods? Or somebody else entirely?

A cold wind swept through the hall and Eska blinked at the chill. The Ice Queen held her body in a music box and her memories in a locked chest somewhere deep within the palace – it was almost enough to make Eska give up hope of ever finding a way back into her past – almost but not quite.

Because Eska knew something the Ice Queen did not. She *could* speak.

She just didn't want to.

Chapter Two
Flint

Flint raced across the Driftlands on a sled pulled by huskies. The dogs strained against their harnesses as they bounded forward, but they did not yap or bark. They ran silently, as if they could sense the boy's fear, and only the runners skimming the tundra could be heard.

Standing upright at the back of the sled, his boots astride on the caribou antlers and his scruff of brown hair flapping about his face, Flint used the moonlight to guide him. Round hillocks of ice, down dips in the snowfall, on and on towards Winterfang Palace. It was a cold night and Flint's breath froze in little crystals on the lynx-fur trim of his parka. But, despite the chill, he didn't have his hood pulled up because that would have meant dislodging the fox pup snuggled inside.

'Look, Pebble,' Flint whispered. 'It's Winterfang. There's no turning back now ...'

There was a shuffle of white fur from inside Flint's hood, then two black eyes emerged. Pebble blinked. They were rushing along the coast now and to their right the snowy cliffs plunged down to the sea. In a few weeks, they'd see beluga whales gliding between icebergs and walruses resting on the shores, but for now the sea was still mostly frozen and, further up the coast, a jumble of domes and towers burst out of the Ice Queen's enchanted iceberg.

Pebble nibbled at Flint's bear-claw earring. The fox pup was used to the trespassing, mishaps and tellings-off that came with belonging to Flint, but he was always well fed throughout each ordeal which meant the ongoing peril was usually worth the trouble.

Flint tapped Pebble's nose. 'Now is *not* the time to be asking for extra food. We've got a handful of Tusk guards to get past, a palace to break into and my ma to free.' He paused. Put like that, the evening sounded rather intense, but then he thought about the items stashed inside his rucksack and the months he'd spent planning in his tree house and he felt his courage return. 'Besides,' he continued, 'I fed you back at Deeproots and you had seconds of lemmings, if I remember correctly.'

Pebble grunted, then turned round and stuck out his bushy tail until it was smothering Flint's face. Flint pushed it away and reluctantly Pebble got the message and manoeuvred his bottom back inside the hood. They sped on.

'The guards will be celebrating long into the night – just like they did last year when the first sun rose after winter.' Flint paused as the sled bumped over a shelf of ice. 'If ever there was a moment to sneak into the palace, it's tonight, when they're distracted.'

But, despite the nights Flint had spent spying on the

palace and preparing for the break-in, there was a tremble in his voice and his eyes flitted with nerves – because Flint knew the stories of the Ice Queen as well as anyone else. She could kill a person just by holding up her staff, or so people said, and no one hiding in Deeproots Forest or the Never Cliffs could miss the sounds that drifted out from Winterfang every morning: the Ice Queen's organ first, then the haunting chorus of voices – the mothers, fathers, uncles, aunts and grandparents of the hidden children – locked inside the palace. They could drive you mad, those voices, and now anyone who heard them raised their hands to cover their ears.

The sled raced on and the palace drew nearer. Flint swallowed as he took in the jungle of gigantic icicles surrounding the base of each of the five towers rumoured to hold the Ice Queen's prisoners. They cast a web of sprawling shadows over the moonlit tundra and for a moment Flint's mittens slackened their grip on the sled. He thought about his ma, trapped inside, and focused on the main palace wall. He'd climb in that way, then sneak through the passageways to the towers from there.

Flint reached back and tickled Pebble's chin as the dogs approached a bank of snow that blocked the palace from sight. 'Tomkin might have shouted down my talk of a rescue mission because he doesn't think I'm ready to be a proper warrior or that my inventions are up to the job. But, when I return to Deeproots with Ma, my brother will soon see what I'm capable of.'

Flint wasn't proud of the fact that he'd lied to his brother. He'd promised Tomkin he'd destroyed all of his inventions back in his tree house because as Tomkin always said: 'A Fur Tribe warrior fights with spears and fists, not with magic and far-fetched contraptions' – but the truth was, Flint couldn't shut his thoughts away. Ever since he was a little boy, he'd been inventing things and now, no matter how hard he tried to stop his ideas, they kept happening, kept growing, kept changing into extraordinary possibilities. Because, unlike his brother and everyone else in his tribe, Flint still trusted Erkenwald's magic. This was partly because of the piece of bark he'd found in the forest over the summer which bore carvings that talked of how to harness magic and use it for good. But also because his mind was attuned to the things most people missed – river stones that shone in the dark, sunbeams tucked behind trees, coils of mist hovering above puddles.

Flint was sure that, if handled correctly, Erkenwald's magic could be stronger than a warrior's spear.

He steered his sled into a hollow in the bank that spread out into a hidden passageway winding down to the sea. The dogs raced into the darkness until eventually the ground levelled out into an ice cavern and moonlight sparkled against the icicles fringing the way out. Flint tethered the panting animals and placed a finger to his lips.

'I'll be back soon,' he told the dogs as he swung his rucksack on to his shoulder. 'Probably.'

One of the dogs whined and Flint reached into a bag on

the sled and pulled out the frozen rabbit meat inside. He tossed it to the dogs and they chewed hungrily.

Then, with Pebble peeping out from his hood, Flint turned from the cavern and crept towards the palace. The fortress glinted in the moonlight and as Flint slipped beneath the bridge that connected the iceberg to the cliff top on the mainland – his sealskin boots practically soundless against the ice – he realised he had been holding his breath for almost a minute. He breathed out.

Immediately, his body stiffened.

Voices.

A cluster of Tusk guards were chattering on the bridge above him and, as Flint listened, he heard mugs clinking together and a fire crackling. He didn't need to look to know they'd be clad in the armour the Ice Queen had sculpted for them – breastplates of ice and helmets forked with walrus tusks. Heart skittering, Flint stole on, using the shadow of the bridge to hide him.

He paused at the foot of the palace to strap a pair of crampons to his boots, then he swallowed as he took in the glinting base of ice that he needed to climb before he got to the arches opening up into Winterfang. Pebble shivered behind him. They would be in full view of the guards on that ice face, an easy target for one of their spears, but Flint had thought this through. He knew exactly what was needed to create a diversion.

He lifted a whistle carved from gyrfalcon bone out of his rucksack and checked for the handful of snowy owl feathers wedged inside it. He breathed a sigh of relief. The feathers were still there, and that was just as well, because his whole invention hinged on them. Gathered under a full moon out on the tundra, then dipped in rainwater collected before it touched the ground, the feathers had magical properties, if Erkenwald's magic *was* to be believed.

Flint clasped the whistle and blew. No sound came out – the feathers muffled it – but eventually they eased out of the whistle and fluttered silently into the sky. Pebble's eyes grew large and Flint bit his lip as they watched the feathers float eerily above the bridge and trail quite some distance across the tundra. Then, when the feathers were a long way away, Flint's whistle sounded.

The guards leapt up and began shouting. Flint grinned. His invention *had* worked. The feathers had carried the sound of his whistle, only releasing the blast when it was a safe enough distance from him. The Tusks rushed down the bridge and away from the palace towards the noise while Flint hauled a bundle of rope from his rucksack. This was the diversion he'd wanted, but he would have to be quick.

He hurled the end of the rope tipped with a barbed hook up against the ice and it held fast, then he tightened the drawstring around his hood to secure Pebble in place, set his crampons to the wall and climbed up towards the arches. Once or twice his boots skidded down the ice, but Flint kept on going, every now and again throwing a glance behind him to check that the guards were still out on the tundra.

Eventually, Flint came to the arches. He crouched just

below them, panting, and Pebble gave a little moan as he peered over the edge of Flint's hood. They were closer to the palace than they'd ever been, just moments away from breaking in, and as Flint thought of his ma and all the nights he'd spent missing her in the forest he hoisted himself up into the arch.

And froze.

There was a face looking up at him, but it did not boast a crown of snowflakes which the Ice Queen was rumoured to wear. This face belonged to a thin pale girl hunched on a pedestal – and it held eyes full of longing.

'Help me.' The girl's voice was a scratched whisper, as if she hadn't used it in a long, long time. 'You have to help me.'

Chapter Three
Flint

For a moment, Flint did nothing at all. He just stared at the girl in front of him. Her body was almost blue from the chill, but she wasn't shivering. She was absolutely still, like a doll. Only her face seemed alive.

'Turn the key in the pedestal. Three turns to the right and half a turn left.'

Flint frowned. The girl's voice was hoarse, and weak, but there was something strangely magnetic about it and, despite the dangers all around him, he found himself drawn to her words.

'Please,' the girl begged. 'It will undo the spell.'

Shaking himself, Flint gathered his rope into his rucksack, slipped off his crampons and dropped down into the hall; he couldn't risk being seen by the Tusk guards. But still he said nothing. Who *was* this girl? Flint's mind raced as he took in her shock of red hair. The Tusks were blond, the Furs had brown hair and the Feathers had hair the colour of midnight. This girl didn't fit. But those eyes – big and bright and blue – brought back memories of the Tusk spies Flint had seen in the forest last month. And, if this girl was a Tusk spy, he wasn't getting mixed up with her. Not when he had a rescue mission ahead of him.

He took a step into the hall and felt Pebble tense inside his hood. The fox pup's ears were trained to sounds most humans missed and Flint listened hard until he, too, could make out a faint tapping noise, like metal clanging, from deeper within the palace.

The girl blinked frightened eyes at Flint. '*Please*,' she said again. 'There isn't much time.'

Despite the pull of her voice, Flint took a few more nervous steps over the ice-crusted floor: past the organ in the middle of the room, below the chandelier spread with candles that burned with bright blue flames, and on towards the silver trees and the doorway leading further into the palace. Somewhere beyond that door was his ma.

'I know I don't look or sound like much,' the girl whispered from behind him, 'but for some reason the Ice Queen thinks my voice is important.'

Flint kept walking, but his ears snagged on those last words because with every sentence this girl uttered he could feel himself being folded further into her story. Her voice, whether he liked it or not, did seem to hold some quiet sort of power.

'I know things from being locked up here in the palace,' she went on, 'and if you set me free I can help you find whoever you've come for.'

The girl stifled a sob and Flint recognised something in

her then: something desperate, despite her stillness, like the beating fear in the eyes of a wounded animal. And it was harder to keep walking than he had expected.

He threw a glance over his shoulder. 'What's your name?'

'Eska.'

'And your tribe?'

There were tears standing in Eska's eyes now. 'I – I don't remember a tribe. The Ice Queen took my memories when she locked me in this music box.'

'*Everyone* belongs to a tribe.' Flint looked her up and down and the hardness closed back around him. 'Tusk probably – we all know the only reason Tusk children roam without fear is because they're the Ice Queen's spies and their parents are her guards.'

He turned away and concentrated on the hall. It was 'detours' like this – a term his parents had come up with for the distracted, almost sideways nature of his adventures – that always got him into such a mess. And these detours were the reason Tomkin had carved the words *Decide Where You're Going And Go There* on the runners of his sled. The trouble was, Flint realised as he tiptoed over the ice, he usually only discovered where he was going halfway through a journey, and when he arrived he was often somewhere he hadn't intended to be. But this was a journey to bring back his ma and he wasn't going to let a stranger who didn't even know her tribe get in the way of that.

He took a few more steps across the room, mumbling to himself as he went. 'Stupid Tusk spy . . .'

But even as he said the words he knew they weren't true. This girl was afraid – *really* afraid – and Flint had done enough hunting to know what fear looked like. What if she really was the Ice Queen's prisoner and knew things Tomkin needed to hear to stage his rebellion? Flint dug his nails into his hands. He could sense there was something more to the girl than what he was seeing . . .

'Find Ma first,' he murmured.

Pebble, though, had other ideas. Wriggling free from Flint's hood, the fox pup dropped down to the ground and ran up to the pedestal.

'Pebble,' Flint hissed. 'We need to go.'

But the fox pup was clambering on to the pedestal now and Flint watched, open-mouthed, as Pebble raised a tentative paw towards Eska. The little animal was usually cautious and untrusting around those he didn't know and yet with Eska he didn't seem afraid. Flint watched as Pebble rubbed his body against the girl's dress and then licked her ice-cold toes before turning to Flint and making a quiet huffing sound.

'We don't even know what tribe she's from, Pebble. Even if she's not working for the Ice Queen, she could be dangerous.' He glanced across the hall towards the door between the silver trees. '*Come on.*'

But the fox pup wove between Eska's legs and turned his twitching nose back to Flint. The boy grimaced. Tomkin had reminded him only the day before about harnessing the mind of a warrior: becoming silent, focused and deadly. He cursed under his breath. What he was about to do was not focused, and it was decidedly undeadly.

He hurried back to the pedestal and placed a hand on the jet-black key.

Eska's eyes glittered and, though her words were faint, she repeated her plea. 'Three turns to the right then half a turn left.'

Flint shot Pebble a withering look. 'It's your fault if this all goes wrong.'

Pebble flicked his tail defiantly, then Flint's mitten closed round the key and he turned it, just the way Eska had said. For a few seconds, there was a grinding sound, like musical notes draining away, then there was a click as the key finally rotated left.

Eska slumped on to the pedestal and for a moment Flint wondered whether he'd killed the girl. A death on top of a detour would be hard to explain to Tomkin. But then slowly, shakily, Eska raised her head. She looked at her hands first, turning them this way and that as if she couldn't believe they belonged to her. And then she flexed her toes.

'Thank you!' she gasped. 'Thank you!'

But, as she struggled to her feet, the whispers began. Flint jerked his head upwards. They were coming from the blue candles flickering in the chandelier.

Come to the hall, the candles have spoken.
The curse on the child has now been broken!

Again and again the flames whispered and Flint's blood curdled. He scooped Pebble up into his hood, then turned to Eska.

'You didn't tell me the candles were spies!'

Eska staggered off the pedestal, then fell to her knees under the strain of using muscles so long locked under a spell. She scrabbled for the wall and hauled herself up.

'I – I didn't know,' she stammered. And then her voice grew harder and she glanced at the arches. 'We have to leave.'

Flint's jaw stiffened. 'I'm here to free my ma and *you're* going to show me how I get through this palace to the ice towers, like you promised.'

Chapter Four
Flint

Eska shook her head. 'You don't know the Ice Queen like I do. We won't stand a chance now she knows I'm free!'

Pebble slid further into Flint's hood as if he could sense that he was largely to blame for this turn of events while Flint's gaze faltered between the arch he had come through and the door leading on into the heart of Winterfang. He stormed across the hall towards the latter, leaving Eska trembling beside the music box. But, as Flint approached the doorway, the silver branches closed over the frame, barring his way on into the palace. And then footsteps sounded from a passageway beyond the door: heels clacking closer, followed by the slow swish of a gown. The stories of the Ice Queen swirled inside him.

She wears a dress made from the frozen tears of her prisoners. She can hex animals under her control with one strike of her staff. She can turn children to ice . . .

Flint thought of the inventions he had packed into his rucksack: his Camouflage Cape, made from the fur of snow hares, then washed in a casket of sunbeams. And his bone-handled Anything Knife, with a turquoise river gem slotted into the handle.

But these inventions had been made to help Flint slip through the passageways unseen, not to fight the Ice Queen, and with an aching heart he realised his rescue mission now lay in tatters at his feet. He raced back towards the arches. Panes of black ice were sliding across them, closing the hall in, window by window. The palace darkened as the moonlight was shut out, but Flint sped on towards the three arches still left open and, grabbing the key from the music box, Eska stumbled after him.

'You are *not* coming with us!' Flint cried as he hoisted himself into the biggest arch and hauled the rope from his rucksack. 'You've already ruined my chances of freeing my ma!'

The footsteps beyond the hall grew louder and the flames began to hiss. Flint flung his barbed rope into the wall then glanced towards the tundra. The guards didn't seem to be out there any longer – perhaps they were inside the palace now, having summoned the Ice Queen about the strange whistle sounding over the ice – and Flint knew that he only had a few seconds to make this escape work. The black ice burst out from the side of the arch and Flint gripped the rope and began to abseil down the palace wall.

But Eska wasn't giving up. She clambered on to the arch in the nick of time, her body juddering from the cold, and Flint watched, aghast, as she grabbed hold of the rope above him as the last of the windows sealed shut behind her.

Flint slipped to the ground, barely using his mittens or his boots to grip the rope this time, and, moments later, Eska clattered down after him, her hands and feet raw from the rope. Then there was an almighty crash as the largest pane of black glass smashed apart.

Flint dragged Eska beneath the bridge. He couldn't leave her now – she'd only give his presence away – and yet his mission was careering sideways. He hauled a bundle of clothes from his rucksack: a pair of sealskin boots and mittens and a parka and trousers made from grizzly-bear furs, and tossed them to Eska.

'They were for my ma,' he growled. 'But you'll need them if we're going to make it out of this alive.' He drew out a large and very soft white blanket next. The Camouflage Cape. 'I didn't need this on the way here because no one knew I was coming, but now thanks to you . . .' He shook his head. 'We need to run – fast – beneath the cliffs and if we stay under this cape we've a chance of making it unseen.'

Flint jumped as a high-pitched cry pierced the night.

'*Eskaaaaaaaaaaaaaaaaa!*'

The voice was sharp and shrill and it swarmed over the Driftlands. Flint slid a look up to the palace to see a woman standing in the tallest arch, a crown of snowflakes glinting on her head. His insides clenched. The Ice Queen's teardrop gown fluttered in the wind and beside the staff she held sat a wolverine, its dark fur a stain against the ice.

Flint turned to Eska, tucking her beneath the Camouflage Cape with him. 'Run,' he whispered. 'Now.'

And, with the sound of the Tusk guards marching out

across the bridge and the Ice Queen's screech echoing across the kingdom, the two children darted out.

They kept to the cliffs, their boots pounding against the ice, their breath pent up inside them, and, though Eska was unstable on her feet, Flint propped her up and they ran on towards the cavern where the huskies waited.

Flint yanked Eska inside the opening in the cliff and the dogs clustered round them, warm and loyal and ready for the homeward journey.

Eska leant against the wall. 'Free from Winterfang,' she panted in disbelief. 'Free at last . . .' The Ice Queen's voice tore across the ice again and Eska edged further inside the cavern.

'Stand on the metal brake between the runners while I attach the dogs,' Flint muttered. 'I don't want them whisking the sled away before we're ready to go.'

Eska hurried over and pressed down with her boot, but, after the Ice Queen's enchantment, her body was no match for the spirited dogs. The brake flung up, the sled jerked forward and Eska stumbled over. But Flint was on it in a second, slamming a hand on to the side of the sled until it stopped.

Eska picked herself up and wedged a foot down over the metal again, as hard as she could. 'That cape,' she whispered, nervously placing her other boot on to the brake to stop it edging forward, 'we never would have escaped without it. And it was made using magic, wasn't it? That's the reason we got away . . .'

For a second, Flint's shoulders squared with pride – it was

the first time anyone had congratulated him on an invention or even been vaguely interested in Erkenwald's magic since the Tusk Chief's death – but then he remembered himself and scowled.

'Shut up and listen to me.'

He stamped his boot over Eska's so that it sank deep into the snow and the sled held firm.

'The cavern widens into a tunnel and when it comes up on the tundra we'll be a safe distance away from the palace. The guards might see the huskies, but if we and the sled are tucked under the cape they'll just look like a pack of wolves running from that distance, and, with any luck, we'll make it to Deeproots without being tailed.'

Eska nodded.

'We must be quick though – we need to get as far as we can while the night hides us.'

Eska nodded again then, avoiding Flint's eyes, she whispered, 'What's Deeproots?'

'*What's Deeproots?*' Flint scoffed as he untangled the ropes that tied the dogs to his sled. 'Only the biggest forest in the kingdom and home to the legendary Fur Tribe. Everyone in Erkenwald knows that.'

'Everyone except me,' Eska mumbled. A spot of colour had returned to her cheeks, but the clothes she wore swamped her body and she looked pitifully frail inside them. 'Will I be safe with your tribe?'

Flint looked up. 'You can't just wander in and join our tribe! There are rules, you know.'

'But …' Eska's voice trailed off. 'I'd be an extra pair of hands about the place. I'd help.'

'It doesn't work like that,' Flint said. 'You have to be one of us from the start.' He tossed his rucksack on to the fur-lined sled. 'Once we're in Deeproots, you're on your own. I don't know who you are, what tribe you're from or why the Ice Queen thinks your voice is so important, but I just missed my chance of freeing my ma because of you. The *only* reason I'm not leaving you here is because I don't trust you not to blab about my whereabouts to the Ice Queen.'

Pebble yapped from Flint's hood.

'*And* because Pebble is playing up.'

Pebble growled.

Flint sighed. '*And* I suppose because you might know things that could help us fight the Ice Queen.'

Satisfied now, Pebble settled into Flint's hood.

Flint shoved Eska off the brake, pushed his own foot down on it and glowered at the ball of white fur curled up in his hood. 'I blame you entirely for this detour, Pebble. You're going to have some serious explaining to do when we see Tomkin.'

Pebble pretended to snore and Flint rolled his eyes, but, when the wolverine's growl juddered across the sea outside, he pointed to the sled.

'Sit down on the furs in front.' Flint lifted the Camouflage Cape over his shoulders. 'And hold the end of the cape up a little so that I can see out ahead of us.' He paused. 'But don't expect any conversations. It's hard to steer a sled, be cross and talk all at the same time.'

'Can – can I just ask your name?' Eska stammered.

Flint scowled. 'Why do you need it?'

Eska blinked. 'In case we do decide to have more conversations.'

'It's Flint.' There was a pause. 'And we won't be having any more conversations for a while.'

Eska nodded meekly, then Flint lifted his foot from the brake and, as the dogs hastened into the tunnel, the wolverine's growl petered out into silence.

Chapter Five
Eska

They emerged from the tunnel and, when Eska eventually plucked up the courage to peek out from the cape and glance over her shoulder, she saw the dark shapes of the Tusk guards spreading out over the Driftlands in the opposite direction. Relief rinsed through her and, as she slipped back beneath the blanket, she felt her pulse unwind. With every stride the dogs took, she was moving further and further away from the woman who had held her captive for so long.

The wooden sled creaked as it rushed over the ice and the cold air funnelling through the cape stiffened the muscles in Eska's face, but, for the first time since being locked inside the Ice Queen's music box, Eska smiled. Because she had escaped – finally – and the landscape she had watched in silence for so long was now alive all around her. Her heart fluttered at the freedom of it all and she wiggled her hands in front of her chest.

'What are you doing?' Flint hissed.

Eska did a little circle with her elbow. 'Getting used to my body again.'

'Well, don't,' Flint spat. 'It's distracting. Sit still.'

Eska stared ahead for a few minutes and tried her best not to be annoying. Then, very quietly, she began tracing her fingers over her arms and legs for a mark from the Sky Gods that might show she was cursed. But she found nothing and so she went back to very subtly circling her elbows instead.

'Snow clouds are gathering,' Flint whispered to himself. 'Our tracks will be covered by morning.'

Eska stole a look at the night sky and as she watched the darkness closing in she tried to work out whether Flint's words were an opening to a conversation or not. She had no reason to trust him – after all, he hadn't planned to rescue her: it had just sort of happened. But, without Flint, she'd still be trapped inside Winterfang, and though she didn't want to irritate him she was longing to talk to someone after so many months of silence. She had to know more about the Fur and Feather Tribe children. Where were they hiding? Might they bend their rules and offer her shelter and protection? Could she team up with them to fight back against the Ice Queen? And, her deepest desire of all, would they know who she really was?

She tucked the music-box key into her pocket, hoping that now she had it the Ice Queen would not be able to use the music box again. For her or anybody else.

'Tell me about those in hiding from the Ice Queen,' Eska said quietly.

'That sounds dangerously like a conversation to me,' Flint replied, urging his dogs on.

There were no fences or roads on the Driftlands, at least none that Eska could see beyond the gap in the cape, and the moonlight was almost completely swallowed by the clouds now, but it seemed Flint knew this wide and lonely landscape – somehow its shapes and rhythms were locked in his skull – and he swerved the sled through a scattering of trees, then down a shallow bank until it skidded out on to a frozen river coated in snow.

'Please tell me,' Eska whispered. 'Because, if you're planning to leave me, I'll need more information than I have now to survive.'

'Why does the Ice Queen think your voice is so important?' Flint muttered. 'It's not like other voices – I'll give you that – but it's feeble all the same. And you don't even know anything.'

Eska was almost afraid of the answer, of the darkness that the Ice Queen said her voice was capable of, but she had the boy's attention now and she wanted to keep it.

'The Ice Queen is feeding on her prisoners' voices.' Eska watched the river race beneath the dogs' paws. 'And, if she can swallow every voice in Erkenwald before the midnight sun rises, she'll become immortal and will rule this kingdom for ever.'

Eska heard the squeak of mittens tightening round the wooden bar behind her, but when Flint spoke his voice betrayed no emotion. 'What's that got to do with you? Why is your voice any more important than her other prisoners'?'

Eska took a deep breath. 'The Ice Queen told me that

the Sky Gods placed a curse on my voice to make it capable of terrible things. She promised to help me – she said she would take away my cursed voice and use it to summon the outlawed tribes, then tear down the Sky Gods so that they could never harm Erkenwald again.'

Flint didn't reply, and as Eska listened to the near-silent sound of snow pattering against the cape she wondered what he was thinking. Could he sense the shame in her voice at the idea that she might be cursed? Was he planning to tip her off the sled and leave her for dead because of it?

The silence was broken by a snigger. 'No one believes in the Sky Gods or their magic any more ... Not after the northern lights stopped and—'

Eska saw her chance. 'But *you* still believe – in their magic at least.' She paused. 'Back at the palace I saw a lot of dark magic, but what if there's another kind of magic out there? One that could be used for good? One that could be harnessed to make secret capes?' She bit her lip. 'Because that's what you did, didn't you? You used magic to outwit the Ice Queen.'

Flint shifted behind her.

'I can't remember anything about my past,' Eska went on. 'The Ice Queen stole my memories. But I get feelings about things – deep in my gut – and somehow I never believed her when she blamed the Gods for the tribes hating each other. I reckon that was her doing.' She paused. 'I think the Sky Gods are still up there and their magic might be something we can trust, after all.'

Although Flint said nothing, Eska could feel his thoughts whirring close to hers. Theirs was a kingdom that had given up on magic and yet here on this sled were two people who believed in its power, even if one was too proud to admit it.

'If the Ice Queen lied about the Sky Gods,' Eska said, 'then maybe she lied about my voice, too. Not about it being important – otherwise she wouldn't have gone to such lengths to steal it – but what if it's not cursed? What if I could use my voice for good?' Her words were gathering pace now. 'I didn't give in to the Ice Queen because I thought that perhaps, if I escaped, I could somehow use my voice – and a little bit of magic – to fight back against her and to free all those prisoners.'

Flint snorted. 'I've heard powerful voices before – warrior battle cries and chief's speeches – but yours? It's odd and unlikely. There's no way it could destroy the Ice Queen.' He paused. 'And, as for using magic, good luck convincing an entire kingdom that it's something they should believe in again.'

Eska found herself looking at the Camouflage Cape. If she knew one thing about magic from her time in Winterfang, it was that it was an unpredictable sort of business that required a good deal of faith to get it going in the first place.

'Not *all* brilliant ideas start off ordinary and likely,' she said.

Flint drove on without speaking, but Eska could sense by his silence that her words had hit home and she let the quiet linger for a while before pressing Flint in a different direction.

'I pieced together bits about the kingdom's landscape from eavesdropping on the Tusk guards, but what about the children in hiding? Tell me about them.'

'Fine,' Flint replied after a while. 'But only because I can't drive the rest of this journey with Pebble biting me on the ear until I've answered your questions.' The fox pup leapt down on to the sled and busied himself between Eska's ankles. 'The Feather Tribe are somewhere in the Never Cliffs,' Flint began, 'though I've not seen them since before the battle last summer. We used to share food around campfires if we crossed paths on hunting trips and once a Feather boy lent me a quiver of arrows when my own was swept downriver, but everything changed when the Tusk Chief was murdered.' He paused. 'We don't speak to the Feather Tribe now – and certainly not to the Tusks. Outlaws keep to their own kind.'

Eska frowned. 'Then how do you learn new things?'

'We've learnt them already,' Flint snapped.

'But if the Feather and Fur Tribes turn their backs on each other then you can't swap ideas or make plans together to free the Ice Queen's prisoners.'

Flint bristled. 'The Fur Tribe have made plans. Lots of them. Just not with the Feathers. They can't be trusted.'

Eska watched the dark speed by. The kingdom she had been longing to explore from the music box was nothing like the place she found herself in now. She had been hoping for friends and answers, but here was discord and secrets. It was a bleaker, colder world than the one she had imagined and she hugged her coat tighter around her.

'And your parents,' Eska asked. 'Do you believe they're trapped in the ice towers at Winterfang?'

Flint's voice seemed tighter suddenly. 'I know my ma is because every morning I hear her voice trail out over Erkenwald. But my pa . . .' His words faltered. 'He was the Chief of the Fur Tribe – the best warrior we've ever seen – but the Ice Queen used dark magic to fight him and he died on the ice during the battle last summer.' Flint fell silent and Pebble scrambled up towards him and pawed at his neck. 'My brother, Tomkin, is Chief now.'

Eska nodded. 'And what will he say when you return without your ma?'

Flint pulled off the Camouflage Cape and tossed it on to Eska's lap. The snow-filled night surrounded them and Eska could make out the dark outlines of trees either side of the river now and, further downstream, a waterfall shrouded in ice.

Flint stared straight ahead. 'He doesn't know I left.'

And even Eska could tell that the conversation had come to an end then.

The dogs ran on and on and as the hours slipped by Eska felt her eyes begin to close. A sharp nudge from behind jolted her awake.

'Keep your eyes open,' Flint muttered. 'Close them in this cold and they'll freeze shut.'

Eska looked ahead to where the river widened, then turned left. Nestled inside the bend there was a small wooden hut surrounded by trees. The larch trunks it had been made from were shelved with snow, but Eska could make out a door and Flint guided his dogs on to the riverbank and pulled them to a stop before it.

'Stand on the brake,' he ordered Eska. 'Properly this time.'

She scurried round to the back of the sled while Flint untied the huskies and tethered them inside a small outhouse to the side of the hut.

'The dogs need a rest,' he said. 'It's another few hours to the Fur Tribe hideout and we're a safe distance from Winterfang now. We'll leave again at first light.'

Eska squinted through the driving snow. 'You mean you're taking me to see your tribe?' The possibility of being welcomed and looked after by others made her heart flutter. She had been abandoned at Winterfang – no one had come forward to rescue her or even say they knew her – but now there was an opening, a chance for friendship.

Flint shrugged. 'I'm taking you to see my brother – briefly. Then I'm leaving you to fend for yourself.'

Eska's heart sank. This wasn't a promise of safety, after all. But she tried to hide her disappointment. It was a small step in the right direction and after Winterfang that counted for everything.

She glanced at Flint. 'You're interested in my voice, aren't you? You think that your brother should know about me?'

'I'm mildly curious,' Flint replied. 'There's a difference. But you'll need to speak to Tomkin first. He's in charge and, if he thinks your voice will help with his battle plans, he'll use it.'

Eska flinched. 'Your tribe are going to *fight* the Ice Queen?'

Flint held his head high. 'One day – yes. We're not staying at home like last time when our parents made us promise to hide until they returned.' He straightened up. 'And it'll be Tomkin who leads us. He's the best warrior in the tribe now Pa isn't around.'

Eska bit her lip. 'You won't win. I know the Ice Queen. It'll take more than spears and shields to force her back.'

'You don't know Tomkin. If anyone can take on the Ice Queen, it's him.' Flint hefted his rucksack on to his back and pulled open the door of the hut.

Eska stood, shivering, by the sled. 'Is – is it safe in there?'

Flint nodded. 'It's an old Fur Tribe food store – there are lots of them dotted all over Erkenwald, if you know where to look.'

He disappeared inside with Pebble, and Eska followed nervously, closing the door against the flurries of snow. It was pitch-black within.

'Keep still, Pebble!' Flint muttered. 'I need to find the caribou tallow and the heather so that we can see what's what.'

Eska squinted into the dark. 'Can I help?'

Flint grunted.

Eska tried again. 'Tell me what I'm looking for, at least?'

'First rule of the wild – know how to make fire. You're looking for a stone dish filled with hardened caribou fat,' Flint said, 'and a wick of heather. That's a plant that grows out on the tundra, in case you don't know.'

Eska felt her way around the wooden walls, nearly tripping over two large wooden objects tucked into the corners of the hut, then her palms met with a stone dish set between these objects.

'Here!' she cried. 'I think it's here.'

Flint fumbled towards her, then stooped to touch the dish. He rummaged in his pocket and drew out two small rocks and for several minutes the hut was filled with the quiet scuffing of metal. Then sparks appeared and he set them to the heather wick and, within seconds, a soft light flickered.

The wooden objects Eska had stumbled on were beds laden with blankets made from the furs of snow hares and Eska looked around to see clumps of moss had been stuffed into the walls to block the cracks in the timber. There was a table beneath the lamp and above it hooks made from antlers.

They sat down on the beds and Flint turned his Anything Knife over in his hands. He said nothing but Eska could tell, when he kicked his boot against the bed leg and Pebble leapt up into his lap, that he was angry at not returning with his ma.

She picked at her nails. 'I'm sorry we couldn't free your ma.'

Flint didn't look up.

'One day I'll repay you for rescuing me from the palace though,' Eska added.

'I doubt that very much.'

Eska glanced at the knife in Flint's hands. The handle

was made of bone and slotted into the hilt was a blue gem which shimmered mischievously. 'That knife,' she said slowly. 'It's built using magic again, just like your cape . . .' She leant forward. 'You're an inventor, aren't you?'

Flint's face hardened. 'I'm a warrior, like the rest of my tribe.'

But the more time Eska spent with Flint, the more she felt that he wasn't like the rest of his tribe at all. From what he had said, the Fur Tribe didn't believe in Erkenwald's magic and yet he clearly did. And while none of them seemed keen to welcome strangers, Flint, despite his reservations, had. To Eska, Flint seemed a strange kind of warrior and she wondered whether she wasn't the only one who felt like an outsider. Maybe Flint felt different from everyone else, too. But his guard was up so she offered her next words as a truce.

'You're a warrior who believes in magic and I think that's the best way to be – because you won't defeat the Ice Queen with weapons alone.'

Flint cocked his head. 'Isn't it time you stopped talking?'

He stood up and walked over to the corner of the room where a spear carved from caribou antler had been stashed. Grabbing it, he headed for the door.

'Get some sleep,' he muttered. 'You look like you need it. And now that the light has returned to the kingdom, you won't get long before dawn is up.'

'Where are you going?'

Flint opened the door. 'To get food – and I'm going alone.'

But Eska didn't roll over and go to sleep. She hurried to

the wall facing the river, pulled out a clump of moss and peered through.

She watched intently as Flint carved a hole in the iced-up river with his spear and then sat down beside it, his back against the rush of snow. Eska waited. And, though her hands ached from the climb down the palace wall and her throat burned from speaking after so many months of silence, she did not turn away. She needed to learn the ways of the wild – fast – and, if there was one thing she was good at, it was watching the world from a distance.

Chapter Six
Flint

Flint woke to the sunlight streaming through the cracks in the moss and the timber. Normally, he would have welcomed the dawn after so many months of darkness, but now it felt like a warning; they didn't have long to halt the Ice Queen's quest for immortality. He swung out of bed and glanced at Eska. She was still asleep and to Flint's surprise, and irritation, he saw that Pebble was curled up in a ball at the bottom of her bed, not his.

She's even bothersome in her sleep, Flint thought to himself, scooping the fox pup into his arms and tiptoeing out of the hut.

The dogs yapped from the outhouse and only when Flint pulled back the mound of stones he'd placed over his catch and tossed them a fish to share did they hush.

The dwarf willows either side of the river were cloaked in white, but the sky above was a brilliant blue and, as Flint listened, he could hear the soft flump of snow sliding off branches and the pop and crack of river ice melting. Spring was in full swing and Flint knew that the river was not to be trusted as a way across the Driftlands when the temperatures began to climb.

He gathered up an armful of branches, tried his best not to think about what Tomkin might say if he declared, when home, that he was a *warrior who believed in magic*, and laid them out of sight behind the hut. Before long he had a fire going and with his Anything Knife he pierced chunks of the second salmon he had caught and held them above the flames to cook.

Eska shuffled through the snow towards him. 'You should've woken me up,' she whispered. 'I would've—'

'—got in the way,' Flint said.

'—helped with the fire.'

Flint shrugged. 'Quicker on my own.'

He held out a scoop of bark laden with fish and Eska shovelled mouthful after mouthful down.

Flint raised an eyebrow. 'You'd think you hadn't eaten in a year . . .'

'I haven't,' Eska replied. 'Not since the Ice Queen locked me in the music box. It wasn't food or water that kept me alive – just her dark magic.'

Flint wanted to ask more. Despite what he might have said, magic, in all its forms, fascinated him. But he was still cross and suspicious of Eska so he caught himself just before the words slipped out and threw her a death stare instead.

Eska was too busy enjoying eating to notice. 'Last night I watched you cut a hole in the river ice, then plunge your spear in,' she said between bites. 'Then it looked like you were muttering something, but from inside the hut I couldn't hear anything. What were you saying?'

Flint looked up. 'You were watching me? I thought you were asleep?'

Eska shook her head. 'I figured watching and listening were probably the best ways to learn about hunting.' She paused. 'I don't imagine I'll be a particularly good hunter – I've not had much experience jamming spears into things – but hopefully I'll pick it up after a while.' Her eyes brightened. 'Like I did with the brake on the sled.'

Flint squinted. The only reason the sled hadn't careered off was because he had stamped his boot over Eska's – there was no way she'd have had the strength to hold it on her own. He looked at her gaunt face and straggled hair and the furs that almost swallowed her body. Nothing about the girl was geared up for the wild and, before he could stop himself, he found he was offering her advice.

'There are rituals attached to hunting and the tribes always honour them,' he said. 'First you thank the North Star, the Sky God who breathed life into Erkenwald—'

He stopped suddenly, catching himself. No one thanked the Sky Gods any more, but he did. Because despite what he had told Eska earlier, he still believed in the Gods. How could he not when he could feel their magic hovering over the kingdom? Flint cleared his throat. He hadn't known this girl long, but it seemed to be annoyingly difficult to steer conversations in the direction he wanted with Eska; her voice had a habit of drawing surprising, and often unfortunate, things out of him. He decided to move on quickly.

'Then you thank the animal itself for giving up its life for you. An animal chooses its own death, you see; it chooses the hunter to whom it will submit.' He ran a hand down Pebble's back. 'There's a bond between animals and tribes out here.'

Eska breathed a sigh of relief. 'That's good to know. Because if the bonds between the tribes are all broken you'll probably want the animals to hold things together.'

Flint narrowed his eyes at Eska. There was a mad sort of logic to her and he wasn't sure whether he liked it. Before he could reply though, Pebble slipped from his side, poked his nose under Eska's elbow and gobbled up the last of her fish. Flint smirked as Pebble waddled back to him and crawled into his lap.

'You've got to watch your food when Pebble's around.' Flint threw a handful of snow on the fire and it fizzled out. 'His appetite is out of control.'

Eska followed Flint back towards the hut. 'How did you and Pebble meet?' she asked, hurrying to keep up. 'Was it on a hunt and Pebble refused to choose his own death? Maybe he felt he had more eating to do before he submitted to a hunter.'

There was a snuffle-grunt from the ball of white fur tucked inside Flint's hood that sounded quite like a chuckle.

'Found him in our camp scavenging for food,' Flint replied, but he made sure he didn't meet Eska's eyes because that wasn't what had happened at all.

Shortly afterwards, they were back on the sled, racing

between the dwarf willows and the drifts of snow as they travelled further and further south. Flint shivered as the first notes of the Ice Queen's anthem floated over the land. The choir was ever so slightly louder with each day that passed and Flint grimaced now he knew why. Had the Ice Queen already stolen his ma's voice? Would he ever be able to get it back for her?

Flint focused on his sled to stop his thoughts spiralling, keeping the river to his right and watching as Eska's eyes travelled beyond that to the mighty Never Cliffs in the distance, a sprawl of jagged peaks locked in the harsh white glitter of snow. Now and then she gasped and pointed at things and mostly Flint ignored her, but when her gaze shifted to the trees a few miles ahead he knew a conversation was inevitable. The trees were not small and straggly, like the willow shrubs around them. They were tall and bold, the type of trees you could start climbing at sunrise and only reach the top of when the first stars showed. And, as Flint saw them, a smile spread over his face, too.

'Deeproots,' he said. 'The start of it anyway. There are spruce trees here older than Erkenwald's glaciers with roots that stretch so far into the earth they reach depths even the whales in the oceans know nothing about.'

Eska gulped. 'So, where exactly will you take me after we've spoken to your brother?'

For a second, Flint felt a stab of regret that he planned to leave Eska in the forest – it would be fun showing someone, other than his little sister, his secret laboratory up in the trees and all the inventions stored in there – but then he remembered his failed rescue mission and the danger of detours and he banished the thought from his head.

'I haven't decided yet,' he said stiffly.

He steered his sled between the willows which had grown denser and taller now the forest was in sight. Then, without warning, the dogs swerved and backed up in their tracks. The sled stopped and Flint peered ahead.

'What is it?' Eska whispered.

Flint secured the brake and stepped off the runners, clutching his Anything Knife in a shaking hand, then he crept over the snow until he was level with the dogs. There was a scuffling sound from behind a willow and a high-pitched cry that made Eska jump. Flint edged forward and there, huddled under the branches of the tree, was a very large bird.

He slipped his knife back into its sheaf. 'A golden eagle,' he said as Eska tiptoed closer. 'Female, it looks like – they grow much bigger than the males – and this one's huge.' He nodded to the wire encircling the bird's talon. It was attached to a chain that had been tied round the trunk of the willow. 'It's got itself trapped in a fox snare.'

The bird flung its body back from the snare, then flapped its wings against the snow. They were vast, those wings, and flecked with brown, black and gold feathers. But the snare didn't loosen and, after another failed tussle, the eagle jabbed at the wire with its hooked beak.

'We have to help it,' Eska whispered.

Flint looked up at Deeproots. Tomkin would have noticed he was gone by now. He'd be worried – and so would his sister, Blu.

'Even if we free the eagle, it won't survive. Its talon's probably crushed and it'll need it to hunt.' Flint tugged at her sleeve. 'Let's go.'

But Eska stayed where she was, crouched opposite the eagle, and the girl and the bird stared at each other for several seconds. Flint had seen eagles before, but never this close. Its eyes seemed to burn like desert sand and there was something in the way it looked at Eska, as if it was seeing things that perhaps he had missed.

Shaking himself, Flint turned away, but a few seconds later the eagle began to hiss and flap. Flint whirled round to see Eska bent over the snare, her mittens laid down on the snow beside her. The eagle's wings thrashed against her back, nearly knocking her over, but she didn't back away. She kept close to the bird, her fingers working at the trap, and for a moment Flint thought how natural Eska looked alongside the eagle. Wild animals were hard to approach, even harder to help, but Eska was right there beside this bird as if, just possibly, she had tended to wild animals before.

He strode towards her. 'What are you doing? Those wings could break your arm!'

The eagle yanked back, shrieking, but Eska had managed to loosen the loop of wire a little, and in a flurry of snow and feathers the eagle burst free, tumbling over itself before stilling a few metres from Eska.

'Go on now,' she panted. 'You're free.'

The eagle blinked at Eska, its golden head cocked to one side, then it limped behind another tree, trailing its tail feathers out of sight.

Eska stood up and looked at Flint. 'Like you said, there's a bond between animals and people out here.'

Flint said nothing for a moment, then he dragged Eska back to the sled. 'Get on. We can't afford any more detours.'

But, although Flint kept his eyes trained on the trees ahead as they raced towards Deeproots, he was sharply aware of two things: Eska had shown she had more knowledge of the wild than she realised and the eagle she had freed was still watching them from back among the willows.

Chapter Seven
Eska

There was a hushed kind of silence inside the forest. Flint's dogs nipped this way and that between the trunks – they knew their path instinctively and they could tell they were almost home – but as Eska was pulled deeper and deeper into the trees she bit her lip. This was a place that smelled of secrets and if she didn't manage to win over Tomkin she'd be left to find her own way here.

She pointed to a line of large, clawed animal tracks leading into the trees. 'What made those?'

'Grizzly bear,' Flint replied.

Eska shuddered.

The dogs ran on and on until eventually the trees grew so close together there was no longer a clear path through. Flint unhitched his sled, then dragged it and his huskies towards a large spruce tree. Eska frowned. This tree looked just like all the others, but, as Flint slid his bear-claw earring out and slotted it into a crack in the wood, Eska's eyes grew large.

There was a click, then a door swung inwards and as it did so Flint's dogs rushed through and Eska watched, open-mouthed, as all seven of them disappeared, their footsteps pattering into silence. She raised a mitten to her mouth. The tree was entirely hollow – you could fit half a dozen people inside it – and there was a lamp burning in a bracket on the far side.

'Where have they gone?' Eska gasped.

Flint grinned and for a moment it seemed to Eska that he had forgotten to be cross with her. He hauled the sled inside the tree and as Eska peered closer she saw him hang it on a hook on the inside wall.

'Have you checked for bears?' she whispered.

'Just get inside,' Flint hissed, and he closed the door behind them. 'Welcome to the Labyrinth.' He motioned for Eska to stay where she was, then he hurried down some earthen steps and returned a few minutes later. 'The dogs sleep in kennels down below – they don't much like heights, except Pebble – but the rest of the Fur Tribe,' Flint winked, 'we go up.'

Eska wiggled her toes inside her boots. Warmth. Safety. And the possibility of friends. Her body tingled at the thought of it all.

Flint grabbed hold of the rope ladder hanging down in front of them and placed a boot on the first rung. He climbed a few steps, then glanced back. 'Don't say we talked about inventions. Or magic.' He paused. 'Or the Sky Gods.'

Eska clutched the rope. 'What shall I say we talked about instead then? If they ask.'

'Spears.' Flint glanced up the ladder. 'And, um, killing things.'

Eska climbed beneath Flint, rung after rung, until she felt sure the tree couldn't possibly go any higher, but on it went, tiny lamps flickering from the wooden walls around them. Eska tried to plan her words as best she could so that Tomkin might listen and understand when he saw her, then she realised how high up she was and began concentrating extremely hard on Pebble's head, bouncing up and down in Flint's hood, to avoid catching sight of the long drop down.

She stopped dead. There were whispers coming from above. It sounded like two boys.

'It's Flint,' the first hissed. 'He's back!'

A second voice echoed down the tree. 'Let me see, Lofty – shift over.'

'*Owwww*, Inch, you're standing on my hand.'

There was a scuffle, then two faces peered over the edge of a wooden platform that ran around the inside of the tree. Eska craned her head to get a better view. The boys' faces were identical – ruddy cheeks, curly brown hair, matching porcupine-quill earrings – perhaps they were twins. But from what she could see they had very different physiques. Where one was long and thin, the other was small and plump.

Lofty and Inch, Eska mused. *It makes sense.*

Inch squinted towards the ladder. 'There's someone else with him!'

There was a pause, then Lofty's voice came hard and low. 'It's a girl. An outsider, by the looks of things.'

Eska's knuckles whitened round the rope, but she kept

on climbing. Then Flint clambered on to the platform and as Eska followed, panting, the twins backed away from the ladder.

The hollow tree closed several metres above their heads and Eska noticed pieces of bark nailed to the walls, each one bearing carved words: *Otter-Tread, Silent-Claw, Lone-Lynx, Spruce-Wanderer, Wild-Paw*. Perhaps the names here belonged to former Fur Tribe Chiefs and Chieftainesses . . . There was a desk, too, sculpted from wood, with bears, lynx and otters carved into the legs, and a lantern framed by caribou antlers. These were beautiful, homely things and Eska felt she could have spent ages looking at them had it not been for Lofty's and Inch's narrow eyes.

The twins hurried behind the desk and sat down on two high-backed chairs.

Flint looked at his boots. 'I'm sorry I asked you to cover for me when I crept out last night, Lofty.'

Lofty raised an eyebrow, then he glanced down at his desk. There were about a hundred names carved into its surface in columns and, beside each of the names, there was a spruce cone sitting in a hollowed-out scoop.

Lofty picked up a cone from a small wicker basket on the desk and plonked it next to Flint's name. 'In,' he muttered. 'And that's the last time I take the register.'

Inch coughed and Flint shifted his gaze towards him.

'And I'm sorry I made you lie to my sister, Inch.' Flint sighed. 'It was all going so well at first. I sneaked past the guards, stole into the palace and then,' he shot a glance at

Eska – the novelty of showing her the Labyrinth had clearly worn off, 'and then *she* got in the way.'

Eska felt her cheeks burn.

Inch frowned. 'What is she?'

'A girl,' Flint replied.

Lofty sighed. 'I can see that. But what tribe?' He looked her up and down. 'Blue eyes like a Tusk ... But red hair?'

Eska took a tiny step forward. 'I'm not a Tusk.' She felt around for the right words. 'Even though I lived in Winterfang Palace, I never once spoke to the Ice Queen. I hate her, like you, and—'

'LIVED AT WINTERFANG PALACE?!' Lofty spluttered. He turned to Flint. 'I'm used to you breaking rules, but asking outsiders from the palace in for a cup of spruce-needle tea?! What were you thinking?'

'I wasn't planning on offering her *tea*. I was planning on taking her to Tomkin.'

Inch's eyes widened. 'Because he's going to be really pleased to see a Tusk spy.'

'I'm not a Tusk spy!' Eska cried.

'Sounds like something a Tusk spy would say,' Lofty muttered under his breath.

Flint drew himself up. 'Eska's not a spy. She was the Ice Queen's prisoner and she knows things Tomkin needs to hear.'

Inch sank his head into his hands. 'This is a disaster.'

Flint sighed. 'Come on – let us through. Blu will be worrying about me ...'

At the mention of Flint's sister, Lofty stood up reluctantly and Eska noticed something carved into the wood behind where he had been sitting. The head of an enormous grizzly bear: two small eyes above a snout-like nose and a wide neck surrounded by a circle of large brown claws. The fur was carved in such detail it almost looked alive and, when Lofty flicked one of the claws beside its ear to the left, all the other claws followed suit, there was a clanking noise like gears slotting into place, and the bear's colossal jaw dropped open. Eska blinked. The way on into the Labyrinth was through a grizzly bear's mouth!

'Tomkin's in the Swingery,' Lofty muttered. 'They all are.'

Flint took a step towards the open mouth but Inch leapt up. 'Wait! We should check her for weapons. For ice blades and axes and spears and ... and more ice blades before we let her through.'

Eska picked at the cuffs of her parka. 'I didn't come with anything like that.'

Flint nodded. 'She's unarmed. And, besides, she's not the kind of girl who would know how to wield a weapon anyway. Trust me.'

Lofty glanced at Inch. 'Scared of a pathetic little girl. Honestly ... I really worry about you with the rebellion coming up.'

Inch sat down shakily. 'I've already asked Tomkin if I can be on register duty.'

Seizing the opportunity, Flint stole through the bear's mouth, and Eska followed. They emerged a moment later before a vast network of wooden walkways and rope ladders criss-crossing through the canopy of the trees. Eska gasped. How big was this secret world up among the branches?

Dotted around the trunks of the spruces were tree houses – about twenty of them in a large circle. Some were square, some rectangular, others oblong or triangular, but each had a door, little shuttered windows and a chimney on the top. Eska gawped in awe. The forest floor must have been forty metres below, but she couldn't see it – the trees' branches were so dense and any gaps between them had been filled with walkways and ladders – and as she looked up she saw that the branches closed over the hideaway, locking it from sight. Even the birds wouldn't know it was here.

Flint slid a glance to Eska behind him and, though he said nothing, she could feel his pride. She hastened after him, in towards the centre of this hidden village, where the biggest tree house sat.

'The Swingery,' Flint said as they approached it. 'This is where we have tribe meetings.'

It was circular, with a turreted roof made from slats of wood, and, as Flint pulled the door open, Eska held her breath. Tomkin would be inside and, if she could just persuade him to listen to her, maybe he'd let her stay, after all.

Hanging from the roof were lots and lots of swings – some simple boards of wood, others slings made from animal hide and hammocks that could hold several people at once – and the floor was scattered with caribou skins. Dozens of children – all clad in brown furs with brown hair and brown eyes – sat on the swings, their heads turned over their shoulders towards Flint and Eska as if perhaps, just moments before, they had been listening to someone at the far end of the room. Eska swallowed. The children were staring at her, in silence, and their eyes were cold.

At the back of the room, a boy stood up on a large swing hanging from ropes studded with leaves. He flicked a knife up in the air and caught it with one hand. Eska felt her knees wobble. He looked so like Flint, only taller and with a harder jaw.

Flint shuffled forward. 'Hello, Tomkin.'

And, at his words, Eska felt her hopes drain from her chest. Because Tomkin didn't look pleased to see Flint at all.

He looked furious.

Chapter Eight
Flint

'Where on earth have you *been*?' Tomkin shouted. Flint winced. But, before he could reply, a small, tubby girl dropped down from a swing and charged through the ropes towards him. Her hair was short and wild about her face, as if she'd cut it herself, in a hurry, without a mirror, or even scissors.

'My brother! You give me happy!' she cried, flinging her arms round Flint's waist.

Flint reddened and for a moment he forgot all about the trouble he was in. Instead, he felt Eska's eyes on him and he wondered whether she could see that Blu was different from everyone else in the tribe, that her eyes were smaller and sloping, like almonds, and that her words came out all jumbled even though she was eight and she should have known better.

But when he glanced at Eska he saw she wasn't frowning. She wasn't raising her eyebrows in disgust either, like some people did when they spoke to Blu. She was just watching carefully, as he'd noticed she often did, without saying anything at all.

'I miss you, brother,' Blu said.

Flint ruffled her hair. 'I'm here now.'

Blu tickled Pebble beneath his chin, then she turned to Eska and shot out a little hand. 'Who you? I'm Blu.'

Eska blinked. 'I'm—'

Her words were cut short by a thump. Tomkin had leapt down from his swing and was striding across the room. He drew himself up before them – a necklace of razor-sharp bear claws splayed around his neck, a large knife hanging from his belt – and Eska found the words drying up in her mouth.

Tomkin jabbed a finger in Eska's direction. 'Who is *she?*'

'She's not a spy, Tomkin,' Flint said quickly. There were murmurs from the swings around them. 'At least, I'm almost certain that she's not. I met her at Winterfang.'

Tomkin's eyes blazed. '*Winterfang?* Why were *you* at the Ice Queen's palace?'

'I was trying to rescue Ma.'

'Of all the reckless, stupid, irresponsible things you've done,' Tomkin spat, '*this* is the worst.'

Blu clung on to Flint's arm. 'Be nice, Tomkin. Be nice to brother.'

But Tomkin didn't even look at his sister. Instead, he narrowed his eyes at Flint. 'You're still inventing things, aren't you? Even though I told you to stop.'

'No ... Definitely not.' Flint grimaced, knowing how hollow his words sounded. He'd never been a good liar.

'You made a bunch of stupid objects that you thought could help rescue Ma,' Tomkin hissed, 'but they didn't work!

They never work, Flint! When will you learn that magic can't be trusted?'

Blu put her hands over her ears.

'You're not an inventor. You're a *warrior*. Like the rest of the Fur Tribe. Or at least you're meant to be.' Tomkin shot a glance at Pebble who was peeping out of Flint's hood. 'And it's high time you dumped that fox pup back in the wild where it belongs. When we found its mother dead last spring, you were told to drown the pup because it wouldn't survive without her.' He shook Flint by the shoulders and Pebble leapt down from Flint's hood and cowered behind Eska. 'You're too old for pets now – and you're too old for me to be rushing around Deeproots, trying to find you.'

Flint shrunk inside his furs. The whole tribe was listening to what a terrible disappointment he was – even Eska now knew it – and the shame burned his cheeks.

Blu let out a whimper and Flint stroked her hair. 'You're upsetting Blu,' he said quietly.

'*I'm* upsetting Blu?' Tomkin spat. '*You* ran away!' For a moment, his eyes softened. 'Imagine if you hadn't come back . . .'

Flint reached out to touch the necklace his little sister wore, the one he had made by attaching a rabbit paw to a loop of willow twine. It was a good-luck talisman, or so the carvings he'd found in the woods claimed, and Flint hoped that it would keep his sister safe.

'I'd always come back, Blu,' he whispered. 'Always.'

Blu wriggled free and poked Tomkin in the stomach. 'Not nice words. Be friends.'

Tomkin sighed. 'We spent months and months building this hideaway, Flint. We can't afford to have the Ice Queen and her spies following your tracks and finding us.'

Flint shook his head. 'It snowed last night; our tracks are covered – until Deeproots at least. I wouldn't put us in danger.'

There were more mumblings from the Fur Tribe, then someone called out, 'What about the girl? Why's she here? We've no room for outsiders!'

Eska took a small step behind Flint.

'This is Eska,' Flint said to his brother. 'I don't really know who she is, but she was the Ice Queen's prisoner and I think she knows things that could help us.'

There was a long and painful silence, then Blu turned to Eska, shot out her hand once again and said, 'I Blu.'

Eska took her hand and tried to smile, but one by one the Fur Tribe stood up on their swings. And that's when the shouting began.

'Look at her eyes!' one girl cried. 'She's a Tusk spy!'

'She's not welcome here!' a boy shrieked.

'She's the Ice Queen's pet!'

'Tell her to leave!'

'We can fight our rebellion without an outsider!'

Tomkin put up his hand and the voices were quelled. 'That's enough. I need to speak with my brother alone.'

Flint turned to Eska, then pointed to an empty hammock beside them. 'Sit there,' he said, 'and don't attempt *any* conversations.'

Eska seemed about to say something, but Tomkin was already marching off between the swings and Flint had to hurry to keep up. The tribe were muttering now, casting fierce looks towards the visitor sitting by the door, but Flint ignored them. He ignored Tomkin whispering to Blade, Tomkin's second in command, as they passed, too, but, as he stooped to enter a small tent made of caribou skins at the far end of the room, he glanced back towards Eska. Blu was chattering away to her and Pebble was hopping between them. He paused for a second. There was something about this girl, something he couldn't put his finger on. She wasn't strong or impressive and yet he was starting to believe that there *was* something special about her voice, something secret and important.

He ducked inside the tent to find his brother sitting on a stool. Barely taking a breath, Tomkin launched into his lecture.

'The Fur Tribe fight with weapons, not far-fetched ideas. And you need to remember that.'

Flint wanted to tell Tomkin about how well his gyrfalcon whistle had worked, and about how he had so nearly managed to reach their ma. But Tomkin raised a hand before those sentences could unravel and, with a heavy heart, Flint filled his brother in on all that he had seen and heard in Winterfang Palace and about the things Eska had told him of the Ice Queen's plans.

'What if Eska could help us?' Flint said.

Tomkin snorted. 'That runt you dragged in? She'd be of

no help to anyone. And a voice, Flint? Even from you, that type of thinking is ridiculous. How could a *voice* beat the Ice Queen? You've been spun a line by that girl.'

'At least speak to Eska,' Flint muttered. He got up to go. 'Just listen to what she has to say, then you can decide.'

Tomkin sighed. 'There's no point, Flint.'

'There might be!' With that, he hurried from the tent to go and find Eska, but, as he wove through the ropes, he noticed how quiet the room was. The rest of the Fur Tribe were crouched on their swings, watching him with slitted eyes, and, when Flint reached the door, he saw that only Blu and Pebble were on the hammock.

Eska was nowhere to be seen.

Flint made a dash towards the door, but a bulky boy clad in lynx furs blocked his way.

'Whose side are you on, Flint?' Blade asked.

And Flint realised then what had happened, why Tomkin had whispered to Blade on his way to the tent.

'You made her leave, didn't you?' he said quietly. 'On Tomkin's orders.'

Blade raised his chin. 'She didn't belong here. Tomkin's right. We can't trust outsiders at a time like this.'

Flint chewed his lip. Back at the food store he had planned to abandon Eska if Tomkin saw no use for her, but then he'd seen her with the eagle – so stubborn and fierce – and something inside him had shifted. There was more to Eska than first met the eye. Yes, she'd messed up his chances of freeing his ma, but did she really deserve to be cast out?

And what if her voice really *was* the key to defeating the Ice Queen? Flint glanced up at the Fur Tribe and tried to read their faces, but one by one they turned away so that he was left looking at a sea of backs.

And then Tomkin emerged from the tent and made his way through the swings towards his brother. 'It's time to grow up, Flint. We need warriors, not dreamers, to bring the rest of our tribe home.'

Blu picked up Pebble and stroked his head. 'Where your friend, Flint? I like friend.'

Flint felt something tug inside him, but he shook it away, remembering instead the humiliation of being shouted at by Tomkin in front of everyone – and he turned his heart in the direction of his tribe.

'She wasn't my friend,' he muttered. 'She was a stupid Tusk spy.'

Chapter Nine
Eska

Eska ran blindly into the twilight, her head full of bears and wolves and cursed anthems. She hadn't wanted to leave the Labyrinth, even when Flint disappeared into the tent and she was left alone with the Fur Tribe and their mutterings – '*She's cursed by the Ice Queen!*' '*She's rotten to the core!*' But Eska was no match for Blade and, when he seized her by the arm and marched her towards the ladder, she'd had no choice but to follow.

Now she kept running. Back in Winterfang, she had always dreamed of escaping and finding the tribes. But the Fur people hadn't been what she was expecting and she felt more alone than ever now. When Blade had grabbed her, she had wanted to call out for Flint whom she had started to think of as a friend, but she hadn't dared. Because she could see the Fur Tribe were turning against him and Flint didn't deserve that.

Eska stumbled over a log and crashed down into the snow. She lay there for several seconds, her eyes shining with unshed tears.

An owl hooted, the darkness drew closer and Eska forced

herself to her feet. She needed to find some kind of shelter before the light vanished completely. Food would have to wait until the morning.

The shadow of a lynx flitted between the trees and, every time a branch creaked or a twig snapped, Eska flinched. But she kept going until eventually she came to a few slats of wood arranged like a wigwam around a tree trunk. It wasn't much, but it was enough to hide her until dawn. And so, gathering up a handful of sticks and moss for a fire, Eska crawled inside.

She reached into her pocket and drew out the two splints of metal Inch had stuffed into her palm as Blade pushed her down the ladder. She hadn't looked to see what they were at the time, though she'd had her suspicions, but as she turned them over in her hand now she felt a lump in her throat. Fire-starters. There *had* been goodness among the Fur Tribe, but their fear of outsiders was so deep-rooted it meant it wasn't as easy to spot as she had hoped.

She struck the metal splints against each other again and again, just as Flint had done back in the food store, but nothing happened and, before long, Eska's fingers felt like rods of ice.

'Please work,' she whimpered. 'Please, please work . . .'

And perhaps somewhere the Sky Gods were listening. Because the flames caught then and, lying on her side in that abandoned shack, Eska watched them flicker until she fell asleep.

*

She woke to the sound of a sleigh skimming over the snow. Stamping out the embers of the fire, Eska waited. The light coming through the slats showed it was dawn already, but something wasn't right. Eska listened for the Ice Queen's anthem, for the voices floating out over the kingdom, but there was nothing. Which could only mean one thing: the Ice Queen wasn't in her palace. She was on the move.

The sound of the sleigh drew closer and Eska hugged her knees to her chest. It sounded different to the sled that had whisked her away from Winterfang. It was louder against the snow – heavier – and, instead of the patter of husky paws rushing through the trees, Eska could hear the pounding of hooves. Her blood froze. Musk oxen. And only one person rode a sleigh drawn by musk oxen. The Ice Queen.

Eska's skin chilled. The Fur Tribe would have brushed away her footprints from the Labyrinth the night before, but once a safe distance away from the hideout they would have left them – which meant the Ice Queen could track her. Eska chewed her lip. She couldn't stay: the Ice Queen had hexed these musk oxen so that they had the strength to run for hours on end. They would find her soon. She had to run, fast, as far as she could.

She lifted back a slat of wood and darted out of the shack into the dazzling sunlight, half running, half stumbling as she pushed through the trees. Her legs were unsteady beneath her and, after a few seconds, a stitch burned in her side, but she forced herself on, one boot in front of the other. She wasn't going back to Winterfang. Not now. Not ever.

Eska scrambled over fallen trees and skidded on patches of ice, but fear made her blunder on. Then she threw a glance over her shoulder. The Ice Queen's silver sleigh was there, fifty metres behind, carving a channel through the trees. The queen's eyes met Eska's and she smiled through thin blue lips, her teardrop gown billowing behind her. Two Tusk warriors, clad in breastplates of ice armour and holding whips and spears, stood on the sleigh either side of her and, in front, four enormous musk oxen with matted black coats and swooping horns churned up the snow.

'Stop! In the name of the Ice Queen!' the guards roared.

Eska dragged her legs on, her heart smashing against her ribcage. She needed the forest to close in, like it had around the Labyrinth, then the Ice Queen's sleigh wouldn't be able to force its way through. But the trees here were growing sparser and smaller and, from behind Eska, a whip lashed and the musk oxen ran faster.

Then, to Eska's horror, the trees stopped. Just like that. And she burst out into the open. In front of her now were the foothills of mountains: rolling valleys that folded in rivers of melting ice and little copses of trees, before eventually climbing up to form the Never Cliffs. The morning sun glittered over the hills and, with a sweeping sense of dread, Eska tried to keep running. But even the slightest incline bit back at her. She didn't have the stamina for the wild and she knew it.

The sleigh raced closer and Eska whirled round to see the Ice Queen, just metres away, standing in front of her cushioned seat, her staff held high in her hands. Eska grimaced and turned to carry on, but the queen's words wrapped round her like a snare.

'You ran away, Eska! Ungrateful child! After everything I did to keep you safe at Winterfang!'

'Keep me safe?' Eska panted as she ploughed up the hill. 'You held me under a curse!'

The moment the words left her mouth, Eska realised her mistake. Fear had made her careless; it had caught her off guard.

'So you *can* speak, you little wretch!' And then the Ice Queen laughed – a bitter laugh that made Eska's skin crawl.

She ran on, hardly daring to look behind her, then something hard and cold slammed into her back and she was flung, face first, to the ground. Spitting snow and gasping for breath, she looked up. A circle of musk oxen closed in, their heads hung low, their black ice horns glinting in the sunlight.

The Ice Queen held up her staff and the musk oxen stayed where they were, thrashing their horns from side to side, then she stepped off her sleigh, leaving the Tusk guards standing either side of it.

'I've come to take you home,' she cooed and the musk oxen parted as she stepped into their circle.

She stooped and slid five long white fingers round Eska's neck. Eska's pulse drummed at the sight of the red ring on the Ice Queen's thumb – she'd heard Slither say it was filled with frozen blood – then, quite unexpectedly, there was a scream from one of the guards.

The eagle had come out of nowhere, a golden bullet racing through the sky and ripping the guards' spears from their hands. The men grappled in the snow for their weapons, but before they could snatch them up the eagle turned and plummeted again, raking its talons across the guards' faces. The men fell to the ground, clutching their bloodied skin, while the eagle beat its mighty wings up into the sky once more.

Ignoring the guards' cries, the Ice Queen grabbed Eska by the scruff of her neck and dragged her towards the sleigh. She stamped her staff on to the snow and the musk oxen obeyed, gathering in line before the vehicle.

But the eagle was careering down again, its body tucked in like a barrel. Eska closed her eyes as the bird plunged towards her – she felt sure that it would never stop – but at the very last moment it spread out its wings and in one sweeping arc it dashed the staff from the Ice Queen's hand, splitting it in two with its talons.

The musk oxen jerked at the ropes that bound them to the sleigh, suddenly waking from the curse that the staff had held over them, and when their ropes snapped, the Ice Queen's grip on Eska loosened just long enough for her to dart free. She scrambled backwards, hardly noticing that something had slipped from her pocket into the snow, then flung herself into a run. Behind her, the Ice Queen screamed as the musk oxen, no longer under her command, charged off into the forest.

Eska ran at the hill, her ears ringing with the eagle's

high-pitched cries, and only at the top did she allow herself to glance back. The eagle was nowhere to be seen now, but the Ice Queen was bent over the snow and, with a shrill laugh, she picked something up and glared at Eska.

'I will steal your voice by force!' she shrieked. 'When Slither sees what I have here in my hand there will be no stopping his contraption!'

Eska's insides turned as she dug her own hand into her pocket. The key to the music box was no longer there. And, while she couldn't possibly know what Slither had created or how the Ice Queen planned to use the key, Eska realised the threat of it all because the queen was stalking off towards the forest, back to Winterfang, with her guards trailing blindly behind her. She could have battled on against the eagle if the bird had returned, but she hadn't and that fact lay like a cold dark stone inside Eska.

She watched the Ice Queen disappear into the trees, then turned back to the foothills. They rose and fell before her like waves and Eska wondered how anyone could remember their way through when every hill looked just like the last. She sighed, then her eyes fixed on a lone tree a little further down the hill.

And there was the eagle. Perched on a branch like a sentinel.

Eska approached slowly and stopped just a few metres away from the bird. And, as she watched the majestic creature, something like a memory, only looser and less defined, stirred inside her. It was a feeling that although she had no obvious place among Erkenwald's people she might just have a place among its animals. The feeling lingered for a second longer and then vanished and Eska carried on looking at the eagle.

It was the same one she had freed from the snare before Deeproots. She could see the wound to its left talon, still red and raw from the trap, but that hadn't stopped it attacking just moments ago. And Flint's words about it struggling to survive with an injured talon seemed almost ridiculous now.

But, even if Eska hadn't seen that talon, she would have known the eagle by its eyes: yellow orbs, fierce like the sun. The eagle blinked, then it launched itself off its branch and sailed across the hills until it was nothing more than a speck in the sky, leaving Eska alone once again.

Chapter Ten
Eska

Eska trudged on through the foothills, squinting into the glaring sun. The snow was melting in places with patches of grass, juniper and rocks poking out and once or twice she jumped as a chunk of snow crunched away from the hillside, then slid down into a hollow. She climbed up on to a ridge. She needed to find shelter, a place to hide should the Ice Queen return, but she was thirsty and hungry and her legs were close to buckling. She picked up a handful of snow and sucked on it, but it tasted stale, like animal sweat, and she spat it back out.

Eska looked out at the landscape before her. There wasn't a living soul in any direction – just the curved backs of the foothills. She sighed. This was a vast and silent emptiness that she knew nothing about. She thought of what Flint might do. He moved quickly, thought quickly and spoke quickly, but Eska did none of those things. She felt tears prick the back of her eyes as she remembered his words to her on the sled: *You don't even know anything.* And he was right. Flint was a part of the wilderness – he understood it – but, as Eska gazed upon it, she felt that it could swallow her whole.

She sat down on a rock, pulled her hood up against the wind and closed her eyes. She was an outcast whichever way she turned. And yet there had been that moment with the eagle on the hillside; somehow things had felt, for a fleeting second, almost familiar.

Eska's eyes sprang open as a noise – a high-pitched cry – sounded from further across the hills.

The cry came again, splitting through the wind, but when Eska threw back her hood she saw only snow-covered hills. She scrunched up her eyes and scanned the foothills and it was then she saw the eagle gliding above the ridges, a dark streak against the deep blue sky.

Eska watched the bird for a few seconds. Perhaps it was hunting for mice or marmots – Flint had said as much back on his sled – but, as she looked on, Eska began to wonder whether that was really what the eagle was doing. It didn't dive down to catch any prey, but it didn't sail off into the distance either. It just soared between the hills, back and forth, back and forth, as if – maybe – it was waiting for something.

Eska looked around. Perhaps it was waiting for another eagle. But no more birds appeared and, as the eagle cried again, Eska thought of Flint's words: *There's a bond between animals and tribes out here.* Her breath fluttered. Was the eagle helping her in return for saving it from the trap? Eska stood up and, because she had no bond with any person or any place, she found herself walking over the hills after the eagle.

She was hungry still and her legs ached more than ever, but something about the bird made her want to follow it and, as Eska crested yet another hill, her heart leapt. Before her lay a valley and in it was a wide, meandering river folded in on both sides by hills. There was a small forest wrapped round one of the hills to her left and beyond, where the river narrowed further up the valley into a ravine, she saw the landscape rise into jagged peaks. The start of the Never Cliffs, possibly, where Flint had said the Feather Tribe lay hidden. Maybe they would offer her protection. Maybe they would be more welcoming than the Fur Tribe and she'd be able to find a way to work with them to defeat the Ice Queen ... It wasn't much of a plan, but it was all she had, though if she was going to make the journey to find them she'd need to learn to hunt and build shelters first.

Eska skidded down the hillside, boots slipping on loose stones and snow, until she came to the river. She knelt beside it, cupping hands into the water where the ice had melted, and gulped the liquid down. It was cool and fresh, like drinking the wind, and when the ripples stilled Eska saw all the red, greens and blues of the rocks on the riverbed. Suddenly the landscape didn't seem as white and as bare as it had done before. The eagle cried above her again. She had been following it for at least an hour now and it seemed to do that every time she stopped to catch her breath – and

Eska couldn't help feeling, or hoping, that it was trying to lead her somewhere.

She walked on through the valley beside the river, keeping the eagle in her sights as it flew ahead, and, just when she felt that she couldn't possibly drag her legs on any further, the eagle landed on a rocky ledge leaning out over the river.

Eska blinked. She had been looking up at the eagle for so long that she had missed what had happened to the river. Before her was a waterfall, shielded on either side by crags and rowan trees, only the water itself hadn't melted up here. It was locked in ice still: a great white curtain built of icicles that hung in spiked ropes.

Eska thought of the organ in Winterfang. The icicles that formed that instrument had been conjured by dark magic – and every day she had trembled at the sight of them – but, though these were just as fierce and splendid, they did not bend to another's power. They were *wild* and gazing at them now Eska wondered whether she had found something as powerful as the Ice Queen.

She glanced up at the eagle, expecting it to fly away. But it simply sat, its eyes fixed on the waterfall level with its perch. Eska looked again, at the rocks either side, capped with polished ice, and at the jagged blue tips of the icicles hanging down. It was so quiet, this waterfall, but Eska sensed it was only holding its breath. One day soon, as the days stretched out and the melting began, it would roar. And, as she was thinking of the rush and pound of water to come, she found herself squinting at the frozen spirals, looking deeper, harder, than she had before. She clambered on to the rocks, aware of the eagle watching her every move, and her heart skipped a beat.

There was a tiny gap between the icicles in the waterfall and, behind that, Eska could see wood, not rock as she had expected. She edged still closer, her eyes glued to the ice, then suddenly the eagle squawked from its ledge and Eska looked down. She was only centimetres away from a sheer drop down to the river.

Carefully, Eska climbed over the rocks until they spread out into a platform beneath the eagle's perch. The waterfall hung like a veil in front of her and she noticed the rocky plinth she stood on extended right under it and that there was an opening in the ice large enough for a person to squeeze through. Eska could no longer see the eagle above her, but she could feel it watching, waiting, so she crept over the stone platform before ducking behind the ice.

Her eyes widened. On her left hung the waterfall, a silent shield, but on her right there was a small wooden door built into the rock face. Eska blinked. Did somebody live behind this waterfall, tucked out of sight from the rest of the world? Was it safe for her to stay? She thought of the Ice Queen and Slither brewing curses to snatch her voice – she needed shelter from their dark magic and this place was about as secret as shelters could come.

She stretched out her hand and knocked on the door. Silence. She knocked again, a little louder this time, but still no one answered. And then Eska reached for the handle, a piece of wood carved into a half-moon, and turned it.

The door creaked open and, as the light spilled in, a smile spread across Eska's face. Nestled into the rocky chamber in front of her there was a table laden with wooden bowls and spoons and boxed in by several chairs. There was a stove cut into the rock, too, and beyond that two beds draped with furs. Eska gasped. Someone had even chiselled a little tunnel into the right-hand side of the rock and a pane of glass had been fitted at the end. Eska wondered whether she might be able to see the eagle perched on its ledge from there, then her gaze fell to the item leaning against the tunnel wall. The best thing of all. A spear.

'I can hunt now,' Eska murmured. 'There'll be fish in the river – and probably bears around, too.' She paused. 'Though I'm not sure I'm quite ready to tackle them.'

She grinned. This had to be one of the food stores scattered over Erkenwald that Flint had mentioned. Somehow the eagle had led her right to it and, though Eska's mind was spinning with the discovery, she didn't rush inside right away. She crept back to the opening in the ice and looked up at the eagle on its ledge.

'Thank you,' she whispered.

Then she looked down at her feet and sighed. She was glad of the hideaway and all that it meant, but she was also sorry that now the eagle had repaid her favour she might not see it again. Eska's heart was filled with longing – for family, friends and a home that she remembered – but a little space inside it had opened up for the eagle and, as she dipped her head before the bird now, she hoped that it understood.

The eagle ruffled its feathers, but it didn't fly away. It just croaked, an impatient noise, as if it was eager for Eska to go inside.

She smiled. 'All right, all right. I'm going.'

She turned back beneath the waterfall, stepping inside the hideaway and closing the door softly behind her. Then she flopped on to one of the beds, shutting her eyes against the sunlight streaming in from under the door. She knew she should take the spear down to the river – it was past midday and she had to eat – but the furs were so soft around her that, within minutes, she was fast asleep.

When Eska woke, the hideaway was dark and cold. She sat up on the bed and her stomach growled.

'I should have gone fishing while it was light,' she muttered, scrambling out of bed and feeling her way down the little tunnel to the window.

She pushed the sack curtains aside and a strip of moonlight fell across the hideaway. Eska pressed her face up against the glass and looked out.

'Please be there,' she whispered.

But the stone ledge the eagle had been perched on was silhouetted against the moonlight – and it was empty. Eska turned away. Of course the bird wasn't there. It had repaid the debt and now it had left. Those were the ways of the wild.

'Hunt,' Eska said to herself. 'You need food. Then a fire.'

For a moment, her mind wandered towards the next day, and the day after that. What was she doing, really? What was her plan? Find the Feather Tribe when not even the Ice Queen, with all her dark magic, could root them out? Use her voice to free the prisoners at Winterfang when she didn't even understand its power and she knew the Ice Queen now had plans to steal it from afar?

Eska looked around her. Inside the hideaway she felt relatively safe, but she'd have to go out soon – to hunt, to get water and then on to find the Feather Tribe – and she'd be completely and utterly alone. The tasks ahead loomed large, but after a few minutes Eska shook herself.

'There's no time for that kind of thinking. I need to work out *how* to survive out here first. Then I can think about what happens next.'

She grabbed the spear. It had been carved from caribou antler and the end was tipped with a slice of flint bound with animal sinew. Gripping it hard, she opened the door.

And screamed.

There was a dark, round shape just in front of her on the rocks. For a second, Eska was rooted to the ground with fear and then the shape hissed and grew as two large wings flapped open and the eagle hurried to the opening in the waterfall before launching up into the sky. It landed, seconds later, on its ledge and Eska breathed out and laughed.

'You scared me,' she said as she crouched in the opening between the rock and the waterfall. And then Eska was silent for a moment as she realised that the eagle wasn't just perched on a slab of stone. There was a large bundle of sticks on that ledge and the bird was settled inside them. Eska gasped. Those sticks were a nest. This was the eagle's home.

'I thought you'd gone,' Eska said. 'Most people seem to take off after they've met me.'

The eagle yapped as if to disagree, then it shifted its weight. Eska watched. The bird was trying to tell her something – she could feel it – but she couldn't read its sounds and signals. Then she happened to look behind her, at where the eagle had been when she opened the hideaway door, and there, laid out on the rock, was a bird as white as milk.

'A ptarmigan,' Eska breathed.

And then she blinked in surprise. The bird's name had come to her just like that – as if she'd always known it – and somehow she knew instinctively that she could use the ptarmigan's feathers to fletch arrows before roasting its meat. Eska stayed very still. Were these memories stirring? Fragments of her past hovering closer? But, when several minutes passed and nothing more came to her, Eska picked up the bird and glanced at the eagle.

'You caught this for me, didn't you?'

The eagle yapped again and Eska dipped her head. Hunting for fish could start tomorrow because now she had food and shelter for the night. She stole back inside the hideaway and lit the stove – and, though there was an Ice Queen set on stealing her voice and a wilderness beyond the waterfall that seemed to shake the night air, Eska smiled.

She wasn't alone now. She had an eagle – a friend – on her side.

Chapter Eleven
Flint

Flint sat in the hammock in his bedroom, watching the long evening light beyond a circular window. A turret leaning out to the side of the tree house that he, Tomkin and Blu lived in, Flint's bedroom was more of a laboratory really. Curved walls were lined with wooden cupboards and inside these were hundreds of bottles, jars, test tubes and funnels filled with bubbling liquids. They were inventions still in progress and Flint always left the cupboard doors open when he was at home; it was important to keep an eye on his contraptions just in case they misbehaved.

He plucked at the silver strands that made up his hammock. He had spun it from moonlight, the gossamer of rare – almost extinct, Flint suspected – ice spiders and after several weeks of experimenting, and consulting the bark which bore the carvings about Erkenwald's magic, Flint had discovered that the strands guaranteed glorious dreams.

He gazed at some of his other creations lining the upper shelves. A football made of caribou hide and stuffed with a knot of wind which travelled so fast when kicked it was almost impossible for any opponent to stop; a clock that read the weather not the time – it poured snowflakes, fluttered sunbeams and oozed mist; a wooden chest in which he had trapped a thunderstorm (with the result that it let out a loud burp every now and again) and a pinch of stardust, and, if unleashed at precisely midnight, the chest rained silver coins for a month.

He sighed. There were lamps lit by sunbeams and rolls of string made from coils of mist. But everything remained locked inside this turret, usually behind closed cupboard doors, so that Tomkin didn't fly off the handle when he saw the inventions still very much existed. Flint swayed back and forth in his hammock and wondered whether it was only magic that Tomkin distrusted. It felt a little as if it might be him, too.

'What wrong, Flint?' came a little voice from among the cushions on the floor.

The cushions were snow clouds dusted with sunbeams that Flint had invented for comfort *and* warmth and Blu was a huge fan. She hurled one at Flint, but missed and several jars toppled off a shelf.

'*Shhhhhh*,' Flint whispered, leaping out of his hammock to check that none of the jars had cracked. He placed them back where they belonged. 'Tomkin's having a meeting in the kitchen with Blade and – I've told you before – you're only allowed to come in and see my inventions if you keep very, very quiet.'

Blu giggled as Pebble chewed on a cushion. It had been

half an hour, at least, since his last meal and the fox pup was already feeling peckish. Blu lifted Pebble into her lap as Flint flopped back into his hammock.

'You sad, Flint. I know you sad.'

Flint turned a magnifying glass over in his hand. It was infused with rainbow essence and could pick up footprints in the snow long after they had vanished from the naked eye. He'd used it earlier that day, reassuring Tomkin that it was the only one of his inventions that still existed and that it was an invaluable gadget when tracking animals for the tribe, but a small and very guarded part of him had been using it for another reason. To track Eska's footprints. Because, no matter how hard he tried to stamp her out of his head, he couldn't.

He thought back to their conversations on the sled. Eska's ideas had been wild and full of cracks, but Flint knew the power of wild ideas. And, despite what he had said to her, the line between angry and interested had been blurring. What if Eska had been right? What if Tomkin needed more than just spears and shields to stage a successful rebellion? But how could he convince a whole tribe to trust in magic again on the word of a strange girl?

Flint shifted in his hammock. He'd allowed Eska to be driven out into the wild where he was sure she wouldn't survive. And, though he'd found her tracks earlier that afternoon, there was now a curfew at the Labyrinth following his unsuccessful mission to Winterfang the day before and Blade had called Flint back before he could follow them for long. So – for all he knew – Eska might be dead already.

Flint swallowed. Outsider or not, she hadn't deserved this.

Blu settled the fox pup on her brother's chest, then wrapped her arms round them both. 'Hug for you.'

Flint smiled.

'Better?' Blu asked as she drew back.

'Better,' Flint replied, ruffling her hair. 'Always better after a Blu hug.'

There was a knock at the door – a quick, no-nonsense rap. Flint leapt up from his hammock and smacked a hand down on a wooden button on the wall. The cupboard doors closed, immediately hiding all his inventions from sight, then he shoved the cushions into a trunk, grabbed a spear and a polishing cloth, and turned the key in the door. Tomkin stood before him.

'Yes?' Flint asked, rubbing the cloth over the tip of his spear.

'Lofty's saying he found the tracks of a sleigh pulled by musk oxen in the forest,' Tomkin muttered.

Immediately, Flint thought of Eska. There was no way she would have escaped if the Ice Queen had found her.

'Blade thinks the Ice Queen was here looking for the girl you took from Winterfang.'

Blu cocked her head. 'Eska. I like Eska.'

Tomkin gave her a stern look. 'No, Blu. You don't. She – and your brother – have got us into a mess.'

Blu frowned. 'Everyone OK?'

'Yes.' Tomkin avoided her eyes. 'But that's not the point.' Blu skipped from the room and Tomkin turned to Flint. 'We need to be careful when hunting. If the Ice Queen found Eska in Deeproots, she'll assume one of the tribes helped her and are hiding nearby. There's no sign of the Ice Queen now, but you can bet she'll send her Tusk guards back to the forest to search the area.' He paused. 'So, I'm telling everyone to select hunting grounds wisely and keep watch at all times.'

Flint nodded. It was an effort to keep his mind on his tribe and hunting when he knew for certain now that Eska was at the mercy of the Ice Queen.

'Any sign of the girl?' he asked as casually as he could.

'No,' Tomkin replied. 'Lofty turned back at the sight of the sleigh marks.'

Flint scrubbed his spear harder, as if somehow that might undo the guilt he felt inside. He was a part of the Fur Tribe, but Eska's words had made him question his place here. Why, when he tried so hard to harness the mind of a Fur Tribe warrior, did he end up feeling more and more like an inventor? And why, when the Feather Tribe might know important things – like how best to fight the Ice Queen – did his tribe insist on cutting themselves off? Flint couldn't help feeling that he was as much of an outsider in the Labyrinth as Eska had been.

'I've doubled the hours on weapon-making and added another fighting session before breakfast,' Tomkin said. 'We'll need to be ready for the rebellion soon – and this time we won't lose.'

With that, he left the room and Flint slumped on to his hammock. He'd been wary of detours after so many failed missions, but he couldn't help feeling that Eska was a detour he should have pursued. Regardless of where it might have led him.

Chapter Twelve
Eska

Eska crouched on a stone in the middle of the river, squinting against the glare of the morning sun. She didn't like being out in the open, especially because, until just a few moments before, the valley had been ringing with the Ice Queen's anthem and Eska kept imagining Tusk guards, sent to drag her back to Winterfang, cresting the summits of the surrounding hills. But none came and she needed to prove to herself that on her first morning here she *could* find food. The water rushed around her, clear and sparkling and, she hoped, full of fish, because she couldn't let the eagle do all her hunting – that would be rude – and who knew how long it planned to stay? Maybe it had other nests.

Eska focused on the water, her spear hovering just centimetres from the surface. There was a cry from somewhere above her: the eagle's call and, so long as the bird was with her, she didn't feel afraid.

Minutes passed and, just as Eska was beginning to think perhaps there weren't any salmon swimming in the river, a shot of silver scales flashed beneath the surface. She launched her weapon, but, in her excitement, it wasn't just the spear she thrust forward. Her whole body went crashing into the icy water, too.

Quickly, she emerged, eyes and mouth wide with shock, and scrambled up on to the bank. The eagle had now landed and stood just a few metres away and, though Eska wasn't sure whether birds *could* look unimpressed, she felt that this one did.

She scowled at it. 'I suppose you'd have known better?'

The eagle glanced at the hideaway, then back to the river and Eska didn't need to speak eagle to understand what that meant. *Get dry. Come back. Try again.*

A short while later, Eska emerged from her hideaway, dry and warm. But it was nearing midday now and she still hadn't caught a fish. She walked along the bank and, just as she was getting ready to jump on to the rock in the middle of the river, the eagle squawked. Eska followed its gaze towards the sun and realisation slowly dawned.

'My shadow,' she murmured. 'It'll scare the fish . . .'

She wandered a little further downstream until she reached a point where the bank was low and the ice had melted from the edge. She knelt down in the snow and waited and, a few metres away, the eagle waited, too.

After several minutes, though, Eska grew stiff and she shook out her legs and changed position. The eagle hissed and Eska went back to waiting. When ten minutes passed and still no fish emerged, Eska thumped her spear down in the snow.

'It's no good.'

But the bird didn't move. It stayed exactly where it was, its feathers tucked into place, its eyes locked on the river. Eska sat despondently beside the bird, the seconds drifting into minutes, and she began to notice the silence around her. The whole valley was cloaked in quietness, but the longer she waited – and listened – the more the silence spoke. Water murmured, river ice groaned, a ptarmigan's wings whirred and a weasel scampered up a tree. She had somehow overlooked all this before. And Eska wondered then whether there was more to being a hunter than being big and strong. Perhaps it was just as important to be still – to listen keenly – and to see into the heart of the things that most people missed.

It took over an hour to catch her first fish, but, when Eska lifted the salmon out of the river on her spear, her face glowed with pride.

'I did it!' she laughed. 'I actually did it!'

The eagle ruffled its feathers and Eska found herself wishing that Flint had been there to see this, too. She tried to remember the ritual he'd told her about.

'Thank you, North Star,' she whispered, holding the fish up in her hands and glancing at the sky, 'wherever you are up there. And thank you, little fish, for choosing to submit your life to me.' She paused. She felt there should be more somehow. 'It was especially kind of you because I was getting really cold and a little bit uncomfortable sitting out here on the snow. So, you came along at just the right moment. Thank you very much and I hope—'

The eagle hissed so Eska decided perhaps it was time to wrap up the ritual.

'—that I have honoured the bond between animals and tribes. Even though I'm not strictly in a tribe. Yet.'

She gutted the fish, as she'd seen Flint do, and, with the eagle flying above her, she walked back to the hideaway.

Eska was surprised to see the bird swoop into the opening behind the ice and watch her, from the platform, as she cooked the fish on her stove. But she didn't shut the door or pretend the eagle wasn't there. Instead, she talked as she cooked, feeling glad of the bird's silent presence.

'If you're going to stick around,' Eska said, 'I'll need a name for you.'

The eagle yapped and Eska suddenly wondered whether it was annoyed.

'Not because you're a pet,' she added quickly. 'More because you're here and I'm here and—' She wanted to blurt out that she was lonely, that she was scared to go to sleep because her heart ached even in her dreams, but instead she concentrated on turning the fish, '—it would be nice to know your name.'

The eagle yapped again and Eska thought she might have misread the sound before because, now that she listened, she could hear the softness at its core.

'It should sound wild, this name.' Eska cut the fish in half. 'The kind of word the wind might use if it could speak.' She looked up. 'Because you're like the wind, you know. Fast and free and fierce.' She thought about the eagle showing her the hideaway and teaching her to fish. 'You're kinder than the wind though.'

She edged forward and placed half of the fish on the rock outside her hideaway. The eagle stayed where it was and it was only when Eska looked away and began to eat her own portion that the bird tucked into its share.

As they ate, Eska glanced at the eagle now and again. The wound from the snare was healing already and, as the minutes drew on, Eska felt something familiar stir inside her. The bird was proud and strong, but it was also protective – of her, at least – and its character felt like a trait she'd once known. A memory flickered then slipped from Eska's grasp. But a word remained, a name that was unmistakably female and that to Eska really did sound like the language of the wind.

'Balapan,' she whispered.

And at the name the eagle looked up and turned round, as if it had been waiting for Eska to say that word from the very first moment they met.

Chapter Thirteen
Eska

Eska could have stayed inside her hideaway for the rest of the day quite happily. But it turned out Balapan was bossy as well as protective and the eagle had yapped outside her door until Eska snatched up her spear and made her way out into the valley again.

Ears pricked for the sound of a sleigh, Eska trudged up the tallest of the hills after the eagle. She paused halfway up, her face shining with sweat, and watched as the eagle soared above her. Balapan's eyes didn't roam the hillside aimlessly as Eska's did. They darted about, from one part of the valley to the next, and as Eska looked harder – deeper – she saw the landscape as the eagle did: the herd of caribou denting the horizon on the other side of the valley; the ghost-like shape of a snow hare darting up a hill; and the footprints of wolves, lemmings and marmots scoring the snow around them.

Eska carried on walking, and watching, and in the hour that followed she found a discarded caribou antler that she realised could serve as a bow to accompany the quiverful of arrows she'd spotted in the hideaway. And she flushed a snow hare from its burrow, which Balapan pounced upon, and Eska decided she would use the animal to make mittens that fitted – the fur for gloves and the sinew for thread.

The wild was still vast and unknowable, but Eska was learning how to carve out her own small place in it. And, though this small place thronged with animals instead of people, Eska discovered, quite unexpectedly, that she was starting to feel a part of it, that she was less alone than she had thought.

She sat on a large rock and thanked the North Star and the snow hare's spirit for a successful hunt, then she turned to face Balapan, who was perched beside her.

'We make a good team, you and me.'

The eagle looked at Eska, long and hard, and in those bright yellow eyes Eska saw something precious, something she had almost given up on. The Ice Queen despised her, the Fur Tribe had driven her out, but this eagle was telling her she mattered.

Eska listened to the rush of river water echoing through the valley. 'I don't belong to a tribe – I don't really know where I fit in exactly – but if my tribe ends up just being you and me, Balapan, that would be enough.'

The eagle shuffled nearer until she was so close Eska could see the vane of each golden feather. Then she watched, hardly daring to breathe, as Balapan leant against her. The eagle felt warm and strong and at its touch a deep-buried chord inside Eska's heart thrummed because to know the closeness of another in a wilderness was to belong, even at the very edge of things.

But, when Balapan flinched, Eska knew something wasn't right.

Scooping the hare into the game bag she had found in the hideaway, Eska crept after the eagle as it flapped to the uppermost ridge of the hill. The eagle crouched below the skyline, with just her head poking over, and Eska did the same.

At first Eska saw only the towering peaks of the ice-capped Never Cliffs in the distance, but when she brought her gaze closer, down into the neighbouring valley, her stomach lurched. A sleigh, much bigger and much, much faster than the one she had seen before in Deeproots, was speeding between the hills.

They were too far away to hear anything, but Eska watched, rooted to the spot in fear, as six more musk oxen pulled the Ice Queen, flanked by a dozen Tusk guards in glistening armour, closer and closer towards the north of the valley. Eska's mind whirled. Was there a path from the neighbouring valley to hers? Could a sleigh pass through the ravine above the frozen waterfall?

She tore down the hillside, wincing as she stumbled on a loose stone and her ankle gave way beneath her. She forced herself up and, limping through the pain, carried on down the hill before weaving between the rowan trees by the river and clambering over the rocks leading down to the waterfall. Balapan slipped into her nest – a lookout should anything happen – and, with her ankle throbbing and her heart hammering, Eska squeezed through the opening in the ice and closed the hideaway door behind her.

Trying to ignore the burn in her leg, she waited, crouched in the tunnel before the window, her eyes wide with fear. She had drawn the sack curtains across the pane that morning, but through the narrowest of cracks Eska looked out now.

There was nothing for a long time and, as the light began to fade, Eska wondered whether perhaps the Ice Queen had failed to find a way through the valley and had given up and gone back to Winterfang. But then, out of nowhere: the sound of a sleigh from the north.

The Ice Queen was coming.

Eska drew back from the window, pinning herself against the tunnel wall. She listened as the sleigh pulled to a halt somewhere nearby and the grunts of the cursed musk oxen rumbled into the twilight. Eska's heart thumped at the clink of the Tusk ice armour, but she kept absolutely still. Then the Ice Queen's voice came, loud and sharp and so close Eska could almost feel the words slipping down her spine.

'I summon you foothills under my hold.
Take the girl and the boy into your fold.'

Eska's breath caught in her throat. *The girl and the boy . . .* Did the Ice Queen mean Flint? Had her candles whispered of his presence in Winterfang? And had Eska put him in danger even without the Fur Tribe taking her in?

The Ice Queen's voice dropped as she addressed her guards. 'The hills will only remain under my command until the midnight sun rises – in eleven days' time. I must achieve immortality before then so I can extend my power over every living thing in Erkenwald for ever: hills, rivers, forests, lakes.' She paused. 'And, once I've swallowed the voices of the Fur and Feather Tribes, I will kill every single one of them so that you, my Tusks, can share in the glory of an Erkenwald ruled by dark magic.'

There were murmurs of excitement from the guards, then the Ice Queen added, 'But if I fail to steal these voices in time I will vanish with the midnight sun and all those touched by my magic – my prisoners, Eska's memories *and* my Tusk Tribe – will perish alongside me.'

The guards were suddenly quiet and the Ice Queen went on. 'I must ride back to Winterfang; Slither's contraption is complete and I want to see if it does what he says it is capable of – but you will stay and search Deeproots. I want that forest patrolled. A boy from the Fur Tribe helped Eska escape and he must be taught a lesson. The girl needs to be isolated and helpless if I am to take her voice before she learns about the power of the Sky Song.'

At the mention of the Sky Song, Eska risked a glance through the window. The Ice Queen was standing on a rock overhanging the river, her fingers wrapped round a staff of glistening black crystal. It was taller and thicker than her previous sceptre and at the sight of it Eska withdrew. The Ice Queen thumped her staff against the rock and the musk oxen lashed their horns against the nearby branches. Moments later, Eska heard the lurch of a sleigh and then, finally, there was silence once again.

She peered out of the window to see the silhouette of the eagle standing up in the nest on the ledge. Eska breathed a sigh of relief, but as she thought of the hills boxing in the valley, dark and tall and bidden to the Ice Queen's commands, she shivered. And what was this mysterious Sky Song the queen spoke of? Did it have something to do with her voice? She reached a hand up to her throat, suddenly frightened by what might lie inside it, then she shook herself and lit a lamp.

Eleven days. . . that's what the Ice Queen had said. Just eleven days until the midnight sun and the queen took power over the whole kingdom. Eska gulped. Even if the Ice Queen failed to achieve immortality in that time the consequences would be disastrous: the prisoners at Winterfang would die and her memories – every single recollection of her past – would be lost for ever. Eska's heart was racing now. There was no more time to prepare; she needed to press on into the Never Cliffs as soon as possible to find the Feather Tribe in the hope that they could help her. But her ankle was pounding and, as she eased off her boot, Eska saw that it was purple and swollen. She cursed under her breath. It would be a few days before the sprain healed enough for the journey onward.

Eska looked at her reflection in the metal of a dagger she had found in the hideaway. A girl stared back at her, but despite the sunken cheeks and straggled hair, this girl's eyes were hard. The Ice Queen said she wanted Eska isolated and helpless, but that wasn't going to happen.

Because she wasn't the timid little prisoner she had been, locked inside the music box at Winterfang. She was out in the wild now – with a golden eagle by her side – and for the first time since leaving the palace, Eska dared to hope that the sum of all that might be enough against an Ice Queen with the power to conjure whole valleys to do her bidding.

Chapter Fourteen
Eska

During the days that followed, Eska bound her ankle with caribou hide and filled every waking hour learning how to face the wild head-on so that she was ready for the Never Cliffs when the time came. She took care of her shadow when fishing; she learnt to spot camouflaged snow hares by the flicker of their eyelids; she got her hunting ritual down to just a few words; she tracked snow buntings and geese to see where in the snow they plucked the mountain cranberries from; and, with each hour that passed, she grew to understand Balapan more. She knew which yap meant 'yes' and which meant 'no'; she could tell the difference between a hiss and a squawk and a cry from the clouds that could only come from an animal that knew it was free.

What she didn't understand though was her voice – how every morning since the Ice Queen's visit her throat felt tighter and sorer than the day before and a strange iciness seemed to linger on her tongue. At first she had put it down to fear, but as the days bled on, and each morning her throat became increasingly painful and the cold in her mouth grew sharper, Eska felt sure the music box key and Slither's contraption were behind things. Was the Ice Queen inching closer and closer to stealing her voice?

On the sixth morning after the Ice Queen's visit to the valley, the morning Eska planned to leave for the Never Cliffs now that her ankle had healed, she woke to an almighty crash.

She sat bolt upright in her bed and reached for the dagger under her pillow. The anthem from Winterfang was drifting through the valley, but Eska listened beyond that. There was another noise – a roaring, churning, raging sound – and it was coming from just outside the hideaway.

Eska leapt out of bed, clasping her knife tight, and strained her ears towards the door. She recognised that roar . . . It was water – gallons of it – pouring down the valley. She edged towards the window and pulled the sacking back. Balapan was still there, tucked up in her nest, because she could tell without even opening her eyes which were the noises to be frightened of. And this ear-splitting roar was nothing to do with the Ice Queen. This was the wild talking.

Eska threw on her furs, then opened the door to her hideout.

The frozen fall was no longer there. Instead, a torrent of water burst over the ledge above her, cascading through the sunlight in a glittering curtain. Eska pushed her hair back from her eyes and peered through the water.

She could see the whole valley, snowy hills spliced into slithers by the waterfall, and she knew that, although her ankle was strong enough for the journey onward now, and with the midnight sun only five days away she needed to press on, she would miss these hills. They'd come to feel a bit like home. She cast her eyes towards the largest hill, the one whose snow still clung in knee-deep layers, and blinked. She could have sworn she saw something dark moving across it. She squinted harder. These shapes weren't moving like animals; they were moving, unmistakably, like humans.

Eska swung her quiver over her shoulder, then crouched in the opening between the rock face and the waterfall. Balapan's eyes were fixed on the hillside. Whoever it was out there, the eagle had seen them, too.

For a while, Eska just watched, but, when two figures swung into clear view round the middle of the hill, she frowned. They were a long way away, but even from this distance Eska could see that they weren't especially tall and they weren't clad in ice armour either.

'Members of the Fur Tribe?' she whispered.

Eska watched the figures slogging through the snow, then she listened to the Ice Queen's anthem and thought of the command the queen had given to her guards. Were the Fur Tribe still safe now that Tusk guards patrolled the forest? She knew she shouldn't care – this was a tribe that had cast her out – but somehow she did, despite what had happened.

She glanced up at Balapan. 'Come on. Let's take a closer look. I need to know that Flint and his tribe are safe.'

Eska strode off. The eagle didn't follow, but the pull of other people drew the girl away from the waterfall. She kept to the rowan trees at first and when out in the open she darted between rocks and ridges. She couldn't risk being seen just in case the figures were in fact Tusk guards.

But when she reached the foot of the largest hill and squatted down behind the boulders at its base, the remains of a long-ago landslide, Eska heard Balapan cry. High-pitched, drawn out, it was a warning.

Eska scoured the hillside for the figures and saw them halfway up, two dots against the snow. The Ice Queen's anthem drifted away, then there was a loud grinding sound and, before Eska could even cry out, an enormous chunk of snow broke free from the summit and began sliding down the hill. The figures ran, but, although they were nimble and fast, they couldn't outpace what was coming. Because this was no ordinary avalanche. This was a hillside under the Ice Queen's control and for some reason it had waited until now to attack.

The snow swallowed everything in its path and as it surged down the hill it seemed to gather itself up into a roaring mass of white. Eska's mouth dropped open. The avalanche was full of faces built from the snow itself – horns and fangs and bulbous noses, hooded eyes, pointed ears and gaping mouths – and they leered forward, spreading jagged wings, as the snow roared around them.

Realising that the avalanche was now only metres away from the figures below, Eska leapt up on to the boulders, her instinct to help overcoming her fear of who these people might actually be.

'Move to the side, not down!' she yelled. 'You can't outrun this!'

But her voice felt sticky in her throat, as if the words were only just struggling out. She darted round the side of the hill and threw her arms up in the air.

'Over here!' she cried. 'Over here!'

The figures swerved towards Eska. But the avalanche was moving faster now, and with a hideous roar the faces in the snow swallowed the figures and continued to tear down the hillside. Without thinking, Eska rushed towards the pulsing wall of snow. She could hear voices screaming from inside the avalanche, then something small was tossed up into the mist. It landed by Eska's boots and she snatched it up. It was a necklace made from willow twine and for a second Eska paused, as if half remembering something, but there was no time to think. If she didn't yank the victims free, they'd suffocate or be dashed to their deaths on the boulders at the bottom of the hill.

She charged on up the mountain, ignoring the spray of ice on her face and the cries of the golden eagle circling above, then she flung her bow to the ground and, as the avalanche reared above her, she fixed her eyes on the figures tossing and turning at its edge, and charged into its throes.

For a second, the world turned white, but Eska knew

she had to act before the snow spun her upside down so she reached out, grabbed hold of an arm and, as the snow raged around her, she yanked hard and, just a split second before she lost her footing completely, she burst free from the avalanche. She pulled back from the figure and gasped.

She was face to face with Flint.

And suddenly she realised who the willow-twine necklace belonged to.

'*Blu*,' Eska murmured as she watched the avalanche storm towards the boulders at the bottom of the hill.

Flint blinked at Eska in disbelief, and Pebble did the same from his parka hood, then he scrambled to his feet after his little sister. But the eagle had beaten him to it and he watched, open-mouthed, as the bird dug its talons into Blu's shoulders. The snow faces snarled and hissed and one or two flung jagged wings towards Blu, but Balapan had her now – she wasn't letting go – and as the avalanche raged on the eagle dragged Blu from its sway.

Eska watched the writhing snow smash into the boulders at the bottom of the hill and, as it spilled out into the river and was carried from the valley, she thought about the Ice Queen's enchantment: *I summon you foothills under my hold. Take the girl and the boy into your fold.* The hill had waited until both she *and* Flint were in the valley so that it could ensnare them both at once.

Flint tore down the hill towards Blu who was lying to the side of the boulders, but Balapan rushed towards Eska and this time the eagle didn't land beside her. She swooped on to the girl's shoulder and, as Eska stood on the snow-strewn hillside, she felt the bird's talons wrap round her bones and she wondered then about her past, about whether she'd ever been held this tight.

Chapter Fifteen
Flint

Flint knelt by his sister and wrapped his arms around her.

'It's okay, Blu. It's okay.' Pebble crawled out of his hood and licked Blu's cheek. 'I've got you now.'

Blu's bottom lip was trembling. 'Snow alive, Flint. It angry. Why the snow angry?'

Flint brushed the ice crystals from her furs. 'It's gone now, Blu. We're safe. It's all right.'

And then he turned to face Eska. She was there on the hillside still, just a few metres above them, but this was not the feeble girl he had helped escape Winterfang. This girl was different. Her stance was tough, her red hair was braided with feathers and plaits, and on her shoulder there perched a golden eagle. It was the same one Flint had seen trapped in the snare before Deeproots – he could see the scar on its left talon – but what on earth was it doing with Eska? And how had she survived in the wild for so long? He scooped up Pebble and stumbled to his feet, but, on seeing Eska, Blu pushed past him.

'Eska!' she cried, clapping her hands. 'My friend! I miss you!'

Balapan launched herself into the sky, unsure what to make of the bundle of fur charging towards her, but Blu wasn't fazed. She flung her arms round Eska and squeezed her tight.

Eska blushed. 'Hello, Blu.'

The little girl drew back. 'Flint looking for you in forest!'

Flint plucked a clump of ice from Pebble's fur. 'Quiet, Blu.'

She scrunched up her nose. 'Flint looking for you, Eska! At night when Tomkin sleeping. And today on hunt. Always looking with his magic glass!'

Flint was suddenly glad that his magnifying glass was tucked away in his rucksack and not out in his palm, searching for Eska's tracks, as it had been only a few hours before.

'We came out to the foothills to hunt ptarmigan, actually. The Tusk guards are patrolling the forest now and we can't access our usual hunting spots.'

Blu smiled. 'We came to find you, Eska. Flint forget.'

Flint scowled at his sister. 'We strayed a little further than previous hunts this morning to, um, find the best ptarmigan ... but we didn't expect to stumble into the Ice Queen's enchantments.' He looked around the valley. 'So, you found another tribe to take you in then?'

Eska glanced at Balapan wheeling above them. The bird was wary of the visitors, but she could tell that these ones meant no harm. 'Yes.'

Flint frowned. 'The Feather Tribe? In the Never Cliffs?'

'No.' Eska picked up her quiver and slung it over her shoulder. 'It's just me and Balapan.'

The eagle cried above them, carving its circles in the bright blue sky.

Flint shook his head. 'You survived out here, in the wild, without a tribe?'

'I've got a tribe,' Eska replied. 'It's just not very big yet.'

'But – who taught you to hunt? How did you find shelter?'

Eska shrugged. 'Balapan.' Then she added, 'The golden eagle.'

'But . . .' Flint's words trailed away.

'She showed me the hideaway, then she taught me to hunt,' Eska explained. 'Fish first, down by the river, then hares up in the burrows on the ridges. Ptarmigan, too, once I'd bent the caribou antler into a bow, strung it with sinew and fletched my arrows.' The words spilled out, toppling over each other in their strangely magnetic way, as Eska negotiated her first proper conversation since leaving Deeproots. And all the while Flint listened, his jaw open. 'We get along pretty well, Balapan and me, so long as I remember to wash up my dishes after hunts. But I suppose washing-up is to be expected in tribes. It's not exactly fun though, is it?' She paused. 'Sorry, I forgot you don't much like talking.'

Flint was too shocked to speak, but Blu simply rolled her eyes. 'Keep up, Flint. Eska good hunter.' She grinned. 'Let's eat Eska food.' There was a growl of approval from Flint's arms. 'Pebble hungry, too.'

And Flint was surprised to see that Eska didn't flinch at Blu's demands or even seem to hold a grudge about what the Fur Tribe had done to her when she'd asked to be welcomed in. She simply handed Blu the necklace she'd found in the snow and nodded towards the river.

'This way to the hideaway,' she said.

Flint was quiet as they walked and while Blu chattered away to Eska he glanced up at the eagle soaring over the valley. It didn't seem to be following them exactly, but he could tell that it was watching their every move. Flint knew about the bonds between animals and tribes during hunts – he'd learnt all about that from his pa – but no one had ever spoken of an animal teaching a person the ways of the wild. And yet somehow Balapan had helped keep the girl alive, against all the odds.

He walked on in silence, but, when Eska led them behind the waterfall to the wooden door built into the rock, Flint couldn't hide his astonishment.

'You – you found the Giant's Beard!' he stammered. 'The waterfall that freezes all through winter and hides Erkenwald's most secret food store . . .'

Eska pulled the door open. 'Well, technically, Balapan found it.'

The eagle settled into its nest on the ledge outside and Blu patted Eska's back. 'This amazing, Eska!'

Flint stepped inside and his eyes travelled over the beds, table and chairs and the little pieces of the wild Eska had collected: red quartz from the riverbed on the windowsill;

pine needles scattered over the floor; and snowy-owl feathers twisted round the base of a lamp.

'It really is . . .' Flint murmured as he closed the door. And then he realised what he'd said and reached for some new words. 'Snargoyles – that's what we ran into back on the hill.'

Eska lit the stove while the others took a seat. 'Snargoyles? So that's what happens when the Ice Queen calls the hills to obey her . . .'

Flint nodded. 'Snow hexed by dark magic does strange things. Lofty said he saw snargoyles in this valley shortly after the battle last year and none of us came back after that.' He paused. 'Until we decided to hunt here today, of course.'

'Without bows or arrows,' Eska said, avoiding his eyes.

Flint shifted in his seat. He couldn't help feeling he was losing control of the conversation, something that often seemed to happen with Eska. He sank into silence as Eska reached for the plucked ptarmigan. She threw one, still raw, to Pebble who squealed with delight and then she knelt by the fire as the meat cooked.

The silence dragged on and Flint's eyes widened as Eska plated up the meat and handed the food around.

'Thank you,' he said, after a while. 'For the ptarmigan and for helping us out with the snargoyles. I don't know what would have happened if you and Balapan hadn't shown up.'

'Just keeping a promise,' Eska said quietly.

Flint thought back to her words on his sled: *One day I'll repay you for rescuing me.* They were words that he had scoffed at and yet Eska had kept to them. Because of her courage and loyalty he and his sister were still alive – and, on realising that, something inside Flint thawed. This was a girl he and his tribe had vastly misjudged.

He took a deep breath. 'I think, maybe, I was wrong about you, Eska.'

Eska smiled then, a wide smile that reached her ears, and Flint found himself wondering whether birthplace, parentage and appearance were really the things that you should list people under. Somehow courage and loyalty seemed like better markers.

Eska launched into all that had happened since leaving the Labyrinth: being chased on to the foothills by the Ice Queen's sleigh, Balapan saving her, the queen's plans to curse Erkenwald and wipe out the Fur and Feather Tribes, and the mysterious mention of the Sky Song.

Flint tried to imagine his beloved forest cursed by the Ice Queen's power: trees rotted through, lynx hexed to obey her, the Labyrinth destroyed and his whole tribe gone. His heart trembled at the thought.

After a while, Blu got up to play with Pebble, but Flint and Eska kept talking through the day and, though he said nothing, Flint couldn't help noticing the change in Eska's voice. Her body was sturdier, even the way she moved was more decisive, but her voice – although still strangely captivating – was undoubtedly weaker. Once or twice, she tried to clear her throat, as if she could tell there was something wrong and was embarrassed by that fact, but it didn't sound like a tickle or a cough to Flint.

Eska leant back in her chair and sighed. 'I still don't know who I am. Or why my voice is important. Or what this Sky Song is. Or even how I'm going to stay hidden from the Ice Queen.'

'I don't think people stop evil by staying hidden.' Flint looked through the window at the afternoon shadows cast by the rowan trees. 'I think they stop it by standing out.'

Eska pulled her hair back from her face and wound it into a plait. 'But the midnight sun rises in five days! How—' Flint gasped and Eska spun round. 'What? Am I doing the conversation wrong again?'

'Look back at the window for a second,' Flint murmured, then he leant forward and peered at her neck. 'You have a birthmark just below your hairline.'

'Oh,' Eska replied. 'Is that good or bad?'

Flint grinned. 'It's big – the size of my fist – and the pattern is so clear I could have drawn it on! It's the Little Bear, the constellation of the Sky Gods!'

Eska's face paled. 'The Ice Queen told me that I bore the mark of the Gods – that it was the proof that I was cursed. I didn't know what she meant, until now.'

Flint shook his head. 'You're not cursed, Eska.'

'How do you know? I've got the mark to prove it!'

Flint shook his head. 'Because since we met you've got me thinking. Two whole armies of warriors weren't enough to defeat the Ice Queen last summer and Tomkin's rebellion will be no different, no matter how many extra training sessions he organises.' He paused. 'I know that Erkenwald's magic *can* be used for good.' His face reddened at the words kept secret for so long. 'And I think your birthmark is a sign that *your voice* is the key to defeating the Ice Queen.'

At the mention of her voice, Eska winced, and Flint couldn't help feeling that she was holding a secret back. She grabbed her spear. 'Raise your knife, too, so that I've got a mirror behind me. I want to see the birthmark.'

Flint did as she asked and as Eska looked at the constellation stamped on her skin she swallowed. 'I was planning to leave for the Never Cliffs today to seek out the Feather Tribe, but then the snargoyles attacked.' She gripped her spear. 'It's too late to go on now but I need to set off at first light tomorrow because time is running out. The Feather Tribe might know something about my past or the Sky Song, and to defeat the Ice Queen I'm going to need to know more than I do now.'

Flint nodded, then he was silent for a few minutes. He knew he should be getting back to Tomkin – this was exactly the sort of 'detour' his brother was always warning him about – but Flint's gut was telling him to go on with Eska. He thought of his ma trapped in Winterfang, and Erkenwald emptied of the Fur and Feather Tribes, and its rivers, mountains and oceans cursed by the Ice Queen. What if, by journeying to the Never Cliffs with Eska, he could prevent all that? What if he could stage a rescue mission that worked not only for his ma, but for all the others prisoners, too, a mission that would make Tomkin proud of him for once?

But there was Blu, currently dangling titbits of food before Pebble who jumped up and gobbled them down. He couldn't leave her here. She didn't have the co-ordination to hunt on her own or the strength to spend nights in the wilderness with no one by her side. But he couldn't tell her to go back to Deeproots – she wouldn't find her way without his help – and going back to the Labyrinth with her would mean risking the Tusk guards and Tomkin's rules. But to come with him, if he went on with Eska? She wouldn't keep up in the Never Cliffs: she wouldn't be able to cope with the dangers around them.

'I want to come with you, Eska,' Flint said quietly.

And Eska nodded as if, perhaps, she could read him a little better than he thought.

'But Blu,' Flint whispered. 'She'd be slower than us. And she wouldn't understand things.'

Eska watched Blu rolling on the bed with Pebble. 'We'll look after her,' she said. 'You, me and Balapan.'

Flint bit his lip. 'It's a big thing looking after her. Bigger than you think.'

Eska nodded. 'I know. But that's what tribes do.'

Flint was taken aback by her words. Not many people had the patience for Blu – and fewer still the understanding – but somehow Eska, an outsider he knew next to nothing about, seemed to have both. And her acceptance stirred something deep inside Flint's heart.

Eska looked around the hideaway. 'We'll leave at first light, after—'

Blu hurried to the window. 'Something there,' she said, frowning. 'Something in the trees.'

Eska looked over Blu's shoulder. 'Balapan's still in her nest, Blu. It's okay. She'd let us know if there was anything to worry about.'

Blu shook her head. 'Something there. I saw it. Big shape.'

Flint drew Blu back to the table. 'Come on, Blu. It was probably just—'

A shiver rippled through Flint because there were footsteps crunching through the snow outside, accompanied by a low, husky breathing. Someone or something was approaching the Giant's Beard.

Eska grabbed her spear with one hand and Blu with the other, then Flint edged forward on silent feet before lowering an eye to a small crack in the door. His stomach tilted.

White fur. An eye as black as coal.

'Erkenbear,' he whispered, his voice laced with dread.

Chapter Sixteen
Eska

Eska ground her words out over her fear. 'We can take it. All of us together. If we—'

There was a knock at the door and Flint leapt backwards. 'Erkenbears don't knock!'

The knocking came again, an urgent pounding against the wood.

Eska swallowed. 'This one does.'

'Open up!' The voice on the other side of the door was a throaty growl. 'I'm a friend.'

Eska slid a glance to Flint. 'You're absolutely positive it was a bear?'

'Yes!' Flint spluttered. 'I saw it!'

There was a loud thud and the door swung open, clattering back against the hideaway wall. An enormous Erkenbear reared before them, its coat shining silver in the early evening light, its mouth a gaping maw of daggered teeth. And suddenly a new scent hung in the air: one of ice and snow and, very faintly, blood.

Blu crawled beneath the table with Pebble, but Flint and Eska stood side by side, their weapons raised.

Eska tried to think as Balapan had taught her. Calmly, boldly. She brandished her spear. 'Come any closer and we'll . . . we'll stick these in you.'

And then a strange thing happened. The bear's head flopped back and a man's face appeared beneath it: a long white beard tipped with ice and skin as gnarled as washed-up timber. Eska peered closer. This was an old man wearing an Erkenbear pelt.

'But . . .' Flint blinked. 'You were a bear outside. I know you were! The way you moved and growled.'

'What an extraordinary thing to say,' the old man murmured. 'My pelt must have confused you.' But as he spoke his breath puffed out into a mist of ice and behind it Eska could have sworn she saw him wink.

Flint rubbed his eyes. 'And now . . . But there are no grown-ups left out here! The Ice Queen took them all to Winterfang after the battle.'

The old man brushed the snow from his furs. 'She didn't take me.'

Eska watched the man carefully. His eyes gleamed like drops of polished night, his beard was as white as his furs and his large, weathered hands could easily have passed for paws. She had seen the Erkenbears out on the ice while locked in Winterfang Palace and watched the skull-crushing blows they could wield. She had heard their grunts and roars, too, and as the old man spoke Eska thought she heard something of that wildness in his voice.

Blu poked her head out from beneath the table. 'What happening, Flint? I scared.'

Flint narrowed his eyes at the old man. 'Who are you? And how do we know we can trust you?'

'Because of your eagle,' the man replied. 'It saw me approach, but it didn't seek to warn you.'

Eska stiffened. 'How do you know that eagle's got anything to do with us?'

'I'm closer to the wild beasts than you might think.' The old man smiled and Eska saw a gentleness in his midnight eyes. He bent down so that he could see under the table. 'I mean no harm, little ones. You can come out if you want.'

Blu scooped Pebble into her arms, but stayed where she was. 'You feed Pebble. He hungry. Again.'

The old man drew a pouch out of a pocket in his furs. Inside were cubes of frozen meat and he placed several before Pebble's paws. The fox pup waddled out of Blu's lap, sniffed the meat and then munched hard before letting out a small burp.

Blu grinned. 'I Blu. Boy is Flint – best brother in the world – and girl is Eska. She my friend.'

The old man straightened up. 'I'm glad to have found you all for I've things to say that you must hear.'

Eska half turned so that she could whisper to Flint. 'We need all the help we can get before we set off for the Never Cliffs and he's right that Balapan would've warned me if there was dark magic in the air. I think we trust him. For now.'

Flint nodded to the old man. 'Take a seat. But if you try anything remember Eska wasn't lying – we'll stick the spears in you.'

They gathered round the table and though it was an old man that sat in a chair opposite them Eska couldn't help feeling as if she was in the presence of an Erkenbear and that made her sit up straight and listen hard.

The visitor leant forward and his pelt shimmered. 'My name is Whitefur, though many know me as the Ever-Wandering One.'

Flint turned his knife over in his hands. 'Which tribe do you belong to?'

The old man raised an eyebrow. 'No tribe that you would know of, boy.'

Flint frowned. 'Everyone belongs to a tribe. Fur, Feather, Tusk. That's how it works.' He glanced at Eska. 'I think.'

Whitefur shook his head. 'Belonging is not about knowing your tribe. It's about trusting people whatever their tribe.' He paused. 'There are many ways to belong.'

Eska's cheeks reddened because, although Whitefur had directed his reply at Flint, something about his words tiptoed close to her heart.

'I walk with the wild,' Whitefur said. 'With Erkenbears and snowy owls, with wolves and drifting caribou. *That's* my tribe.' He looked at Eska. 'And I know who you are, child.'

Eska's pulse thumped.

'You're like me. A Wanderer. Someone with an unbreakable bond to the wild.'

Wanderer. Eska turned the word over in her head.

'You don't slot into a tribe perhaps, but you fit in with the wild. You're a part of it. Just look at the bond you share with that eagle.' He paused. 'There are only a handful of us scattered across the land now and, when the Ice Queen took you, we feared the worst.'

Eska leant forward, hungry for the truth. 'Took me from where?'

'From your mother and father.' Whitefur looked down. 'They were Wanderers, too.'

Eska's heart fluttered as the pieces of her past gathered closer.

'Wanderers hear and see things others miss,' Whitefur went on. 'And we knew, from the way the whales sang and the wind blew that night last spring, that the Tusk shaman, under the influence of the Ice Queen, killed the Tusk Chief. But, when your father visited the Fur and Feather Tribes and tried to explain the truth, they wouldn't believe him. He tried to tell them that the only way to defeat the Ice Queen would be to fight back using Erkenwald's magic, but mistrust and suspicion had already started working their way into people's hearts and minds and, before long, the bonds between the tribes, and the people's belief in Erkenwald's magic, had crumbled. When the day of the battle came, the Wanderers fought alongside the Fur and Feather Tribes, but we were small in number and unable to conjure enough magic to force the Ice Queen back.'

Eska bit her lip. 'My parents fought in the battle?'

Whitefur nodded. 'And you did, too. You've been wielding bows and arrows since you were tiny and, no matter how many times your parents tried to persuade you to stay hidden that day, they couldn't keep you from their side – you were adamant that you wanted to fight.'

He looked down and was silent for a few moments. 'Your mother was killed out on the ice, by a wolverine bewitched by the Ice Queen.' The old man's eyes softened. 'She loved you, Eska. With a fierce kind of love that could rattle mountains.'

Eska felt the room sway. She had had a mother, one who'd loved her, but knowing that had come too late. Beneath the table, two little arms wrapped round her legs. Blu couldn't really understand what was going on, but she could sense Eska's sadness and she held on tight.

Whitefur sighed. 'Blackfina, she was called, and she was as much a part of the sea around Erkenwald as the whales that glide through its waves. She understood the underwater songs of orcas and narwhals and she swam down into the depths with the seals.'

Eska tried to take it all in and when she closed her eyes she saw a woman standing on the cliff top above the ocean. Her long red hair streamed out in the wind and, above her, a flurry of kittiwakes cried. The memory slipped from her grasp and Eska's heart surged with longing.

'Eska's father,' Flint said quietly. 'Is he alive?'

The old man nodded. 'Wolftooth still lives.'

Eska slumped back in her chair because there it

was – *hope* – the knowledge that she had a person out there to call her own.

Flint glanced at Eska. 'We need to find him.'

But Whitefur shook his head. 'He's a prisoner in Winterfang Palace.'

Eska gasped. Her father had been so close to her – all those lonely days and nights in the music box – and yet she had never known.

'What happened?' Eska asked. 'Why did I end up alone in that music box?'

'Because of your voice and all the possibilities inside it. From the moment you were born and we saw the mark of the Sky Gods on your neck, we Wanderers knew you were special. In the days when the Sky Gods still danced at night, we used to hear them singing, too, and they sang of a child with a voice so powerful it could save Erkenwald if darkness came.'

Flint turned to Eska. 'See,' he said softly. 'You were never cursed; you were marked to stand out.'

Eska felt the weight of Flint's and Whitefur's words. For a long time she had hoped she might be able to use her voice for good instead of evil, but now she could feel the Ice Queen stealing it from afar and if Flint and Whitefur knew that maybe they'd give up believing in her and she'd be all alone again. Eska shifted in her seat. The thought of her voice being more powerful than the Ice Queen's staff and anthem and endless dark magic seemed to be growing horribly unlikely.

Whitefur went on. 'The Ice Queen, a fallen star from the Little Bear constellation, was jealous of you from the very start, Eska, and she and her shaman had the deadliest Tusk warrior and a pack of wolverines seek you out at the battle. The wolverines wrenched your mother away from you and when your father realised he had lost Blackfina he held you close to him and tried to fight on. But the Tusk warrior was fighting with dark magic on his side and I remember watching, powerless to help, as he dragged you and your father to the palace.'

Whitefur met Eska's eyes. 'The queen threw your father into the ice towers and you were shut away in her music box. Later, we Wanderers heard your father's voice singing in her choir, but not yours, and we assumed you had been killed. Until a few days ago, when, in the dead of night, your eagle found me while I was hunting on the Driftlands. It flew round and round until I realised that it was flying in the same pattern each time it circled – the shape of the Sky Gods' constellation – and I knew it was a sign that you might still be alive. I watched the direction the eagle flew off in, then I followed, and when I arrived in this valley a few days later I remembered the Giant's Beard, one of Wolftooth's favourite food stores.'

Eska brushed a hand against the table leg. Had her pa sat at this very table? Had he slept in the bed she lay down in each night? The possibilities tingled inside her, then she thought of her ma dying to protect her in the battle at Winterfang and a lump lodged in her throat.

'I never asked for any of this,' she said quietly, 'for a voice so dangerous and terrible it got my ma killed and my pa locked up.'

Whitefur ran a hand through his beard and little specks of ice floated to the ground. 'Dangerous, perhaps. Terrible, no. You have a gift, Eska. Your voice has the power to do great things if you use it wisely.'

'But my voice is getting weaker!' Eska blurted out.

She looked down. Whitefur deserved to know the truth – he was helping her find a way back to her past – and so did Flint. Eska realised that now, despite what it might mean for her.

'Every morning when I hear the Ice Queen's anthem, I feel something cold inside my mouth – like icy fingers trying to reach down my throat and pluck at my words.'

Whitefur growled and beneath the table Pebble scurried behind Blu.

Eska went on nervously. 'When I escaped from Winterfang I took the key from the music box with me but out in the foothills, the Ice Queen snatched it back.' She paused. 'It's cursed and I know that she planned to give it to her shaman, Slither, so that he could finish a contraption designed to steal my voice.' Eska sniffed. 'At the moment, the Ice Queen can only weaken my voice but it won't be long before she finds a way to take it completely.'

Eska waited for the disappointment that was bound to follow but where that could have been she found loyalty instead.

'Then we have less time than I thought,' Whitefur replied. 'We must act quickly.'

Eska glanced at Flint.

'Knowing that the Ice Queen has found a way to steal your voice doesn't change things,' he said. 'We're still in with a chance, however small, of saving Erkenwald.'

'But how can my voice hold back an Ice Queen, a terrifying shaman *and* an army of Tusk guards when it's growing weaker by the day?' Eska cried.

Whitefur's eyes glittered. 'A voice is a mighty thing, Eska. When everything is taken from you – your family, your home, your friends, your dignity – you still have a voice, however weak it sounds.' The light from the lamp on the table made shadows flicker on the rocky walls as night folded round the hideaway. 'And *your* voice has the power to silence the tribes, command animals and shake the skies – if you can prove that you are the rightful owner of the Sky Song.'

'But we don't even know what it is,' Eska whispered.

Whitefur smiled. 'Many years ago, the North Star blew the legendary Frost Horn to breathe life into Erkenwald and the Sky Song was the tune the Sky God played on that horn. It was a tune infused with the very greatest magic and the Gods meant for you, the child chosen by them, to find it one day, and to sing it so that hope might come to Erkenwald when darkness closed in.' He sighed. 'But the Ice Queen wants your voice so that she can use it for a very different tune, one full of dark magic that will call the Fur and Feather Tribes in, then tear down the Sky Gods.'

131

Flint took a deep breath and Eska realised that he, too, was struggling to understand now. 'How do we find the Sky Song if it's just a melody?'

'How?' asked Blu from under the table, though the word didn't carry any understanding. It was just an echo, a reminder that she wanted to be heard, too.

'The Gods used to sing of Eska's quest.' Whitefur drew himself up and as he looked at Eska his words came deep and growled. 'You must find the forgotten Frost Horn and blow it from the stars before the Ice Queen steals your voice. Only then can you unleash the Sky Song and bring hope back to Erkenwald.'

Chapter Seventeen
Flint

Flint snorted. 'Find something that's forgotten and then blow it from the stars? I was all for trusting in Eska's voice but what you're suggesting is downright impossible. It doesn't even make sense!'

Whitefur stayed very still. 'And there I was thinking you were an inventor. Someone who believed in impossible, illogical things.'

Flint narrowed his eyes. Up until an hour ago, he had thought all Erkenwald's grown-ups were imprisoned at Winterfang and yet here was Whitefur, an adult walking free and armed with all sorts of surprising knowledge. 'What do you know about my being an inventor?'

Whitefur shrugged. 'I can see the magnifying class poking out of your rucksack – infused with rainbow essence, I assume?'

Flint gasped. How could Whitefur know that, unless . . .

'I'm guessing you found the Wanderer's Shield, into which the earliest Wanderers carved their knowledge of magic.' He paused. 'We thought it had been lost years ago.

133

I'm glad it's been found by someone open to Erkenwald's wonders.'

Flint's eyes widened at the realisation of what he had stumbled across. Then he sniffed. 'Yes, well, I'm not doing any more inventing because it keeps getting me in trouble.'

'Brilliant ideas often meet with scorn,' Whitefur replied, 'in the beginning, anyway. But you'll show them, boy. You'll show them all when you find the Frost Horn.'

'*If* we find the Frost Horn,' Flint mumbled.

Whitefur clasped his hands together. 'We Wanderers believe that after the North Star breathed life into Erkenwald he hid the Frost Horn somewhere in the kingdom so that its magic might hover over the land long after he left. No one has ever found it but I've heard it said that the songs of the Feather Tribe talk of this horn. And it's my belief that if you can find these outlawed children they might be able to help you.'

'Do you know where they are?' Eska asked.

Whitefur shifted. 'I think they've gone into hiding in the Lost Chambers, a warren of secret passageways inside the Never Cliffs, but I don't think anyone has ever found them either.'

'So we're searching for two things no one has ever found?' Flint said.

'Following magic is almost always a complicated affair.' Whitefur paused. 'But if you can find the Feather Tribe and win their loyalty they will talk to you about the Frost Horn.' He glanced at Flint. 'You'll need the Fur Tribe on your side, too, eventually, because only when all the tribes unite will we beat the Ice Queen.'

'Unite the tribes?' Flint nearly choked on his words.

Eska blew out through her teeth. 'So, *if* we find the Lost Chambers, *if* we make friends with the Feather Tribe and *if* we then locate this Frost Horn, we've got to blow it from the stars?'

Blu poked her head out from under the table. 'Stars long way, Eska.'

Whitefur smiled. 'Yes, a long way away, but possible to reach, with magic on your side.'

Blu clambered out and placed her chubby hands on her hips. 'What you talking about? And where's cup of tea? Pebble and me thirsty.'

Whitefur nodded. 'I quite agree, Blu. Impossible things are often easier to believe after a mug of tea.'

Eska set about brewing some pine-needle tea and roasting a rabbit she'd caught the day before while Blu padded up to Flint and leant close to his ear. 'What happening, big brother?'

Flint put an arm round her waist. 'We've got to find something, Blu.'

'Find Ma?' she asked hopefully.

Flint shook his head. 'Not yet but soon.'

Blu picked at her dirt-clogged nails. 'Miss Ma, Flint. Miss her. Love her.'

Flint nodded. 'Me too.'

And then, into the quietness of the hideaway, Blu began

to cry – little snivels that choked her throat and made her shoulders shake. 'Ma,' she sobbed. 'Want Ma.'

Whitefur stood up and bent down on one knee, holding out his hands.

'Blu,' he whispered. 'I have something for you.'

She wiped the tears from her face.

'Come,' he said. 'Give me your hands.'

Blu looked at Flint who nodded. Then, very slowly, Blu walked towards Whitefur and held out her hands. The old man wrapped them in his, as if they were precious little stones, then he closed his eyes and drew in a very deep breath. His chest and shoulders rose beneath his furs, his old, cracked lips drew tight and then he opened his mouth and let his breath out. Tiny flecks of snow spread from his lips into a cloud of falling silver that glinted in the lamplight and showered around Blu.

Eska looked up from the stove and gasped. 'What is it?'

'Diamond Dust,' Flint whispered. 'It occurs when snow freezes to ice as it falls … only Erkenbears have breath as cold as this.'

Blu blinked into the dancing flakes, her face full of awe, and Whitefur continued to breathe out, his eyes still closed, as the Diamond Dust filled the hideaway, scattering glitter around Flint and Eska. And they laughed then, at the touch of ice on their faces and the sight of magic working for them alone.

Whitefur opened his eyes and the Diamond Dust vanished. Then he smiled. 'It will protect you on your journey through the Never Cliffs. At the time when you need help most, say my name.'

'You're an Erkenbear, aren't you?' Flint said quietly, trying hard to make sense of things, because the lines that divided all that he knew – tribe and non-tribe, animal and human – seemed to be blurring. He frowned. 'I don't understand how but you are. I know you are.'

Whitefur stood up and winked at Flint. 'You do say some very strange things.' He glanced at the stove. 'Now, Eska, how about that pine-needle tea?'

They talked long into the night – of Eska's parents and the times before the Ice Queen's rule, of the battle and the choir of stolen voices – and it was several hours later that they emerged from the hideaway on to the ledge behind the waterfall.

Whitefur bent down and picked up a bundle of long, thin objects. He handed them round. 'Skis and poles. I found them in a food store out on the Driftlands and I brought a set for each of you. They have strappings for your boots and you'll need to fix them fast because up in the Never Cliffs you can't afford to put a foot wrong.' He glanced at the eagle looking on from her nest. 'Does she have a name?'

Eska nodded. 'I call her Balapan.'

Whitefur smiled. 'Like Blackfina's song ... Your mother had a beautiful voice and many a night, when we crossed paths, I heard her sing to you round the campfire. Songs of orcas in the deep and eagles in the skies. *Balapan*, she used to call the king of the birds, an old Erkenwaldian word for the wind because she felt that only eagles – and the Gods – really knew the power of the skies.'

And, at those words, Eska's soul shook. A week ago in the Giant's Beard she had found her way back to a memory of her ma and, though the Ice Queen might have used dark magic to steal her past, it was clear that some things, like love, were stronger even than an Ice Queen's curse.

'I must go now,' Whitefur said. 'Tusk guards are patrolling Deeproots and I want to make sure the Fur Tribe stay safe.'

Flint smiled at the thought of Tomkin discovering that an Erkenbear Wanderer – who was most definitely magical, and therefore completely illegal in his brother's eyes – was keeping watch over Deeproots.

Whitefur looked from Eska to Flint to Blu. 'Good luck in your search for the Lost Chambers. And remember, you have the wild on your side and the wild doesn't play by ordinary rules.'

The group watched as the old man slipped out on to the rocks lining the river and, as they peered through the gap beneath the tumbling waterfall, they saw him walk under the starlit night. But when he was past the rowan trees, some way down the river, he stooped to all fours and his rhythm changed, from the measured gait of a man to the thundering power of a beast. Flint blinked. Ever since meeting Eska, his world had begun to shift and, while at first these changes of perspective had rocked him, now he was beginning to see that things weren't as black and white as he had thought. And as he turned back inside the hideaway he understood a little better. Eska had a tribe after all – one made up of eagles and Erkenbears – and, day by day, it was growing.

Chapter Eighteen
The Ice Queen

Meanwhile, in a frosted turret in Winterfang Palace, the Ice Queen sat on a throne built from walrus tusks. They jutted above her head and shoulders, a fan of pointed ivory, and beside her sat a wolverine, purring darkly. She let her fingers glide along the staff across her lap, then she raised her head to the other person in the room.

'You have done well, Slither.'

The shaman's face twisted into an ugly smile as he eyed the statue in the middle of the turret. It was a life-size model of a child – the eyes, nose, hair and limbs all chiselled out of glass – and, though Eska was miles and miles away, to the Ice Queen and Slither it felt as if she was standing right there on the floor in front of them.

'I believe the contraption is working as we wanted it to,' Slither replied. 'There are signs on the glass to prove it.'

He pointed to the spidery lines spreading out from the hollow in the statue's throat and the Ice Queen's blue lips quivered as she took them in. Then she stood up and stalked towards the statue, raking her staff across the frosty tiles. She held her crown of snowflakes high, then lifted the black key from the chain around her neck and slotted it into the hole in the statue's throat.

Her eyes flickered towards Slither. 'The magic in this turret only works when I play the organ – it is fuelled by my growing strength – so I shall play the organ in the evenings as well as the mornings from now on.' She paced towards the window and looked out at the stars. 'Because we only have five days before the midnight sun rises.'

Slither's scalp tightened. 'We must be careful not to move too quickly. Magic used in haste often crumbles. Perhaps we could—'

The Ice Queen cut across him. 'I need Eska's voice drained from her body before she realises she can claim the Sky Song for her own. So, when you hear my choir sing, I want you to turn and turn and turn.'

She left the room, the wolverine by her side, and, as the organ sounded a moment later and the prisoners' voices sailed into the night, Slither wound the key again and again and more dark veins seeped across the statue, scarring it through with black.

Chapter Nineteen
Eska

At dawn, they packed rucksacks full of food and flasks of water and for a moment Eska felt sad that they were leaving the Giant's Beard, the place she and Balapan had come to call home, but then she remembered Whitefur's words. She had a pa to rescue now – and the Sky Song to discover.

The Ice Queen's choir had sung all through the previous night and on into the early morning and, though it had stopped now, the fact that the anthem had sounded for so much longer than usual made Eska and Flint exchange anxious glances. The Ice Queen's power was growing and Eska's voice was getting weaker still. She couldn't see how it would be strong enough to silence the tribes, command animals and shake the skies . . . She had tried to pick out the individual voices when they sang, desperate to recognise her pa's voice, but no recollection came and she sat behind the waterfall, her hand on Balapan's back. She could feel the bird's heartbeat, sure and steady, beneath her feathers and somehow that made her feel stronger.

'Can you lead us to the Lost Chambers?' she whispered. 'Like you led me to the Giant's Beard?'

Balapan yapped and ruffled her feathers, then she charged towards the waterfall and Eska gasped as she shot through it and spiralled up into the air. Eska crossed the river to join Flint and Blu and with their skis and poles strapped to their backs they followed the eagle up into the ravine and then on through the gap in the hills which led out of the valley. The river snaked west, then ran towards the sea, but Balapan hurled her cry across the sky, beckoning them north, on into the heart of the Never Cliffs.

At first the land climbed gently, but before long the hills built themselves up into jagged mountains and, though Pebble kept nibbling Flint's ear for food and Blu stumbled in the deeper snow, the group trudged on. After an hour though, they collapsed on the top of a mountain and shared their water round.

'They go on and on,' Eska panted as she looked out over the ridges that scored the horizon.

Flint nodded. 'They're called the Never Peaks for a reason.'

Eska swallowed a mouthful of water. 'Do you think most people feel like this before a quest?'

'Like what?'

Eska considered. 'Small.'

Silently, they watched the mountains – the slopes of ice, banks of scree and frozen waterfalls that hung like tapestries of frost – then they listened to the *whrum* of Balapan's wings above them.

'If you count us all together,' Flint said eventually, 'you, me, Blu, Pebble *and* Balapan, we're not so small.'

Eska nodded. 'Sort of tribe-sized when you think of it like that.'

Blu picked up a handful of snow and smoothed it between her mittens. 'We go home see Tomkin now. I love my brothers.'

Flint sighed. 'No, Blu. I told you, remember? We won't see Tomkin until we've found the Frost Horn.' He nudged her skis towards her. 'We need to get your skis on so that we can find a quicker trail through the mountains.'

Blu stared at the skis. 'Don't like them.'

Flint slotted her boot into the first binding. 'You need to let me put them on, Blu. We've got a job to do, remember?'

Blu narrowed her eyes and then, to Eska's surprise, she threw her snowball in Flint's face. 'Not doing skis,' she snapped. 'Don't like skis.'

Flint wiped the snow away. 'You love skiing, Blu. I've seen you zip through Deeproots after me and Tomkin.'

Blu turned away. 'No.'

Flint lowered his voice. 'Now you're just being difficult.'

Eska could see Flint trying to cling on to his patience, but, when Blu folded her arms and pouted, his anger spilled out.

'Fine,' he muttered, flinging her poles into the snow and tightening his hood around Pebble. 'If you're going to play difficult out on the Never Cliffs, I'm going to play difficult, too.'

And, with that, he strapped his boots to his own skis, grabbed his poles and set off down the mountain at breakneck speed. Eska didn't know much about tribe behaviour – perhaps flinging poles around and pouting was perfectly normal – but she knew, from spending time with Balapan, about loyalty and so she crouched next to Blu.

Her voice was quieter than Flint's, more scratched and far less sure of itself. 'You can hold my hand for the first bit – if you want – but you're probably going to be a lot better at this than me.'

Blu prodded the snow with her mittens. 'I good skier. Speedy speedy. I like fast. Ask big brother.'

But Flint was already shooting down the mountain, his skis slicing wide arcs in the powdery snow. Eska watched. He looked graceful, like a bird skimming the surface of a river, but also slightly furious in the way he jabbed his poles into each turn.

'Come on,' Eska said. 'Let's go after him.'

Putting on the skis was easy enough, but, as Eska poled her way towards the edge of the mountain with Blu, she swallowed. She'd never skied before. There was no way she'd keep up with the others . . . Balapan yapped from above and Eska knew what that noise meant: it was a call to move faster, to keep going. She lifted up her hood so that the fur was snug around her cheeks and then, gripping Blu's mitten, they set off.

Blu, it turned out, only needed to be held for a second. As soon as her skis picked up speed, she let go of Eska and sailed on down the mountain after her brother. She wasn't graceful like him – tucked into a wobbly crouch, she looked rather like a runaway cannonball – but she was getting down the mountain. Which was more than could be said for Eska. She couldn't seem to find the nerve to point her skis downhill. Instead, she swerved across the side of the mountain with shaking knees, watching nervously as Flint pulled up on a ledge and Blu careered over a little bump, then clattered into him. They were hugging, poles and pouts evidently forgotten, and Balapan yapped again. The eagle was getting impatient now and so, drawing in a deep breath, Eska tilted her skis down the hill.

Her eyes streamed, her legs wobbled and, for a few seconds, Eska forgot to breathe. Then her calves grew sturdier and her thighs tightened as she felt her way into the snow. Moments later, she was leaning into the slope, shifting her weight from one leg to the other as she carved her mark into the mountain.

She grinned. This was something she *had* done before. The pace, the balance, the thrill of winding deeper into the wild. Some patterns of behaviour, it seemed, couldn't be unlearnt. And as she swished through the snow a memory burned in her mind: she was smaller than she was now, much smaller, and she was making her way down a snowy mountain, her little skis framed by two larger ones that belonged to the man holding her up from behind. She could feel the softness of his wolf furs. She could hear the sound of his deep voice urging her on. She could smell the warmth of campfires and pine needles on his breath. And she knew, without a shadow of a doubt, that this was her pa. He had taught her how to ski.

The memory vanished and Eska pulled up in front of Flint and Blu, showering them both with a spray of snow.

Blu grinned. 'You good, Eska. Better than Flint.'

Flint pulled Blu's hood down over her eyes at that, then he turned to Eska. 'You did well.'

Eska blushed. 'This is something I've done before – with my pa. I can feel it.'

'I wasn't talking about the skiing.' Flint glanced at Blu who was feeding Pebble a clump of snow, then he undid the straps of his skis and hoisted them on to his back. 'Though you're not bad at that either.' He looked at his sister again. 'It gets hard sometimes.'

Eska nodded. 'I know.'

'Especially since Ma and Pa left and Tomkin became Chief. Most of the time it's just me and her. Not that I'm complaining. It's just—'

'—hard sometimes.' Eska swung her skis on to her back. 'You'd make a good eagle, you know.'

Flint laughed. 'Why's that?'

'Because you're protective – and patient.'

Flint chewed his lip. 'Some of the time.'

They traipsed up the next mountain and Eska wondered, as she glimpsed Balapan disappear inside a cloud and then burst out the other side, how much longer they'd have to go before they saw signs of a tribe hiding among the cliffs.

They shared out some of the food Eska had cooked the night before, then they made their way on and on through the mountains – into the endless spring light – until eventually a late dusk fell and they came to a lake covered in black ice. Like a stain of ink, it squatted before the surrounding peaks, blocking the way ahead. There was no sparkle, no glint, no reflection of evening clouds on the ice – just a cold dark mass of black – and, at the sight of it, Pebble growled.

'Devil's Dancefloor,' Flint murmured. 'Pa used to tell us stories about it. He said it was one of the deepest lakes in all Erkenwald and that the reason it's black is because years ago the Feather Tribe grew frightened of the storms that raged through the Never Cliffs so they trapped the largest of the thunderclouds down inside the ice.' He paused. 'It's just a story though.'

Eska watched Balapan soar above the lake. 'We've got to cross it, haven't we?'

'Your eagle seems to think so.' Flint squinted. 'And I can just make out a narrow path on the other side, winding on through the mountains.'

Eska bent down to unstrap her skis. 'If it's black ice covering the lake, it'll be frozen solid so it'll hold us. Right?'

Flint unfastened Blu's skis. 'Absolutely.'

But, as they approached the shoreline, nobody said a word. Not even Blu, who watched the Devil's Dancefloor with narrowed eyes.

Cautiously, they placed their boots on the ice and Eska waited for its creak and groan, but this was a slice of the wild that didn't talk. It lay silently beneath them and as they walked out on to it, the sealskin soles of their boots stopping them from slipping, they looked left and right and sometimes over their shoulders. Because, although none of them said it, each felt that perhaps someone or something was watching them.

It was only when they were in the middle of the Devil's Dancefloor that the noises started. At first it was the drawn-out moan of ice and it made the group bunch closer and rise up on to their tiptoes. But then another sound came: a restless rumbling from beneath the ice that spoke of thunder gathering many miles away.

Eska's insides clenched. 'Go quietly,' she whispered to Blu and Flint. 'And keep your eyes fixed on Balapan.'

For a few seconds, Flint and Blu did just that, then the rumbles grew, like an enormous engine throbbing into life. Eska noticed Flint's hold on Blu's hand tighten and she looked down. The lake was no longer a block of impenetrable black. It was mirror-clear and beneath its frozen surface things were moving. Long, thin arms that seemed to be made from trails of smoke reached up towards the ice and beat their fists against it.

Eska felt her legs sway. There were faces below the arms, masks of grey with gaping mouths, and they were calling with hungry voices:

'The Ice Queen came and cast her curse
On thunderghosts and much, much worse.
Come dance with spectres locked in ice.
Your whispers, though, won't quite suffice.
One word out loud is all we need
To drag you down and fill our greed.'

Eska gulped. So the stories Flint's pa had told him were true; the Feather Tribe *had* locked a thundercloud inside the lake, but now the Ice Queen had manipulated it to do her bidding.

Eska kept her voice low as she turned to Flint and Blu. 'Whatever you do, don't raise your voices above a whisper.'

She put a finger to her lips to check that Blu had understood and, when the little girl nodded, the group kept walking. But when two large fists pummelled at the ice between her boots Blu couldn't stop her fear spilling out.

'I scared, Flint!' she cried. 'Scared!'

What happened next happened fast. The ice beneath Blu's feet fell away in one swift slice and she shot down into the lake. Where she had been standing the surface closed up to form a shield of solid ice and then it was not only the fists of the thunderghosts beating below.

Blu's small hands raged against the ice while wisps of grey swirled around her.

Chapter Twenty
Flint

Flint fell to his knees, pounding his knuckles against the ice, and beside him Pebble raked his claws over the surface again and again. But the ice didn't shift. It remained locked over Blu like a depthless seal and all around her the thunderghosts twirled. They were dancing now, their voices delighted cackles, as Blu's eyes clouded with terror.

'No,' gasped Flint. 'Not this! Not this!'

He threw back his head as a wail full of love and loss and anger rose in his throat, but in the nick of time Eska clapped a hand over his mouth and looked into his eyes.

'Don't cry out,' she whispered. 'Don't let the thunderghosts take you, too. Think, Flint. Think. What do you have in your rucksack that could help Blu?'

Hardly hearing, Flint laid his palms on to the ice over his sister's hammering fists. He'd put Blu in danger because *he* had wanted to prove to his brother that he could set things right and find their ma. The shame and longing beat inside him and tears streamed down his cheeks. 'I can't lose her, too,' he whispered. 'I can't.'

Balapan landed by his side and began pecking at Flint's rucksack, desperately trying to wrench it open.

'You won't lose her because you're a thinker,' Eska urged Flint. 'A problem solver. Now, *think* your way out of this.'

Flint shook his head. 'Most of my inventions don't even work,' he whispered. 'Tomkin's right – he's always been right – I can't control magic. I can't even keep my little sister safe. I'm useless.'

Eska thrust the rucksack into Flint's lap. 'Tomkin doesn't know what you can do. He didn't see how the Camouflage Cape helped us escape from Winterfang.'

Blu slammed her fists against the ice, and the thunderghosts let out a rumbling laugh.

'Help your sister,' Eska murmured. 'I know you can.'

And so, with shaking hands, Flint tipped the objects from his rucksack. The Camouflage Cape spilled over his lap, but he brushed it aside. His Anything Knife clattered against the ice, but he ignored that, too, and it was only when he held up a small glass bottle filled with golden liquid that he stopped searching.

'Maybe this,' he whispered. 'Bottled sunlight mixed with firefly glow. It's hotter than fire, if mixed right.'

Still trembling, he poured it over the ice above Blu. At first the pool of golden liquid simply lay on the ice and Flint's tears rolled faster, then the invention began to bubble and hiss and a second later it burned through the ice to reveal a thrash of limbs below.

'Blu!' Flint gasped.

There was a clamour of thunder and more scrabbling limbs, then Flint and Eska hauled Blu out of the lake and the black ice folded over the hole, sealing the thunderghosts back where they belonged.

Flint held Blu close. 'I'm so sorry,' he sobbed. 'I'm so sorry. I never should've let you leave Deeproots.'

Blu clung to her brother's waist, gasping the air back in. 'I love you, Flint,' she panted. 'I love you more. I stay with you.'

Flint squeezed her tight, right close to his heart, then after a while he wiped the tears from his face and looked up at Eska.

'Sorry,' he whispered. 'I didn't expect all that to come out.' He blushed and looked away. 'Tomkin says crying is a sign of weakness.'

Eska raised an eyebrow. 'Tomkin also says you're not an inventor – and look at what you did just then. You rescued your sister from thunderghosts, despite how terrified you were!' She paused. 'So, really, tears are just a warm-up for courage.'

Flint looked down, trying to ignore the thunderghosts moaning beneath the ice. 'I'm not sure I'm going to make a very good warrior though. Too much—' he looked at Blu, searching for the right word, '—gentleness.'

'I don't think you have to fight with weapons to be a warrior,' Eska whispered. 'You could fight with love and tears and inventions instead. That would probably be just as good.' She thought of the way Balapan was – fierce and tough and definitely wild – but there was a gentleness there, too, even if it wasn't easy to spot at first.

Eska stood up. 'I think *gentleness* is a mighty word because you have to be strong of heart to be kind.'

And Flint smiled then because, although Eska's voice didn't sound like much, she often found the words that mattered.

The group hurried over the Devil's Dancefloor, only too glad to leave the thunderghosts behind, but, as they stepped out on to the snowy path through the mountains ahead, Flint cast a worried look at his sister. She was shivering badly and the light was fading fast.

'We have to find shelter and a place to rest for the night,' Flint said. 'Blu needs dry clothes, a fire and warm food.' He scoured the banks of snow either side of him. 'The grizzlies hibernate in the Never Cliffs so if we find a bear cave we can bed down there.'

'With the bears?' Eska shifted. 'Or will they have finished hibernating?'

Flint rolled his eyes. 'It'll just be us. Now, come on, before we lose the light completely.'

It took them an hour to find a bear cave in the end and it was Eska who spotted the opening between a cluster of trees on the mountainside. They helped Blu inside the rocky den and, while Pebble snuggled close to her, Flint lost no time in gathering kindling for a fire and branches for bedding and Eska prepared the remaining ptarmigan. Before long, they had a fire flickering and the colour returned to Blu's cheeks, and though the Ice Queen's anthem rolled out again that night, even louder than before, and Eska's voice was ebbing away, Flint refused to be afraid. Because their strange little tribe was together still – and they had a plan – and through the short night he knew that Balapan would keep guard.

They left the cave early the next day, with the notes of the Ice Queen's anthem ringing in their ears, and journeyed on through the Never Cliffs under a sunless sky: hiking slopes so steep they bent into a crawl, traversing ridges so narrow they hardly dared breathe and skiing through valleys so vast and white it was almost impossible to tell which way was up or down against the clouds.

Flint paused, panting, before the summit of yet another mountain. 'I can see how the Ice Queen never found the Feather Tribe . . .'

Eska and Blu pulled up beside him.

'We'll find them,' Eska said. Then she nodded to Balapan wheeling above them. 'Remember the Ice Queen didn't have the wild on her side.'

Blu pointed to the snowy overhang a few steps further up the mountain. It was lined with enormous icicles that hung down in turquoise fangs.

'Don't like them. Horrid,' Blu said, shrinking inside her furs.

Flint looked at the row of ice daggers and shuddered. Something about them did feel oddly sinister. 'Let's keep going until we get over the top of this mountain, then we'll strap on our skis, find a safe spot for food and—'

His words were cut short as one of the icicles dropped into the snow at his feet. It stuck in the snow like a lance.

Flint shook himself. 'Skis on now. Let's get some speed around the side of this mountain.'

Blu frowned. 'You said top of hill for skis.'

Flint eyed the fringe of icicles. 'Not any more. Something doesn't feel quite right about this slope.'

Another shard of ice fell from the overhang and, from Flint's hood, Pebble whimpered. And then more and more followed until the entire row of icicles was raining down like a flurry of spears. A barrier of criss-crossed ice lay before them and, up in the sky, Balapan screeched.

Flint's flesh crawled. This was a mountain bidden to obey the Ice Queen and they were right in the midst of it.

Yanking Blu's boots into their bindings, Flint tried to ignore the strange clicking, clattering sound coming from below the overhang. But when Eska looked up and gasped, he couldn't ignore it any more and he watched, pulse thrashing, as the shards of ice gathered themselves up into a figure the size of a very tall tree. Its body glittered, its fingers were long, sharp slices of ice and all around its gaunt head barbs of frosted hair jutted. But it was the mouth that made Flint tremble: a dark cave strung with glinting icicles. The figure blew out – a deep, heaving breath as if waking from a long slumber – and his ice teeth rattled.

'He's – he's real!' Flint stammered.

Eska recoiled. 'Who is?'

Flint tightened his hood round Pebble, grabbed Blu's hands and pushed with his poles. 'Needlespin!' he yelled. 'The ghoul that haunts the Never Cliffs!'

Chapter Twenty-One
Eska

Jamming her poles into the snow, Eska led the way round the side of the mountain.

'Ski! Fast!' she cried.

Down they went, undoing hours of hard climbing, but that didn't matter now because Needlespin was scuttling closer, wielding a silver-spiked ball and chain, and, though Balapan dived at him again and again, he barged her out of the way – and stormed on.

'Visitors?' he cackled. 'Running away so soon?'

His voice was full of spiked edges and at the end of every sentence the words snapped off like broken ice.

Eska turned panicked eyes to Flint.

'Keep going!' she shouted. 'Keep going!'

But Needlespin was gaining on them, closing the children in between two mountains. Eska scanned the slopes for a crossing point until her eyes rested on a fallen boulder covered in snow that was wedged between the mountains.

She took in the vast drop below it – several hundred

metres, at least – then she found herself pointing towards the boulder with her ski pole. It was the only way.

'Across there!' she bellowed, nipping from the mountainside on to the boulder.

Blu followed with Flint close behind.

'You think I won't leave my mountain?' Needlespin screeched.

And he leapt over the gap between the slopes as if he was jumping over a puddle. He landed in a crouch and his icicled limbs creaked. Then he looked up, his teeth jangling. 'Not when I've been given orders by the Ice Queen to hold you here.'

Eska's mind whirled as they skied on down the next mountain. She thought about the inventions stashed inside Flint's rucksack and the quiver on her own back, but there was no time to reach for anything like that because Needlespin was now swinging the ball and chain above his head.

'Ice!' he shrieked, thumping the spiked ball down into the snow. 'More ice!'

And Blu, Flint and Eska screamed because, beneath their skis, they felt the mountain harden into a slope of bruised ice. Their skis lost grip, their poles clattered against the surface and, like three runaway marbles, they shot down the mountain.

Balapan plummeted, too, but she was thinking faster, seeing faster, bending the wind to suit her own purpose and missing the treetops and jutting overhangs by the slightest turn of her feathers. The eagle called out above a lip of ice.

Eska summoned up her voice until it was as loud as she could make it. 'Point your skis towards Balapan!'

'That's a jump!' Flint screamed. 'We'll soar for miles! Blu won't manage the landing!'

But Eska was tilting her skis towards the eagle now, towards the mound of glittering ice scooping up to the next mountain, and, with no better ideas, Flint snatched Blu's hand and steered his little sister after Eska. Pebble's eyes grew large as they neared the lip.

And, close on their heels, Needlespin sniggered. 'You can't outrun me, children! Wherever you go, I'll find you!'

His words echoed through the Never Cliffs, but Eska, Flint and Blu careered on and then – one, two, three – they were soaring off the ice lip, climbing the height of the mountain opposite, in the air.

They landed with a *poof* in powder snow, a tangle of skis, poles and limbs, before a cluster of trees dripping with icicles.

Flint twisted round to face Blu. 'Are you okay?'

Blu's bottom lip was wobbling. 'I scared, Flint. Scared.'

Eska glanced around. 'I think we've lost Needlespin ... Maybe he could only cross those first few mountains?'

Pebble scrambled out of Flint's coat and peered closer at a tree behind them. He took a few steps forward and the silence throbbed. Then, as Balapan veered towards them, Eska spotted a movement within the trees. A silver-blue eye flicked open between the branches, an icicled claw curled round a trunk and then, as Pebble clattered back towards Flint, Needlespin burst out from behind a tree.

'Did you miss me?' the monster spat.

He lumbered towards them and the group scrambled to their feet and launched their skis down the mountain. But they could hear Needlespin's ball and chain whirring in circles and as it spun above him a torrent of icicles shot out from the silver spikes, narrowly missing the children's furs.

'Ice spears!' Blu cried.

Flint clutched her hand for a moment. 'Keep going! Just keep going!'

But Eska had learnt to listen when the panic crowded in – to eagles, to the wild and to the quiet beat of her heart. *Whitefur*, it was saying. *Remember what Whitefur said to you back in the Giant's Beard.* And, as she darted between trees and swerved round humps and dips in the snow, she thought of her hideaway behind the waterfall and how a man who might or might not have been an Erkenbear had filled it with Diamond Dust.

'Whitefur,' she whispered. 'Whitefur.'

Flint shot her a glance as he stooped beneath a branch. 'What?'

'Whitefur,' Eska said again as one of Needlespin's icicles whizzed past her ear. '*At the time when you need help most, say my name* – that's what Whitefur said!'

And as Needlespin roared behind them, his teeth jangling like hollow bones, Flint and Eska shouted Whitefur's name. Again and again they bellowed it and at first Needlespin simply laughed and hurled out another batch of icicles.

Then a curious thing happened. Tiny flecks of shimmering silver puffed out into the air around Flint and Eska and no matter how many times Needlespin pitched his weapons he couldn't hit the boy or the girl. The icicles simply bounced off the shell of sparkling snow and clattered to the ground.

'Whitefur's Diamond Dust,' Eska breathed. 'It's protecting us!'

Then she watched, aghast, as Needlespin charged down the mountain behind them and tossed a spear at Blu. It struck her on the elbow and she cried out in pain. Flint swerved towards her, taking a little of her weight.

'Say Whitefur's name, Blu. It will help you!'

Blu leant into her brother's side as they skied. 'Don't understand. Don't understand.'

'Yes, you do, Blu. You do. Trust me. Say Whitefur's name.'

'White – Whitefur,' she stammered.

'Yes, Blu! Again – louder this time.'

Blu flung the Erkenbear's name out into the Never Cliffs as Needlespin's spear careered towards her. 'Whitefur! Whitefur! Whitefur!'

The icicle crashed to the ground and all around her the Diamond Dust danced. Blu, Flint and Eska flew on down the mountain, shooting off bumps and veering round trees.

'Now what?' Flint shouted to Eska.

'Follow Balapan.'

And though Needlespin scuttled over the snow towards

them, flinging his ball and chain against the trees, they followed the eagle – until it circled a cliff edge with a terrifying drop beneath. Flint turned to Eska as they raced towards it.

'No,' he breathed.

Balapan plummeted down and then tucked her wings in just before she hit the snow. She soared up into the sky again and, with one eye on the snow and one eye on her eagle, Eska tried to understand what Balapan was saying.

'Pull up at the last minute,' she panted, tucking into a ball to quicken her pace. 'And grab whatever you can to stop yourself from falling. Trust me!'

Behind them, Needlespin's voice hacked through the air. 'Over you go! Splinter splat! You'll be easier to guard with broken bones.'

Eska, Flint and Blu were level now and, as they sailed towards the cliff edge with Needlespin just metres behind, they yanked their weight sideways, slipped off the edge and then clung to the tops of the trees immediately beneath.

Needlespin charged over the lip, his arms wide, ready to crush the children in his icy grasp, but they were nowhere to be seen. And as the monster leapt into the air he realised his stride had been too big – too greedy – because he'd overshot his prey and the trees they clung to and far, far below, snaking through the cliffs, was the one thing that could break him.

Black ice.

The frozen river loomed like a shadow and Needlespin picked up more and more speed as he hurtled towards it, limbs flailing. Then there was an almighty crash as he hit the ice and Eska, Flint and Blu, clutching at the branches of the trees beneath the ledge, watched the broken pieces of Needlespin's body rattle across the river.

Chapter Twenty-Two
Flint

An eerie silence followed and for a while all Flint, Eska and Blu could do was stare at the river below them. Then the Diamond Dust slipped away through the trees and Flint put an arm round Blu's shoulders.

'That was close,' he panted.

'I think mentioning Needlespin before we set off from the Giant's Beard would have been helpful,' Eska replied.

Flint glanced at Blu. 'I didn't want to scare her.'

Blu looked down through the branches and wailed.

Eska rolled her eyes. 'Because finding out this way was so much better ...'

Flint turned to Blu and hauled her on to a sturdier branch. Then he looked at Eska. 'You and Balapan saved us back there. We'd never have survived all that without you.'

Eska grinned then she looked around. 'Maybe don't tell Tomkin we got Blu jammed into the top of a very high tree.'

Blu pulled at a branch. 'We tell Ma.'

Flint laughed. 'Let's kick these skis off and climb down.'

Balapan was waiting on a rock at the foot of the trees and as they clambered through the lower branches Flint watched as she swooped to Eska's shoulder and leant against the girl's cheek. Eska stretched up a hand and ran it over the eagle's wing and Blu shuffled through the snow towards the eagle.

'Want to hug Bala.'

It was the name Blu had started using for the eagle and neither Eska nor Flint had corrected her.

'I'm not sure eagles are very good at hugging,' Eska said softly. 'Animals are a bit different from humans.'

Blu tilted her head. 'Animals hug. Just not with arms.'

And, as she raised her little hand towards Balapan, the eagle loosened her wing and brushed it against Blu's palm.

'There. Hug. See?'

Flint ruffled her hair. 'I'm proud of you, Blu. You were brave just now. Really brave.'

They shared out some mountain cranberries and water, then they strapped on their skis and looked down at the river winding on through the Never Cliffs. A cluster of tundra swans were feeding on algae where the afternoon sun had thawed the ice, but other than that the landscape was absolutely still and, just as Flint was about to suggest they get going, Eska gasped.

'The river,' she said quietly. 'Before the mountains close it in, there are lots of little tributaries branching off from it. And, well, if you squint hard enough, the river almost looks like a giant feather . . .'

166

Flint peered at the scene below and his eyes widened. 'You're right.'

'Feather Tribe close,' Blu said.

Flint thought about it. 'I once heard that the Tusk Tribe used to stand on the cliff tops to the north of the kingdom, then look down at the icebergs and read messages in their shapes.' He paused. 'Maybe the Feather Tribe use landmarks as signs, too. Blu's right; I think they *are* close ...'

The three of them skied quickly down the mountain and rather than crossing the frozen river – the episode with the thunderghosts was still fresh in everyone's minds and Needlespin's remains lay scattered across it – they hastened along beside it, following its curve and jumping over the tributaries which snaked out into the mountains. They glanced around, eagerly searching for any signs of civilisation, while Balapan flew overhead. And, when Pebble realised that Needlespin was no longer a threat, he leapt down from Flint's hood and joined in the hunt.

The fox pup bounded ahead, sniffing at the snow and padding carefully across the tributaries, but, when the mountains closed in again and just the main river ran on through a narrow gully, Pebble started barking.

'*Shhhh*, Pebble,' Flint hissed. 'We can't afford to draw attention to ourselves.'

But still the fox pup barked and Flint noticed then that he was pawing at the snow on the mountainside to their right.

Eska frowned. 'What is it?' she whispered. 'What has he found?'

'I think he's caught a scent and wants us to follow it.'

Flint hurried closer to Pebble and noticed a shelf of rock hanging out above the path, a few metres above the fox pup. In a swish of feathers, Balapan landed on it, then she stayed very still.

'Something about this mountain is important,' Eska said slowly. 'Both Pebble and Balapan know it.' She took a step beneath the ledge and her eyes widened. 'Look at this!'

Strung from the tip of the ledge right down to the base of the mountain was a giant spiderweb laced in ice. It hung in delicate spirals, each loop coated in dashes of frost as thin as silver eyelashes, and Flint knew, as he gazed upon it, that magic was involved. Then he saw how: the centre of the web was a cluster of ice and on it sat a spider. It was the size of a fist and as clear as glass.

'An ice spider,' Flint murmured. 'They usually spin ice unless it's a clear night, then they spin moonlight.' He paused. 'It's beautiful, but how is it going to help us?'

They watched quietly as the spider left the middle of its web. Then Flint understood – the web was not complete – the spider was spinning still and the gossamer it spun did not fill the spaces left with ordinary loops. Words were appearing, silver words that shone in the twilight.

'It – it's trying to tell us something,' Eska breathed.

No one dared speak until the spider had stopped and two words glistened in the web.

CHIN DOWN

Flint turned to Eska. '*Chin down?* I don't understand.' He threw his hands up. 'We've only got three days to stop the Ice Queen and we're faced with an ice spider spinning nonsense! We need to find the Feather Tribe!'

'*Chin up,*' Eska said. 'I heard you say that to Blu when you were trying to encourage her to keep going through the Never Cliffs this morning.'

Flint turned away from the web and looked on down the path through the mountains. 'Yeah, well, this spider got it wrong then because it's saying *Chin Down* which makes no sense at all.'

He grabbed Blu by the hand, but to his surprise he found her reluctant to move on.

'Come on, Blu. We've no time for this!'

But his sister didn't move. She kept her head down and her eyes fixed on the base of the mountain. 'Chin down,' she said. 'Put chin down, Flint. Look.'

Flint tucked his chin into his chest and followed Blu's gaze then he saw what she was looking at – something they would have missed completely had Blu not listened to the spider's instructions. There, nestled into the base of the mountain, was a very faint, dome-shaped crack in the snow as if, perhaps, someone had opened a way into the rock not so long ago.

Flint and Eska brushed the snow away until they found what they had been looking for: a door carved into the cliff face with a small skull acting as a handle.

'A bird skull,' Flint breathed. 'Snowy owl, it looks like.'

And then his face broke into a grin. 'The snowy owl is the symbol of the Feather Tribe. I think we've found the way into the Lost Chambers!'

They turned to see the spider drop to the ground then it scuttled down the path, on into the mountains. But as it went they noticed it didn't leave a trail of thread or tiny pricks where its feet marked the snow. It left footprints. Human footprints. And as Flint looked at them he remembered Whitefur's words: *Good luck in your search for the Lost Chambers. And remember, you have the wild on your side and the wild doesn't play by ordinary rules.*

'That was a Wanderer, wasn't it?' he whispered to Eska. 'Like how Whitefur was an Erkenbear but also a man. That spider – it was . . . I don't know what it was! But it was one of your kind, I'm sure of it.'

Eska's eyes were wide. 'Do you think one day I'll learn how to shape-shift into wild creatures?'

Flint smiled. 'Wouldn't put it past you.' He looked at his little sister. 'You were right to trust that spider, Blu; to wait until you understood what it was saying.'

Blu nodded. 'I clever.'

And though Flint was used to waiting for Blu, used to her dawdling behind and not understanding, this time *she* took his hand and, shivering, led him into the mountain.

Eska followed with Balapan on her shoulder. They were in a passageway large enough to stand in and balanced on the rocky ledges either side of them were halved eggshells of every colour imaginable – speckled green, turquoise, mottled purple, gold – and inside each one a candle flickered.

Flint pulled the door shut behind them, then his eyes travelled over the eggshells as they walked on. 'Peregrine, pintail, lesser snow goose, red-winged sparrow, mountain bluebird. This is the Feather Tribe all right! Only they would know where to find the eggs of birds like these.' And then he gulped as he remembered the reception his tribe had given Eska. He slid a glance at his friend who was looking equally nervous. 'Just leave the conversations to me,' he said.

Eska nodded, then she laid her hand on Balapan's talons and Flint thought it looked a little like the bird and the girl were walking hand in hand.

Pebble hurried ahead, but, after a few minutes, he stopped and cocked his head to one side. Because blocking the way ahead was a large bird with a long, scooped neck and a fan of white feathers that filled the entire tunnel. It looked like a peacock and yet its colouring was different; this bird was as white as freshly fallen snow.

Flint blinked in disbelief. 'That's a moonflit!'

Eska gulped. 'Is that good or bad? I didn't come across them in my training with Balapan.'

Flint rubbed his eyes. 'Neither. It's just – unlikely. Impossible even ... These birds have been extinct for centuries!'

Eska peered closer. 'Look at its feathers. Each one has a circular pattern on it.'

Flint nodded. 'Eyes, our ancestors used to say, because

moonflits can see beyond ordinary things – into hearts and minds and—'

Blu squealed as the white markings flicked a fraction to reveal hundreds of grey, staring eyes.

'I don't know how the Feather Tribe got hold of this creature but I think it's acting as a guard,' Flint whispered. 'I think if the moonflit lets us past it means it trusts us.'

Very slowly, the feathered eyes opened and closed and then the bird lowered its tail feathers into a sweep of white and backed into the shadows so that the group could see what lay beyond. Darkness. A space so black there was no difference between blinking and keeping your eyes wide open. Flint lifted Pebble into his hood, then, holding Blu's hand still, he shuffled forward.

Eska tiptoed after them. 'Is it a dead end?'

Blu moaned. 'I want home, Flint. Tired. Cold.'

Flint squinted into the black, but, just as he was about to speak, there was a creak and then a click behind them. And he knew immediately what had just happened. A door in the dark had been closed.

They had walked straight into a trap.

Chapter Twenty-Three
Eska

Eska felt Balapan leap from her shoulder, but as she reached out with scrabbling hands they met with wooden bars ahead, around and behind. Eska gulped. They were locked inside a cage. She swung her skis down to grab her bow and heard Flint unsheathe his Anything Knife.

Then a voice in the dark spoke. 'Who are you?' It was a boy who sounded only a little older than Eska and Flint.

'Two – two of us are Fur Tribe,' Flint stammered. And then he paused and added hopefully, 'Fur Tribe warriors and—'

'Need fire,' Blu whimpered. 'Cold toes.'

Another voice slithered out of nowhere. A girl this time and her tone was frostier than the boy's. 'They don't sound like warriors to me. I vote we let our arrows fly.'

'I'm a Wanderer,' Eska said. 'Wolftooth's daughter. He came to you before the battle at Winterfang.'

Her words were met with a deathly hush, then the girl's voice came again and each word was coated in hate. 'You're not welcome here. *Your* father is the reason ours are gone. If he hadn't come and stirred up ideas of fighting the Ice Queen, maybe ours wouldn't have left the Never Cliffs.' She paused. '*You're* the reason we lost our tribe.'

The boy spoke again. 'Easy, Rook. Remember the moonflit. It let them pass.'

But there were murmurings now – dozens of voices clamouring in the dark.

'Get her out!'

'She's got no right to be here!'

Eska's ears churned with the all too familiar sounds of a tribe turned against her and she felt the hopes she'd harboured on her journey through the Never Cliffs sift slowly away.

And then Rook's voice came, cool but loaded: 'We should kill her . . .'

Eska's pulse skittered and the voices grew into a knot of angry hisses.

'How dare she show her face?'

'Our parents are gone because of her!'

'She's probably working for the Ice Queen now!'

Eska shrank inside her furs and from Flint's feet Pebble whimpered. Was it to be like this everywhere she went? Walls of loathing that she couldn't break down?

The voices rose louder still, the threats grew darker, and Balapan leapt back on to her shoulder. Eska felt the eagle's talons dig down to her bones, then Balapan cried out, a sharp screech that echoed through the mountain. The voices fell silent.

'Lights,' the boy in the darkness commanded. 'Bring up the lights.'

A scraping sound followed, of metal striking stone, then, one by one, lamps emerged on rocky ledges until, finally, a giant atrium came into view. Enormous dreamcatchers studded with quartz and strung with snowy-owl feathers dangled from the roof while the cavern floor was scattered with loose feathers: red ones striped with black, white ones dashed grey, large black ones, oval downy ones and small electric blues. And there were branches, too, fashioned into chairs and tables in among the feathers. It was like a giant nest.

But even more extraordinary were the Feather Tribe themselves. The cavern walls were full of scoops and bulges and inside every one was a large wooden birdcage, like the one Eska and her friends were trapped in, but the doors to these other cages were open. Crouched within were boys and girls, all with black hair and dark skin, and clad in wolf furs with colourful feathers splayed out in a fan over their shoulders and chests. They were armed – each with an arrow poised on a bow – and every single one was pointing at Eska and her friends.

'You have a golden eagle?'

It was the boy they'd heard speak first and he was standing in the biggest of the birdcages, one tucked into the middle of the far wall. He climbed down the ledges, his electric-blue shoulder feathers glimmering in the candlelight, before striding across the cavern floor. He stood before his prisoners, but his face was softer than Eska expected it to be.

'We only want to ask about the Frost Horn,' she said quietly.

Flint nodded. 'We don't mean any trouble.'

'I had a dream that you would come,' the boy said. 'A girl with a golden eagle asking about the songs we sing of the long-forgotten Frost Horn.'

Eska lowered her bow and, with Balapan still perched on her shoulder, she gripped the bars of the cage. 'Yes,' she breathed. 'Your songs – that's why we've come!' She glanced down at Blu. 'And to find proper shelter for our friend; she fell in the lake and the thunderghosts nearly drowned her.'

There was a snort from behind the boy as a girl with narrow eyes and a fan of black feathers over her upper body slunk forward.

'Lies, Jay. Don't listen to her. No one could outwit the thunderghosts now that the Ice Queen has them in her power.' She paused. 'And there's something strange about her voice. I don't like it.'

Eska recognised the girl as the one who had spoken with such malice a moment ago and she knew she had a choice: back down, as she had done in the Labyrinth, or stand up and try being brave. 'It's not lies,' she said shakily. 'Flint rescued Blu from the lake with one of his inventions.'

The boy, Jay, frowned. 'Inventions?'

Flint blushed and then mumbled something into his chest, but Eska pressed on. 'Yes. When he said he was a warrior earlier, he meant to say that he's an inventor.' Her voice was rough and gravelly, thanks to the Ice Queen's magic, but she gathered up her words nonetheless. 'One of the best that Erkenwald has ever seen.'

Flint slid a glance to Eska. 'You really are terrible at conversations.'

But Jay didn't wrinkle his nose or scoff at Eska's words. He just nodded, then he looked at the girl beside him. 'There *is* something different about her voice, but I'm not sure it's something we should fear.' He paused. 'And we could do with an inventor in times as dark as these. What do you think, Rook?'

Rook circled the cage, her dark eyes never leaving Eska's. Then she shrugged. 'Suit yourself. But you know what I think of your visions ... Just because you dreamed of a moonflit protecting us and one turned up to show us the entrance to the Lost Chambers doesn't mean that we should let an inventor, a Wanderer and,' she looked down her nose at Blu, 'a snivelling little nobody into our tribe – especially when they go banging on about the Frost Horn, which we all know doesn't exist.'

Flint raised his chin at Rook, his eyes hard, and Eska could feel the anger on Blu's behalf boiling inside him.

She reached out a hand and held his arm. 'Not now, Flint. We need their help.'

Rook's words dripped on. 'They'll weaken the Feather Tribe, Jay. Mark my words.'

She sloped off into the shadows and Jay turned back to his prisoners.

'The moonflit trusted you earlier and that's enough for me, whatever Rook says. But, before I tell you anything about us, I need to know how you found the Lost Chambers when even the Ice Queen and her guards failed to.' He paused. 'Prove that you're against the Ice Queen and her dark magic.'

And so Flint and Eska told Jay of their escape from Winterfang, of the sleigh chase through Deeproots, of Whitefur's words about the Sky Song and the Frost Horn and, finally, about the ice spider who had helped them find the Lost Chambers.

Jay nodded when Eska and Flint finished speaking. 'You're a true Wanderer, Eska. Your bond with the golden eagle proves it. And I can sense the power in your voice – despite what the Ice Queen is doing to it.'

Balapan's talons squeezed Eska's shoulder gently and she felt a quiet sense of pride.

'My parents are the Chief and Chieftainess of the Feather Tribe,' Jay said. 'And, though they're locked up in Winterfang, they told me to listen to my dreams – the gift every Chief of the Feather Tribe is blessed with – and I'm listening to them now.' He lowered his voice and looked straight at Eska. 'I want to help you.'

And those last five words cradled Eska in warmth because there was an opening now – a little space in this tribe for Eska and her friends.

Jay took a key from his pocket and turned it in the birdcage lock. The door creaked open and Eska, Flint, Pebble, Blu and Balapan stepped out into the atrium. But, from the shadows of an alcove, Rook narrowed her eyes and turned a sharp white fang over in her hands. It was the one she had stepped on a few weeks ago while out in the open, the one that had caused her foot to turn black before she pulled it out and the one that belonged, undoubtedly, to a cursed wolverine. And only one person had the power to hex wolverines . . .

Chapter Twenty-Four
Flint

Jay glanced at Blu, then cupped his hands round his mouth. 'Pipit!' he called. 'Take Blu here to the hot springs. She needs a warm bath.'

Blu clung to Flint. 'You come, too. My brother. Bath.'

Flint ushered Blu towards Pipit, a little boy with dreadlocks and green spotted shoulder feathers. 'I need to talk with Jay. Go along now, Blu.'

But Blu shook her head. 'With you. Big brother. And Pebble.'

For a moment, Flint ground his teeth, then he remembered Blu's face beneath the Devil's Dancefloor and how far she had come from all that she knew and loved. And he saw what was really important.

'I won't be long,' he said to Eska and Jay and as he walked, hand in hand with his little sister, after Pipit, he couldn't help feeling that something about Jay was oddly familiar. He racked his brains as he crossed the cavern, but his thoughts were broken by a voice from the shadows.

'Strange kind of warriors,' Rook muttered.

Flint tensed as he heard the words, but he kept on walking, out of the main atrium and along another tunnel that widened into a very different chamber. It was smaller than the first and when Flint saw that it was filled with a dozen bubbling hot springs jutting out from the rocks he forgot his anger. He grinned at Blu and moments later they were submerged in the steaming water. Even Pebble found himself kicking about in a smaller pool and Flint wondered then at all the things he'd seen since meeting Eska. It had been a detour worth following, after all.

They dried themselves with feathered blankets, then slipped back into their furs and returned to the main chamber, where the tribe were sitting round a long table piled with food. Balapan watched from a ledge up among the dreamcatchers, only shifting her gaze to snatch at the mice she found scuttling through the cavern, while Flint and Blu took a seat next to Eska, up by Jay at the head of the table. The Feather Tribe ate quietly, now and again stealing glances at the newcomers and sharing thoughts in guarded whispers.

Jay swallowed a mouthful of food. 'We plan to hide here for as long as it takes for the Ice Queen's rule to crumble. We're quick-moving and we're quiet. We can stay one step ahead of her and the Tusk guards in the Lost Chambers.'

Eska fiddled with her fork. 'The Ice Queen's rule isn't just going to crumble if she fails in her plans – not without me finding this Frost Horn and claiming the Sky Song. Because when the midnight sun rises she and all her prisoners at

Winterfang will perish.' Jay's face paled and Eska went on. 'Staying hidden isn't an option. And, when I blow the horn, I'm going to need help. I'm going to need your tribe to stand alongside me, to fight when the time comes.'

Flint winced. Eska had gone straight in and now there was no turning back. 'The battle at Winterfang was lost because our parents didn't really know what they were up against,' Flint said quietly. 'They tried to fight an Ice Queen with spears and bows, but that's not enough. We need to call upon,' he lowered his voice, 'magic this time. Upon the Frost Horn, the Sky Song, your dreams—'

'—and Flint's inventions,' Eska said firmly.

Flint cringed into his furs. They hadn't even reached the main course and he and Eska were already talking about magic and inventions.

But, before Jay could reply to any of this, another voice answered from the end of the table. Rook. She flung her bowl aside and stood up, her eyes scanning the rest of her tribe.

'That Wanderer there wants us to stand alongside her and fight! With *magic*? The very thing that tore this kingdom apart! She thinks that with the help of *our* songs, she'll find the forgotten Frost Horn and use it to defeat the Ice Queen!' Rook gestured around the cavern. 'She wants us to risk all this for the sake of a magic that no one believes in any more!'

There were mumblings from the Feather Tribe as Rook's poison worked deeper.

'So, what do you say, Jay? You've always told us to lay low, out of sight and out of danger.'

Jay said nothing for a while then he cleared his throat. 'I wonder, Rook, whether Eska and Flint are right. Hiding away until the midnight sun passes isn't the answer any more – not when it means risking the lives of all our families trapped in Winterfang.' He paused. 'Maybe we do in fact have a fight ahead of us – and, if so, we might need to start trusting in Erkenwald's magic again.'

The candlelight glimmered over Rook's feathers. 'We were managing fine before your guests showed up. What if they were tailed here by Tusk guards? What if the Ice Queen finds us?'

The Feather Tribe exchanged anxious glances.

'Or,' Rook spat, 'what if fighting means the end for us, like it did for so many of our parents?'

The boys and girls huddled round the table nodded.

'We might be eaten by wolverines!' cried one.

'Or cursed by the Ice Queen's shaman!' said another.

And, before long, the tribe had erupted again: shouts, threats, fists banging.

Rook sat down and smirked at Jay. 'And *that* is what happens when you let outsiders in.'

Jay tried to bring everyone back to order – to make them understand that their tribe wasn't something fixed and closed, that it was open to strange dreams, Fur people and even a girl with a golden eagle by her side – but Rook's words had stirred the Feather Tribe's fear and it brought the worst of their hearts out into the open.

Blu raised her hands to cover her ears and Eska turned frightened eyes to Flint.

'What do we do now?' she said in a cracked whisper.

Flint thought back to Whitefur's words. 'Tell them about your voice.'

Eska reached a hand up to her throat. 'My voice is nothing compared to all their shouting. Nothing.'

Flint shook his head. 'Then tell them about the Sky Song's power. Tell them about the things that Whitefur said your voice can do when you find the Frost Horn.'

'Silence the tribes, command animals and shake the skies,' Eska whispered.

'Good,' Flint replied. 'Now louder. *Much* louder.'

Beside her, Jay leant forward. 'Tell them, Eska. They might be my tribe, but they're not listening to me. Perhaps they need to hear it from someone else.'

Eska looked at the raging crowd. 'I – I don't think it'll work. There's too many of them and my voice isn't big enough!'

Flint shook his head. 'You just need one person to listen, then others will follow.'

Eska stood up, her knees shaking, and cleared her throat.

Flint thought of the Ice Queen winding away Eska's voice and he knew that when the anthem came again they'd hear it, even though they were in the middle of a mountain, and that afterwards Eska's voice would be weaker still. But, for now, she had words, and she needed to speak them with all the force left inside her. 'Tell them, Eska,' he said firmly.

'The Sky Song isn't something that belongs to worn-out legends!' Eska cried.

A few children looked up at her, but most continued to jeer and shout.

'Keep going,' Flint urged.

'It's the tune the North Star played on the Frost Horn to breathe life into Erkenwald all those years ago!' she shouted. 'And it's the only thing that can defeat the Ice Queen now!' She paused. 'I may not remember anything from my past, but I know this: we only have three days to stop the Ice Queen cursing Erkenwald and wiping out the Fur and Feather Tribes for ever, but, together with my friends and the help of Erkenwald's magic, I will find the Frost Horn and claim the Sky Song. And, when I do, I will use my voice to stop the Ice Queen and put an end to the divide between tribes!'

Some of the Feather Tribe heckled and, for a second, Flint wondered how on earth Eska was going to break through their distrust and hatred, but then he noticed that others were listening and Eska was forging on.

'I will silence the tribes, command animals and shake the skies!'

More heads turned to listen and Balapan leapt from her perch and circled in the air above them all.

'I may not have a whole tribe behind me,' Eska cried, 'I may not have words that you think amount to much now – but I won't give in. I won't back down. I have a voice and I'm going to make it count!'

She had the tribe's attention now. The chamber was absolutely silent.

'Because we have a kingdom to protect and families to bring home and, even in the face of an Ice Queen whose anthem reaches every corner of Erkenwald, *our voices matter more*. I *will* find the Frost Horn and I *will* blow it from the stars and, as one tribe, we *will* beat the Ice Queen.'

Balapan's call rang out then, like a shuddering battle cry, and suddenly the Feather Tribe were on their feet, whooping and cheering.

And Flint smiled at Eska. Some people collected shields of bark; others collected eggshells and feathers. But Eska? She collected people.

Blu ran round the table and hugged Eska tight and at their feet Pebble began chasing his tail and yapping excitedly.

Jay raised an eyebrow at Rook. 'And *that* is what happens when you let outsiders in.'

Then, to Flint, Eska and Blu's surprise, the tribe began to sing, a slow, lilting tune that reminded Flint of the way the wind soughed through the trees in Deeproots. And, with every word that sounded, Flint realised that this was a tribe who, contrary to Rook's words, did still believe in magic.

'Up north before the Groaning Splinters
The Grey Man stands up tall.
He's been there now for many winters
Though snow and hail does fall.

The cliffs are steep; we can but warn.
Gravestones are often laid.
So those who search for the lost Frost Horn
Must seek the Grey Man's aid.'

And, though the Ice Queen's anthem began as soon as the Feather Tribe finished singing, weaselling its way into the depths of the Lost Chambers, it was a soulless drone compared to what Flint, Eska and Blu had just heard.

Flint reached down and ruffled Pebble's head. 'We have a lead now. We need to find the Grey Man before the Groaning Splinters, the icebergs way up north.'

Eska rubbed her throat as the Ice Queen's anthem wound its way round her windpipe, leaving her voice almost threadbare. 'We'll leave as soon as it's light.'

Jay nodded. 'We're behind you, Eska. When you find the Frost Horn and blow it from the stars, we'll know to come out of hiding to help you.' He paused. 'I don't suppose either of you has a plan for how to reach the stars?'

Eska hung her head and Blu blew through her lips, but Flint looked at Jay with glittering eyes.

'I have an idea,' he said.

Eska stepped forward. 'An invention?'

Flint avoided her eyes. 'Possibly.' He fiddled with his cuff. 'I don't like talking about my ideas until I've properly thought them through. Just in case they don't work.'

Jay nodded. 'What do you need? Is there anything we can help with?'

'As a matter of fact, yes.' Flint picked up a snow-goose feather from the ground. It was white and large and he ran a finger up and down its length. 'How many of these do you have?'

Jay grinned. 'Thousands.'

'Can I take some?'

Jay picked up another and pressed it into Flint's hand. 'You can take them all.'

And it was then that Flint recalled where he had seen Jay before. Years and years ago, when he was little more than a scrap, his pa had taken him hunting and out on the foothills before the Never Cliffs they had shared food with the Feather Chief and his son.

Flint tilted his head towards Jay. 'I remember you,' he said.

Jay was thoughtful for a moment and then he smiled. 'Round the campfire when we were very small,' he said slowly. 'We ate snow hare and caribou before everything,' he paused, 'changed. You had lost your quiver of arrows in the river that day and I lent you mine.' Flint nodded and Jay reached out and put his hand on Flint's shoulder. 'From this day on, you and your tribe will always be welcome here and if we cross paths hunting we will stop and eat and share stories.'

Flint felt a heaviness inside him lift at the warmth of Jay's words. Erkenwald was that little bit closer to the kingdom he remembered before the Ice Queen arrived and turned it upside down.

But, while Flint, Eska, Blu and the Feather Tribe busied

themselves collecting snow-goose feathers and clearing away dinner, Rook brushed past the moonflit in the entrance tunnel. She clutched the wolverine fang in a hot, angry fist and with the sound of the Ice Queen's anthem ringing in her ears she stalked out into the starless night.

Chapter Twenty-Five
Eska

Eska woke to the Ice Queen's anthem – and the sound of a birdcall. She pushed back the feather quilt, stretched inside the cage she had slept in and opened her eyes. Balapan was still crouched on the ledge outside it, but Eska knew the call she had heard hadn't belonged to the eagle.

A short, sharp yap came again from the entrance tunnel. It was the cry of a snowy owl. Eska had heard a similar call from her hideaway behind the Giant's Beard, but something about this one was slightly different. And then Pipit burst into the cavern and Eska remembered his words from the night before: the snowy-owl call was a signal used by the Feather Tribe. A warning that danger was nearby.

'The moonflit!' Pipit cried as the Feather Tribe sat up in their cages. 'She's crying! And her tail's tucked up and shaking!'

Jay scrambled up the ledges until he came to an empty birdcage not far from Eska's. 'She's gone!' he gasped. 'Rook's gone.'

The Feather Tribe leapt out of their cages and reached for their bows and arrows.

'She's – she's gone to the Ice Queen, hasn't she?' Eska stammered.

Jay's face darkened. 'Perhaps. Something inside Rook changed a few weeks ago. She came in from a hunt and her thoughts were darker, her words sharper.' He shook his head. 'But I don't believe Rook's to blame. I think it's the Ice Queen – somehow she got to Rook.' Jay glanced towards the tunnels on into the mountains. 'You must leave now. Your skis won't be much use on the ice flats, but we can lend you a sled and some dogs from the outchambers. Ride fast across the Driftlands until you find the Grey Man; there's no time to spare if the Ice Queen knows where you are.'

Flint gathered up his sack of snow-goose feathers. 'What if Rook tells the Ice Queen where the entrance to the Lost Chambers is?'

'I've ways of charming the door and changing its location,' Jay explained. And then, after a pause: 'You're not the only one who kept believing in magic when the rest of the tribe turned their backs.'

Grabbing Pebble from the food store, where he was helping himself to a third breakfast, Flint, Eska and Blu tore through the candlelit passageways after Jay. They ran past chambers filled with furs, bows and arrows, until eventually they came to a small cave that contained ten yapping dogs. Balapan flew up to the highest ledge she could find and peered down.

The dogs were bigger than Flint's had been – wolfish grey

coats and strong, muscled legs – and they crowded round Jay, their tails wagging, as he harnessed them to a fur-lined sled. There was space enough for Eska and Flint to stand on the runners and Eska nudged Blu towards the seat in front.

'For you,' Eska whispered. 'A little throne.'

Blu clambered on. 'Happy.'

Pebble swaggered up to the dogs, desperate to be part of the pack, but Flint lifted the fox pup into his arms, dropped him on to Blu's lap, then wedged his sack of feathers at her feet. 'Working dogs don't eat three breakfasts before a run, Pebble.'

He climbed on to the back of the sled, but Eska hesitated for a moment and looked at Jay.

'You will come, won't you?' Her voice was little more than a scratch. 'When I blow the Frost Horn?'

Jay nodded. 'I'll come. The whole tribe will. I give you my word.'

Pulling her hood up, Eska mounted the sled beside Flint. Words, she was beginning to realise, were like glue. They held promises and friendships together. And though her own words were coming apart she hoped that Jay's were enough to rouse his tribe when her call came.

'Thank you for everything,' she whispered.

Jay smiled, then he put his hand on a slab of rock on the chamber wall. 'Once I open the door here, you'll be out on the Driftlands.' The dogs shifted their weight, as if they could sense the journey ahead. 'Ride fast across the ice and follow the river until it reaches the Groaning Splinters. You'll find the Grey Man there and, though our ancestors talk of a wise old man, it's my bet he'll be in pieces in light of what's been going on. The Ice Queen's reign won't have been kind to folk like him.'

He pushed against the slab of rock and it crunched forward to reveal a door out of the mountain. Almost immediately, there was a sharp cry and a flap of feathers as Balapan glided into the world beyond. The cold slipped into Eska's lungs and she squinted into the silver mist that hung over the Driftlands.

'Spring hasn't reached the north yet,' Jay said. 'But you'll find the ice makes your travels swift.' He clasped Eska's and Flint's hands, then he ruffled Blu's hair. 'Until we meet again, good luck.'

And, before Eska, Flint or Blu could reply, the dogs lurched forward, hauling the sled out on to the ice and it was several seconds before Flint gathered them under his control.

He steered through the mist. 'How are we going to find the river in this? I can barely see the Never Cliffs behind us let alone Balapan in front!'

Eska peered through the wisps of white. They hung like floating ribbons over the ice, masking the morning sun, and, though the Ice Queen's anthem had now trailed away, every time Eska heard a new sound – the wind moaning, a musk ox grunt – she spun round. The mist was a cloak and the Ice Queen and her sleigh might appear from under it at any moment.

Flint nudged Eska. 'Well, how are we going to find it?'

'I'm thinking, Flint,' Eska replied. 'I need quiet for that.'

Flint tapped his mittens on the sled and Eska tried to ignore him. And, as they raced away from the Never Cliffs, Eska thought carefully. Animals needed water to survive so any wolves or musk oxen that prowled the Driftlands would head to the river if they could break a hole in the ice.

'Follow any animal tracks you find,' she said. 'They'll lead us to the river.'

But as Eska's eyes flicked downwards it was not footprints that she saw. All around them now, only just visible through the mist, were caribou antlers, shed from the animals themselves the year before. They lay on the ice like stiff white claws.

'That's odd,' Flint murmured. 'Normally, the hares, lemmings and voles gnaw away at the antlers after they've fallen from the caribou.'

Eska shifted her weight. 'Why would those creatures suddenly stay away?'

'Look – on the tip of every antler.' Flint swallowed. 'I think the smaller animals did come; they just never left . . .'

And as Eska peered more closely she noticed the tiny animal skulls hanging from the antler tips. Blu tucked her legs up to her chin, Pebble burrowed his head into her furs, and in front of them the dogs' ears cocked this way and that. It was like a graveyard of antlers around them and Flint did his best to weave a way through, but, when his sled crunched over one, the wind died away completely and the silence that followed pulsed.

'The Ice Queen's dark magic has been here,' Flint whispered. 'This whole place feels cursed.'

'A taste of what's to come for the kingdom, if we can't stop her . . .' Eska shivered. 'Ride faster.'

Flint urged the dogs on and in the distance they heard a wolf howl.

Eska tensed. The sound was low and lingering, like wind moaning through a chimney, and as it rang out the skulls on the antler tips rattled. Then it died away and, a few moments later, the sled was free of the antlers and Eska glimpsed Balapan's silhouette through the mist.

She pointed down to the snow. 'Wolf tracks leading east.'

They followed them until they came to the river, a silent snake winding its way north, a few minutes later.

'This Grey Man – what do you think he's like?' Eska asked.

Flint flapped his reins and the dogs sped on. 'Old, if the Feather Tribe have been singing songs about him for generations – and unhappy, because the Ice Queen doesn't look kindly on Erkenwald's magic.'

Eska nodded. 'We can cheer him up, especially when he learns that you're an inventor and you might know a way of reaching the stars so that I can blow the Frost Horn.'

Flint glanced at Eska. 'You know inventions don't always work.'

'Yes.'

'So, you understand this one could be a disaster?'

'Yes.'

'So, why aren't you more worried?'

'I'm terrified,' Eska said quietly. 'But sometimes all you can do when you're scared is hope.'

The mist thickened without them noticing at first. It was only when the dogs grew twitchy, shying at bends in the river and flinching at frozen trees, that Eska felt her heart quicken. Then the wind picked up, heaving and groaning and stirring the mist so that it rose around them like a slow-creeping wave. The dogs stopped before Flint drew them in and though they were large, strong beasts they whined like newborn pups. And, when Balapan appeared through the hazy screen and swept low beside Eska, she knew something wasn't right.

Blu turned wide eyes to her brother. 'I scared, Flint.'

Before Flint could reply, the wind blew harder, whipping the snow and ice up into its swell until a churn of flakes tore around them and the world seemed to dissolve into white. The dogs backed up towards the sled and Balapan's wings juddered as the wind gathered pace and strength.

Eska shielded her eyes with her arm as the snow beat against her. 'This storm is brewed with the Ice Queen's magic! Keep going!'

Flint whipped the dogs on, but as the wind shunted the snow and ice against the group the dogs yanked at their harnesses before snapping free and bounding away into the endless white. The sled ground to a halt again and the blizzard raged with newfound fury, sending needle-sharp ice against the children's faces.

Flint rushed towards Blu and lifted her, Pebble and his sack of feathers from the sled. The group could barely open their eyes in the face of the storm, but Eska managed to, just a crack, and that was enough to see a square shape – a snow-covered food store perhaps – a few metres in front of them.

'There!' she cried. 'Shelter!'

Balapan spiralled into the sky and yapped, but her cries were drowned by the smashing of the gale, and Eska, Flint and Blu staggered towards the hut. They yanked the door open and it clattered back against the wall then they stumbled over the threshold and hauled the door shut.

Chapter Twenty-Six
Flint

I t was still and quiet inside the hut, despite the wind and
the snow roaring across the Driftlands, and Flint noticed
a rickety table with a stool beside it and a heap of furs
bunched in a rocking chair in the corner. There was nobody
inside that he could see, but the place felt homely, a welcome
escape from the menace outside.

Flint tickled Pebble's chin, then bent down beside his
sister. 'Are you okay?'

Blu brushed the snow from her face. 'Don't like hut. Not
nice.'

'It's better than being outside in the Ice Queen's storm,'
Flint replied, but he noticed that Pebble didn't leap down
from his hood to explore as he usually would.

'Where's Balapan?' Eska whispered. 'Didn't she follow us
in?'

Flint's eyes caught on a dark shape huddled on the
windowsill outside. The eagle's wings were folded tight
against the barrage of snow and wind.

Eska eyed her cautiously. 'Do you think if Balapan didn't come in then—'

Flint grabbed Eska's arm. 'Look at the walls!'

Eska gasped.

In the hurry to find shelter no one had noticed that this was a hut made entirely of bones.

Flint glanced around, his shoulders bunching higher as he took in the mesh of white bones surrounding them, then he listened to the *tap-tap-tapping* of Balapan's beak against the window, a small but fierce sound amid the gusting blizzard. 'We need to leave,' he hissed. 'Now. Because I don't think this is an old food store at all; I think it's a hut cursed by dark magic!'

Eska shot to the door and yanked the handle, but it wouldn't budge. She threw her body against it. Still it wouldn't move and, at the realisation that they were trapped, Blu shuffled closer to Flint.

And that's when the wolves began to howl – hollow moans that rose into the storm and echoed with malice.

'Wild wolves don't sound like that,' Flint whispered.

Eska gulped. 'They're bewitched, aren't they?'

Flint put a shaking arm round Blu as the howls droned on into the storm.

'We can't just stay here and wait for the wolves to come for us,' Eska spluttered. 'We need to get out!'

As if in response, Balapan flung her weight against the window. But this pane wasn't made of glass: it was a slab of cursed ice and, no matter how many times the eagle barged into it, it wouldn't break. The wolves howled again and Flint watched in horror as Balapan launched herself off the windowsill and disappeared from sight.

'Has – has she left us?' he cried, rushing to the window.

Eska followed. 'She can't have done – she'd never abandon us!'

And while Flint and Eska pressed panicked palms up to the glass Blu hurried to the corner of the hut. Unseen by the others, she crouched low and whispered to the eagle whose talons she could hear wrenching the bones away from the outside.

Blu peered through a tiny gap that the eagle had opened up. 'I see you, Bala. I help.'

She pulled at a bone and as it fell away the whole hut groaned and then juddered and a much larger bone from the ceiling clattered down, smashing the rocking chair behind her in two. Flint whirled round and then gasped as he saw what was happening.

'Balapan and Blu!' he cried, snatching up his sack of feathers. 'They're creating a hole for us to escape out of!'

He and Eska darted towards the corner of the hut and, kneeling beside Blu, began scrabbling at the walls. A cluster of bones thumped down, missing Flint's head by a fraction.

'Careful, big brother,' Blu said. 'Hut fall. Big bang. Slowly, slowly with bones.'

And, though the wolf howls clamoured closer and Blu's, Flint's and Eska's hands were tingling with nerves, they pushed gently against each bone they wanted to move until finally there was an opening large enough to crawl through.

'Now!' Flint cried, ushering Blu out first. 'Quick!'

He followed close behind with Pebble in his hood and just as Eska lifted her body through the gap after him the whole hut creaked to the side, then the bones thundered down into a giant heap of rubble behind them.

'Balapan,' Eska panted as she clambered free from the debris.

She held the eagle against the storm and Flint hugged his little sister, but there was no time for praise. They didn't have any dogs to pull their sled away. Even running would be hard because the snow blocked out the sun and shadows so that all that remained was a depthless white. And still the wolves howled. They sounded terrifyingly close now and Flint cursed as he realised Whitefur had only sworn to help them in the Never Cliffs.

Balapan tore up into the sky and Eska grabbed Blu's hand. 'Run!' she croaked. 'Follow Balapan!'

Flint seized his sack of feathers, then grabbed Blu's other hand and together they sped from the rubble of bones, heads down as they charged through the blizzard after the eagle. And though the snow battered their faces and the wind punched their furs, they struggled on.

But the Ice Queen's dark magic was on to the group now and, as the storm pulled back for a moment, three sleds drawn by enormous midnight-black wolves raced into view. Blu shrieked in horror as the pack of slathering animals, pulling twelve Tusk guards clad in ice armour and tusked helmets, advanced. Then the blizzard closed in again and the sleds vanished.

Flint, Eska and Blu ran blindly after Balapan. *Did the eagle know a place where they would be safe?* Flint wondered. *Or was she fleeing, too, in the knowledge that the dark magic was finally closing in?*

The wolves bayed and the Tusk guards bellowed, but the noises didn't seem to be coming from behind them now. The din was all around: a bawling, roaring, screeching ruckus. Flint listened to it and saw Balapan hovering above them, then he realised, with sickening dread, that there was nowhere left to run, nowhere left to hide.

He stopped and drew out his Anything Knife, and Eska pulled down her bow and arrows, then they waited. But the wolves didn't approach. The din grew steadily louder and as Flint and his friends huddled together they realised the roaring sound did not belong to the wolves. Theirs was a strangled yowl while louder than that, fiercer than that, was the throaty growl of another animal.

Flint turned to Eska. 'There's something else out here on the Driftlands.'

Eska nodded. Even Blu seemed to understand. And, as the group listened to the roars and clashing of spears, Flint realised that someone, or something, was fighting their battle.

The air rang with the sound of the fight: roars so deep and fierce and wild that the very blizzard seemed to shake. The wails of the men were nothing beside those roars – merely empty cries that knew the end was in sight – and then, finally, there was silence. Even the wind died to nothing, as if it was no longer bound under the Ice Queen's control. No guards cried out. No beasts roared. The only sound to break the stillness was a slow, heaving pant. Then the mist lifted and Flint, Eska and Blu saw clearly.

Twelve Tusk guards lay strewn on the ice and surrounding them – and Flint, Eska and Blu – was a ring of enormous Erkenbears. They faced inwards, their soot-black noses pointing to their kills, their bodies planted like boulders.

Flint's blood coursed. 'This is either an excellent situation to be in – or a dreadful one.' His eyes darted from one bear to the next. 'It's very hard to tell which.'

'The wild doesn't play by ordinary rules,' Eska murmured.

Flint gulped. 'In which case, they won't be that fussed about what they eat – Tusk guards, wolves, US!'

He watched Balapan rising, coil after coil, into the sky, the tips of her feathers fluttering in the wind. The eagle didn't cry out or yap to warn them of danger. She simply flew, until she was almost lost in the clouds, then she let her call go, and, one by one, the bears threw up their heads and roared.

The sound of the bears and the eagle tore across the Driftlands and as Flint glanced at Eska he felt a strange tingling fill his body. She was surrounded by the wild – *her* tribe – and for a moment it felt like the animals were singing just for her. The Erkenbears fell silent and Balapan flew without calling. Then, very slowly, Eska stood up. The bears took a step closer, claiming the ice with their heavy paws.

'I hope you have a plan,' Flint moaned.

Eska walked closer still, edging towards the largest bear in the circle, until its ragged breath ruffled her hair. Then she stopped.

'Whitefur,' she whispered, her voice so quiet it barely sounded at all. 'You came for us, didn't you?'

And, at that, the mighty bear dipped his head.

Flint staggered to his feet. '*Whitefur?*'

The Erkenbear didn't stand up on two feet and shake back his pelt to reveal a man inside, but something about the way the animal looked at Flint, the way it looked right into his soul, made him feel sure that this was their friend.

Blu picked herself up and ran towards him.

Flint gasped. 'Blu! No!'

The little girl threw her arms round the Erkenbear's neck, burying her head in his soft white fur.

Flint blushed. 'You can push her off if you want, Whitefur.'

But the Erkenbear simply wound his head round and tucked Blu closer to his body. Eska lifted a hand to Whitefur's pelt and as she did so the first few notes of the Ice Queen's anthem began.

Flint shivered. It couldn't be later than midday – the choir had only finished singing a few hours ago – but the midnight sun would rise the day after tomorrow and Flint knew the Ice Queen was bent on swallowing all the stolen voices before then. He watched as Eska tried to ignore the anthem and focus on the Erkenbear before her.

She stroked his neck. 'Thank you, Whitefur. If you hadn't—' Eska tried to clear her throat to allow her words out, but no matter how many times she swallowed her voice wouldn't sound above a whisper.

The Ice Queen's anthem droned on – louder now that she had swallowed so many of her prisoners' voices – but it made Flint think of the contraption Eska said the Tusk shaman had made. Was it fuelled by the anthem and now that the choir sang more often was it coming close to draining Eska's voice completely? He watched Eska's eyes fill with tears and then the circle of Erkenbears dropped their heads low. Flint bit his lip. Could the Erkenbears tell that the Ice Queen was winning?

'We won't manage to get the Frost Horn in time,' Eska whispered. 'Will we?'

But Flint's gaze was now fixed on the Erkenbears, on the way that they were standing. Heads dipped, one foreleg stretched out ahead and the other tucked under their bodies.

'Eska,' he said slowly. 'The Erkenbears aren't giving up. They're bowing.'

'Bowing?' Eska whispered. 'Why?'

Flint's eyes shone. 'Because you're in their tribe. And they know, just as I do, that you're the one person in Erkenwald who can still set all this right.'

Chapter Twenty-Seven
Eska

When the Erkenbears pulled back from their circle and gathered together a little way from the group, Eska opened her rucksack and shared round the grayling and boiled eggs Jay had packed for them. She knew the Erkenbears were on their side, but something about their size and smell made Eska and her friends eat with one eye on their food and one eye on the bears. Only Pebble seemed unfazed by their presence, chomping and burping his way through his meal as if he was indulging in a feast in Deeproots.

The afternoon sun burned through the clouds and Eska knew that this break in the weather was just what they needed to travel north. She glanced at the Tusk sleds, smashed to pieces by the fight, but the Ice Queen's anthem had gone quiet for a while and without it droning on Eska found she could think more clearly.

'We need to find the Grey Man,' she whispered. 'But we've no way of getting north. Other than walking.'

Blu scoffed. 'Bears.'

Flint shook his head. 'They're not for riding, Blu. The wild's not like that.'

The group watched as five of the Erkenbears sloped away, spreading out in all directions over the ice, until just Whitefur and one other bear remained.

'I wonder,' Eska whispered.

She stood up and walked towards the two Erkenbears, then she leant in close to Whitefur. She didn't use words – somehow it didn't feel right, in the same way that if you were going to climb a mountain you wouldn't stop to ask its permission – instead, she ran a hand down the bear's neck, then scooped a fistful of fur into her hand. Whitefur dipped his head and Eska hauled herself up on to his back.

And as Eska sat astride the Erkenbear she remembered Whitefur's words inside the Giant's Beard – *Your voice has the power to silence the tribes, command animals and shake the skies* – and smiled. She had silenced the tribes. Well, one of them, anyway. And now she was commanding the animals. She squinted into the sun. Suddenly shaking the skies didn't seem quite so impossible, after all.

Grabbing his sackful of feathers, Flint edged over to the second Erkenbear with Blu. He gave a polite little bow, then glanced at his sister. 'I think you should curtsey before you climb up.'

Blu looked disgusted. 'Wild not like that, Flint.'

And, seizing the bear's fur, she hoisted herself up. Wedging Pebble into his hood, Flint climbed on after her, then he slotted the sack into Blu's lap and wrapped one arm round it and his little sister, and clung on to the Erkenbear's neck with his other.

'They'll take us to the Grey Man,' Eska whispered. She glanced at Balapan soaring above them, then she looked across to Flint. 'Ready?'

Pebble barked and Flint gave a shaky nod. 'Ready.'

The Erkenbears lumbered forward, pounding over the ice with their giant paws, and at first Eska jostled around on the bear's back, desperately trying to stay upright. It was only when she raised her knees so that she was bent low over Whitefur's neck that she found the bear's rhythm. And then she didn't move like a girl but a wild thing, pressed close to the heart of beasts. So *this* was what it felt like to move like a bear, Eska thought, to swallow the ground underfoot rather than stumble breathlessly across it. She grinned. It was like running with the strength of a waterfall on her side.

On and on the bears raced – over ridges of snow, across iced rivers and through copses of winter-bare trees – while Balapan flew above. They never tired, never slowed, never stopped once. Eventually, the coast came into view.

'The Groaning Splinters,' Flint murmured as they neared the snow-blasted cliff tops. 'We're close to Tusk territory now . . .'

From the Erkenbears' backs, Eska, Flint and Blu looked at the giant icebergs, floating like half-toppled houses on the turquoise sea. Eska shivered. Further east, along the coast, and thankfully out of sight from where they stood now, were the Tusk Tribe igloos and the cursed iceberg that was Winterfang Palace.

Eska slipped from Whitefur's back on to the snow. The cliffs in front of her dropped vertically to the sea – their only hope down them was if they found the Grey Man – but as Eska looked around she could see no sign of a tall old man who had braved many winters out on the northern coast. She walked round to face Whitefur and held his heavy jaw in her hands. 'Where is the Grey Man?' she whispered. 'Do you know?'

She half hoped that Whitefur would show his human form and trade words instead of grunts, but the wild never bent the way you wanted it to. Whitefur rubbed his head into Eska's shoulder and she knew that this was goodbye – for now – that he had taken her to the right place and it was up to her, Flint and Blu to do the rest.

'Thank you,' she whispered against the din of the kittiwakes and guillemots chattering from the cliffs. 'I wish my words were louder so that I could really tell you how grateful I am.'

Whitefur stood on the cliff top with Eska, then he dipped his head, and, together with the second bear, he hastened back across the ice, into the heart of Erkenwald once again. Balapan swooped down and landed on Eska's shoulder.

'It won't be long before the Ice Queen steals your voice completely,' Flint said to Eska. 'And just two days until the midnight sun rises. So, where on earth is this Grey Man?'

'Over here,' came a tart reply.

Eska jumped. The voice belonged to a man with a high, almost weedy voice, which might have gone unnoticed had Flint been talking more loudly.

'Well, don't just stand there gawping,' the voice squeaked. 'I've got a headache, a broken leg, a sore back and a sprained knee. I very obviously need help!'

Blu clutched Flint's hand. 'Who this? Who there?'

The voice came again, even higher – and crosser – than before. 'No one comes my way for almost a year and then you three show up, like a trio of gaping buffoons.' There was a sigh. 'I'm right under your noses, you know.'

Eska glanced at the little mound of snow in front of her. 'You don't think . . . ?'

Balapan leapt down from her shoulder and Eska brushed a handful of snow aside to reveal a heap of small rocks. The reedy voice sounded again. It was louder this time and it came straight from the rocks themselves.

'Why are humans always so confoundedly stupid?!'

Flint stared at the rocks. 'How – how can they be speaking?'

'Like this,' the voice snapped.

Blu bent down and lifted up a long, thin rock.

'Do you mind?' the voice muttered. 'That's my arm.'

Eska's eyes widened. 'Jay's words about the Grey Man . . .' She forced her voice on. '*He'll be in pieces in light of what's been going on.* In pieces. The Grey Man is literally in pieces!'

The rocks looked decidedly fed up, if rocks could look that way. 'Clever clogs.'

Flint blinked. 'The Ice Queen must have torn him down

in the battle. Maybe we need to build him back up into a person so that he can help us!'

The voice sighed. 'Yes, you do. Before the sun sets, too, because I have absolutely no confidence in your working in the dark.' There was a pause. 'So, would you be so kind as to pass me my arm?'

Ignoring the Grey Man's demands, Flint lifted an oval rock from the pile and placed it in the snow. 'This could be a face,' he murmured. 'If you squint at it hard enough.'

'Of course it's my face, you bumbling idiot!' the voice inside the rock barked.

Balapan raked her talons across a rounder rock.

'Do be careful! That's my bottom. It's gone rather numb after all this lying down in one place, but I am still fond of it. In fact, I'd say it's one of my best features.'

Down on their hands and knees, Eska, Flint, Balapan, Blu and even Pebble worked as quickly as they could to piece the Grey Man back together.

'Put your back into it!' the rocks squeaked. 'I mean, put *my* back into it! And my hands – I'll be needing them if you want me to help you!'

And, although the conversation was somewhat stressful and Blu seemed determined to place the Grey Man's foot on top of his head and Pebble spent far too much time using his tail to flick stones at Flint's bottom, they did, eventually, manage to cobble together a figure with the rocks. There was a moment of silence as the group looked at their creation arranged in the snow.

'Now what?' Flint hissed.

The Grey Man lay there in the vague shape of a man. His face was a blank stone still – there was no mouth, no nose, no eyes – and yet the creaky voice came again.

'Now this,' it chuckled. 'Finally, this.'

As he spoke, the snow around him whipped up into a flurry then the stones began to move. They ground together like rusty joints, then the Grey Man stood up and on the stone that was his head a face showed. An old, wrinkled face, carved into the rock itself and spotted with lichen.

Two grey eyes blinked. 'Am I tall and splendid?'

Eska squinted. The man came up to her knee.

'But the Feather Tribe song ...' Flint mumbled as he glanced towards the Grey Man. 'It said he was tall. And he needs to be if he's going to help us find our way down the cliffs to the Frost Horn!'

There was an awkward pause.

'I knew it!' the Grey Man wailed. 'I'm small, aren't I?' He raised a rocky palm to his forehead. 'Oh, dismantle my legs; lop off my head! Cast me off the edge of the cliff!'

Blu reached out a hand and patted him on the head. 'You being silly now.'

'That wretched Ice Queen!' the Grey Man snivelled. 'When she cast me down, she stripped me of my devilishly attractive height. She said there were no room for giants in *her* Erkenwald.'

Flint's jaw hardened. 'Well, this isn't *her* Erkenwald. It's *ours*.'

And this time Eska didn't have to prompt Flint to rummage through his rucksack for an invention. He ripped the bag open and pulled out a stoppered bottle. Under the fading light, Eska saw a jet-black liquid within the glass that every now and again flickered gold.

'What's that?' the Grey Man asked suspiciously.

'Bottled lightning,' Flint replied. 'A few drops can drastically increase an object's size or speed.'

'Are you sure, boy?' The Grey Man wagged his finger at Flint. 'Because I might have an allergy to it and I really don't want—'

Blu, it appeared, didn't have much patience with the Grey Man's allergies and, before he could get any more words out, she grabbed the bottle from Flint and began tipping the liquid over him.

Flint snatched the bottle back before she could drain the whole thing. 'I need the rest of it for something else, Blu. Something important.'

For a few seconds, nothing happened and then the Grey Man gasped. He was growing, before their very eyes. The rocks that formed his body swelled to become boulders, the stones that were his fingers stretched out into plinths and the rock that was his head grew until it was as big as a door.

The Grey Man cricked his neck and his voice came forth in a deep boom. 'I had forgotten how splendid it feels to be a giant!'

Blu patted Flint on the back. 'You best inventor.'

Flint beamed.

'We've come for the Frost Horn,' Eska whispered to the Grey Man.

'Well, of course you have! I didn't think you'd dropped by with the Erkenbears for a cup of tea!'

'So, how do we get down to the shore without dying?' Flint asked.

The Grey Man waved a hand casually. 'Oh, it's just a hop, skip and a jump. Would you like to ride on my shoulder or my head? Both will be equally uncomfortable.'

Chapter Twenty-Eight
Eska

They chose the Grey Man's shoulder – partly because it was a flatter surface, but mostly because, when Blu tried to scale the giant's nose to reach his forehead, the giant had sneezed and Blu had been coated in a thick layer of slime.

Eska, Flint, Blu and Pebble sat on the Grey Man's shoulder with the sack of feathers, silently envying Balapan gliding above. The sky ahead was pink and the sea around the icebergs almost purple as the light finally faded. Eska swallowed. Somewhere out there was the legendary Frost Horn and time was running out to claim it.

The giant strode back quite some way from the cliff edge.

'We're sort of in a hurry,' Eska whispered. 'Aren't you going the wrong way?'

'You must never underestimate the wrong way!' the Grey Man thundered. 'Because more often than not it turns out to be the *right* way ... Just with a few more bends in the road!'

Flint nodded warily. 'Yet another detour ...'

The giant spun round and Eska and her friends clung to

the rocky crevices in his shoulder. Then the Grey Man took an enormous stride forward – then another and another – and Eska dug her fingers into the cracks in the stone.

'Hold on!' the Grey Man hollered. 'It's been a while since I made the jump and I've no idea if my back will hold out during the descent!'

A look of horror washed over Flint's face, but Blu grinned.

'*Wheeeeeeeee!*' she shouted as the giant leapt from the cliff. 'I tell Tomkin I jump with giant!'

They plummeted down, down, down with Balapan at their side – past the puffins, kittiwakes and guillemots crammed on to the rocky ledges – and Eska's stomach lurched.

'And run from wolves!' Blu giggled.

The horror plastered across Flint's face deepened and then they landed on the snowy beach with a very large, and slightly painful, bump.

The Grey Man dusted a clump of lichen from his leg. 'Not bad, considering.'

Eska breathed out and as she watched Balapan preening her feathers nearby she thought how much less complicated life would be if she was an eagle. Still, they had made it down to the shore, a drop many of the Feather Tribe had died attempting, and before them now was the sea – dark purple and loaded with icebergs. There were harp seals and bearded seals dotted here and there on the flat icebergs nearby, but further out, on the bridges, leaning towers, columned arches and pyramids chiselled out of ice, there was nothing at all. Eska thought of her ma suddenly and wondered whether she had stood on this beach and swum in the waters that broke over it.

The Grey Man lifted the group from his shoulder and set them down by the shore. They listened to the creak and jostle of the icebergs moving.

'The Frost Horn,' the giant said quietly. 'You'll find it among the last of the Groaning Splinters.' He paused. 'I would say more but the truth is I don't know any more. I just remember, many moons ago, that the greatest of the Sky Gods left it there after breathing life into Erkenwald.'

Flint glanced at the driftwood lying about the beach and swung his sack of feathers to the ground. 'I have a plan, a rough one, for when – *if* – we get the Frost Horn.' He sighed. 'But how do we even get out to the furthest icebergs in the first place? That's a jungle of ice – we'll need a kayak to steer us through!'

The Grey Man knelt down beside them. 'Or just a very convenient wind ...'

He didn't explain any more and minutes later the last of the colour drained from the sky and night crowded in. Eska's skin prickled. There would only be a few hours of darkness – the nights were getting shorter with every day that passed – then dawn would break and they'd be just one day away from the midnight sun ...

'You can't go on now,' the Grey Man said. 'It's too dark and you'll need a rest and food.' Pebble snuffled in agreement. 'But I'll take you at first light.'

The Grey Man stepped back and only then did Eska notice

the abandoned igloo behind him. The slabs of snow were slightly misshapen – battered over the months by the winter storms – but it was a good enough shelter for the night and the group hurried towards it.

'I'll keep guard through the dark,' the Grey Man said, settling himself down on a rock by the shore. He dropped his legs into the water and smiled. 'It's good to be home . . .'

Flint and Blu laid out furs inside the igloo while Eska clambered up the cliffs with Balapan. The eagle cracked open the gull eggs and drained the yolks there and then, but Eska pocketed as many as she could carry and stole back to the igloo. She crept inside. This was a former Tusk home and yet, in the hour she had taken to forage for eggs, her friends had transformed the snowy dome.

Flint had a fire going and above it Blu had hung the magnifying glass infused with rainbow essence and, though from the outside the igloo looked just like a dark shape huddled at the foot of the cliffs, inside it glowed every colour possible. Turquoise danced over the roof, purple flickered across the floor and gold shone on the walls.

'It's beautiful in here,' Eska whispered. 'A pocket of Erkenwald not yet ruined by the Ice Queen.'

Flint cracked the eggs on to a flattened stone he had placed above the fire, then he looked at Eska.

'We're going to find the Frost Horn,' he said. 'However far out on the Groaning Splinters it is.'

'But it's not just finding the horn, is it?' Eska whispered. She thought of Rook leading the Tusk guards towards the

Lost Chambers. 'It's everything that comes after that – blowing it from the skies, getting the tribes to fight with us, stopping the Ice Queen from changing Erkenwald for ever.' She looked down. 'So many things to hope for.'

Flint nodded. 'But think back to where we've come from. The music box, the Giant's Beard, the Never Cliffs and the Grey Man outside guarding our sleep. It's going to be okay.'

'We find Ma,' Blu said.

It wasn't a question. It was a fact. And Eska realised then that hope moved quickly. It could burn inside you one minute and then, just when you thought you'd lost it, you'd find it shining in the hearts of your friends. She looked around the igloo. So long as one of them remembered to bring hope with them, perhaps things would turn out all right.

Chapter Twenty-Nine
Flint

As the sun rose over the horizon, big and pale and flooding the Groaning Splinters with light, Flint, Blu, Eska and Pebble knelt on a flattened iceberg. The Grey Man strode out into the sea, nudging the iceberg forward, and Flint stifled a yawn. He knew Eska hadn't noticed him creep out of the igloo in the night, but, if he carried on yawning like this, she'd start to ask questions – and some things were better left unsaid, especially while the Ice Queen's anthem was going on and Eska's voice was little more than a wisp of breath.

Flint glanced at Balapan circling above them. 'She has an unfair advantage in this quest,' he muttered. 'Wings make *all* the difference.'

The Grey Man walked on for a while longer, then he paused before a maze of iced bridges, arches and spiral columns.

'I'll leave you here,' he said. 'It seems like a perfectly reasonable place.'

'But we need to get to the furthest of the Groaning

Splinters,' Eska whispered. 'We're not even among them yet!'

Flint nodded. 'It's not as if the wind is going to carry us on. It's as calm as a millpond this morning!'

Blu jabbed a little fist in both Eska and Flint's sides. 'Listen to giant. He know way.'

The Grey Man smiled at Blu. 'For someone so small, you're actually rather wise.' He stood back from the iceberg. 'And now for a spot of *convenient* wind.'

He took a deep breath in and his stone body crunched as his chest swelled, then he bent down, level with the iceberg the children sat on, and let his breath out. The iceberg drifted across the water, steered by the giant's breath, and the group swung round as they realised what was happening.

'You're really not coming with us?' Flint cried.

The giant's breath continued to push the iceberg out even though the Grey Man now stood up tall. 'I cannot stay any longer; there is someone I need to speak with.' He paused. 'But you will find the Frost Horn and together you will blow it from the stars.'

Flint wondered whether it would be impolite to point out that the time for overdue catch-ups with friends was probably not now, just hours from the Ice Queen's dominion over Erkenwald, but there was something in the giant's eyes as he said goodbye – something kind and honest and wise – and Flint didn't press the matter further.

'Thank you,' Eska whispered.

And, though the sound didn't reach the giant waving from

the shallows, Flint could tell that he knew the shape of those words because he smiled.

The giant's breath steered the iceberg on towards the Groaning Splinters and, had Flint's and Eska's minds not been filled with images of the Ice Queen wiping out the tribes and tearing down the Sky Gods if they failed to find the Frost Horn, they might have marvelled at the spectacle before them – at the spires, domes and caves of glittering blue ice. The iceberg drifted beneath an arch and on towards a row of spiked peaks.

'Does it seem a bit too quiet to you?' Flint asked after a while. 'If you ignore the Ice Queen's anthem . . .'

He listened for the cries of the birds from the cliffs, but there was nothing now. He looked back towards the flatter icebergs where the seals had been resting. They were gone, too . . . The iceberg glided on and Flint watched Balapan dipping low between the Groaning Splinters as if, perhaps, she had seen something. He reached for his Anything Knife and Eska gripped her quiver.

Then a sloping brown head slid above the surface in front of the iceberg the group huddled on. Amber eyes, whiskers curling from a dark wet nose and two sharp white tusks hanging either side of a drooping mouth. One by one, more brown heads appeared until they surrounded the iceberg in a dark circle.

Flint swallowed. 'Walruses.'

The giant's breath nudged the iceberg forward, but the largest of the walruses lifted its blubbery body out of the water a fraction more until it blocked the path through and the iceberg ground to a halt.

'They'll let us past, won't they?' Eska whispered.

But, when the largest walrus shook his blubber and let out a juddering roar, Flint knew these were not ordinary walruses. Like the wolves back on the Driftlands, these were now brutes cursed to obey the Ice Queen.

Flint fumbled with his knife as a walrus thumped its enormous body on to the ice and stabbed at the children with its tusks. Blu screamed and Flint jammed his boot into its head then, as it reared backwards, Eska sent her arrow into its blubber. The walrus sank out of sight, but the others drew closer.

'Have you got an invention in your bag that can help us?' Eska gasped.

Flint's eyes widened as he remembered he had left his rucksack back in the igloo. The Grey Man had warned against extra weight on the ice and Flint hadn't wanted to lose the snow-goose feathers he'd carried this far in the depths of the icy sea. He brandished his Anything Knife as another walrus shunted its hideous body against their iceberg, then Balapan dive-bombed the beast and it drew back for a second.

'They're trying to topple the iceberg!' Flint cried.

He pulled Blu behind him and plunged his Anything Knife into the neck of a walrus whose tusks were just centimetres from Eska's leg. The beast let out a low grunt-whine, then it vanished beneath the surface.

The air shook with the Ice Queen's anthem and the roars of the walruses as they hacked the iceberg with their tusks, clawing closer to their prey, but Flint and Eska were in the hunt now, their aim sure, their weapons poised to kill, and Balapan was wielding her wings and talons above anything that came close to Blu.

Before long, just one walrus remained. The largest of the herd. It disappeared beneath the surface and when Flint glanced down he could see only the water and the undersides of turquoise icebergs.

'Has it gone?' Eska whispered.

The quietness dragged on and Flint lowered his knife, then there was an almighty boom from beneath as the walrus thrust its weight into the middle of the iceberg. It juddered. It groaned. And Flint's eyes widened.

Then it crunched in two, Flint and Blu on one side – and Eska on the other.

The walrus slid through the water towards the iceberg that Flint and Blu were stranded on and, though Balapan hurtled down to try and distract it, the walrus merely batted the eagle away and, narrowing its yellow eyes, made a beeline for the iceberg.

'Keep going!' Flint yelled to Eska. 'Use your bow as an oar until you reach the furthest of the Groaning Splinters! Then find the Frost Horn!'

The walrus slashed its tusks into the ice by Blu's boot and when Flint wrenched his little sister away he looked up to see Eska frantically trying to paddle towards them.

Flint brandished his knife and the walrus held back for a moment.

'Turn round and keep going!' he shouted again. 'This is your chance, Eska – I can fight the walrus!'

For a second, Flint saw Eska falter, then she turned her terror-stricken face away and inched towards the last of the Groaning Splinters before the wide stretches of ocean.

Flint took a deep breath, then he turned back to face the walrus.

Chapter Thirty
Eska

As Eska approached two glistening columns of ice, she turned briefly to catch a last look at her friends. But what she saw made her insides roil.

A shattered iceberg. Water pulsing red. And one fur mitten floating on the surface.

Balapan screeched from her shoulder and surged into the sky, circling the crimson water again and again. Eska stood up – the horror drumming her bones, the anthem swirling in her ears – but, when Balapan landed at her feet with her head bowed, she threw back her head.

'Nooooooo!'

The wail was a whisper – as she knew it would be – then suddenly the anthem cut to silence and, though Eska's mouth was still open and her throat still thrummed, the word stopped. Just like that. Eska's eyes widened and she scrabbled at her throat, then she swallowed hard and made to cry out again. But this time no sound left her body. Not even a whisper. And the reality of the situation dawned on her.

Flint and Blu were gone and the Ice Queen had stolen her voice.

Eska fell to her knees and wept. She had failed her friends. She had failed her parents. And now she had failed Erkenwald. Balapan wrapped her wings round her, but she couldn't stop the tears. The Ice Queen had her voice and how long would it be before she used it to call the rest of the Fur and Feather Tribes under her command and tear down the Sky Gods? Eska sobbed silently for Flint and Blu. There was nothing left worth fighting for now.

The iceberg carrying the girl and the eagle drifted slowly on. Eska clutched at her throat and tried to find that hope she'd felt before, but it was gone, almost as if Flint and Blu had taken it into the depths of the sea with them, and, when she did finally look up, she saw that she was inside a tunnel carved from blue ice.

It curved over her head like a ceiling of turquoise jewels and it was only then that Eska realised how far she must have floated. She glided out of the tunnel and as she glanced down something caught her eye. Black and white shapes speeding beneath the water – sleek bullets with blunt heads.

Orcas, Eska thought.

A pod of these whales was nudging her and Balapan's iceberg forward and though to Eska it seemed that her fight was over, it appeared the wild had a different opinion. And because of her unshakable bond with Erkenwald's animals Eska looked ahead one more time, despite the grief that rocked inside her, to the last of the Groaning Splinters.

The final iceberg was a curve of white and it reared out of the sea like a slice of the moon. The orcas pushed Eska and Balapan on into a bay in front of it and then all but one of the whales vanished into the deep. The remaining orca surfaced and Eska held her breath at the sight of something so huge and fierce and wild. She looked into the whale's eye and felt a memory hover close.

A woman with long red hair was rocking her back and forth while singing a lullaby about orcas and eagles. The memory slipped away and another surfaced. She was running now, hand in hand with her mother along the beach – and they were laughing. More memories of Blackfina flooded in: paddling a kayak beneath the stars, roasting fish inside an igloo, diving into the summer waves.

Eska gazed at the orca for several minutes, then she remembered the other name for this whale, the name her ma had taught her when she was a tiny girl.

Blackfin.

And suddenly it felt, to Eska, that while the Frost Horn might be miles away her mother's spirit was close. The orca sank into the water and Balapan nestled into her side, but Eska could tell that the whale had not gone for good. Because a song began then, but not one composed of stolen voices like the Ice Queen's anthem. This song was wild – it was the call of the whales – and the ocean around Eska hummed with it.

The whales sang with clicks and cries and long, drawn-out notes and Eska's tears for Flint and Blu and all that she'd lost slipped from her cheeks into the water. And, as they fell, something rather extraordinary happened.

Another whale spiralled up from the depths, one with a speckled back, a white belly and a long, twisted tusk. A narwhal. The rarest of the whales and, if Eska's memories of her ma's words were true, it was known throughout Erkenwald as *the unicorn of the sea*. Its tusk broke the surface first, sparkling in the morning sun, and Eska blinked.

The narwhal dipped its head as if it had expected to see Eska all along, then it laid its tusk down on the iceberg in front of the girl. Balapan ruffled her feathers in anticipation and, hardly daring to breathe, Eska looked at the tusk. It was as long as her arm and wider at the end fixed to the whale's head. She leant a fraction closer and saw a symbol carved into the ivory around the tip.

It can't be . . . Eska thought.

But it was. A carving of the Sky God's constellation, just like the birthmark on her neck.

But why would a narwhal bear the mark of the Sky Song? Eska wondered.

Balapan took a small step forward and dipped her head and Eska, not wanting to seem impolite, dipped hers, too. Then the narwhal shook its body and pulled back from the iceberg, sinking into the sea. Its tusk, however, remained on the ice and Eska realised then that the North Star had given something very precious to the rarest whale in the kingdom.

The tusk was the long-forgotten Frost Horn.

Eska's eyes grew large as she picked it up. She had found

the Frost Horn, but it had come too late for her poor friends, Flint and Blu. The lump in her throat grew. Perhaps now that she had the horn though there was still time to stop the Ice Queen from using her voice? And, as the orcas pushed Eska and Balapan's iceberg back through the Groaning Splinters, Eska knew that her fight wasn't over yet because here, in her hands, was hope.

Chapter Thirty-One
Eska

The orcas pushed the iceberg on, but when they came to the blue ice tunnel again they left, as soundlessly as they had arrived, and Eska's head filled with images of what she had last seen there: Flint urging her to go on to the last of the Groaning Splinters; Blu's terrified face as the walrus thrashed close; the sea swaying red. Fresh tears bloomed and for a moment Eska felt so numb and empty she couldn't move, then Balapan leant close to her and she took a deep breath, laid the Frost Horn by her feet and paddled back between the remaining icebergs into the open water.

The midday sun was dazzling, but through its glare she could just make out the igloo back on the snowy beach. She didn't have a plan yet, but she hadn't heard her voice echo out over the kingdom so maybe, just maybe, there was still time for an idea to work itself out. But blowing the Frost Horn from the stars? She wasn't an inventor, like Flint, so how was she going to climb up into the sky? A tear trailed down her cheek as she thought of Flint and Blu, and then her heart quickened. Back on the beach, through the haze of sunlight, something was moving.

She squinted. *Not possible*, a voice inside her whispered. And then, *Please let it be possible . . .*

She dug her bow into the water again and again, pushing through the stream of sunlight until she burst through – and there, on the beach, were two people. A little girl dressed in furs playing with a fox pup on the rocks near the end of the bay and a boy with a mop of tangled brown hair disappearing inside the igloo.

They were alive! Somehow Blu and Flint had survived the walrus attack and were waiting for her to return with the Frost Horn. Eska flung up her arms to get their attention – then, out of the corner of her eye, she saw something else.

A skin-boat was rounding the headland into their bay, a Tusk guard at its helm, and he was just a few metres from the rocks where Blu was cuddling Pebble.

Eska opened her mouth to shout out, suddenly forgetting her voice had been stolen, and when no sound came she threw up her hands. But Blu was facing the wrong way – she couldn't see Eska or the Tusk guard approaching. Mind whirring, Eska seized the Frost Horn and blew as hard as she could. Nothing happened. Would the horn *only* sound if blown from the stars?

Balapan pecked at her furs. *Stay low*, the eagle was saying. *Stay hidden. Don't do anything that might draw attention.*

Eska steered behind a solitary iceberg, then she peeped round to scan the beach for Flint. He was inside the igloo still and, as the Tusk guard silently pulled up his boat and edged over the rocks towards Blu, Eska's body stiffened with fear. She was defenceless. No match for the guard and the weapons she saw glinting in his boat.

She made to move – anything to try and warn Blu – but then she realised that if the guard saw her, too, he'd raise the alarm and there could be more Tusks further up the coast. They'd take them both, then they'd destroy the Frost Horn and there would be no hope of beating the Ice Queen.

Eska watched in horror as Pebble launched himself at the Tusk guard to try and protect Blu, but he was booted into the snow as the guard clamped a hand over Blu's mouth. Pebble struggled up and ran at the guard again, but the man simply seized the fox pup by the snout and dragged both him and Blu towards his skin-boat before binding and gagging them.

The guard began to row back round the headland, not thinking to check inside the igloo. And, though Balapan was pressing all her weight against Eska, trying to hold her back, Eska couldn't just watch as Blu and Pebble were led away. She steered the iceberg into the open and stood up, shouting empty words and waving her hands. Blu's eyes met hers, wide and scared, but the Tusk guard was facing the other way, rowing hard along the coast in the direction of the Ice Queen's palace.

Confident now that the guard hadn't seen Eska, Balapan soared into the sky after the boat. The eagle shrieked as she approached the headland and at the sound Flint rushed out of the igloo. He saw Eska floating towards him and he threw up his hands and cheered, then he glanced across the beach to where Blu had been playing. He started forward, suddenly realising that his little sister was gone, then his face paled as he took in the eagle bulleting after the tail of a skin-boat gliding round the headland.

'No!' Flint screamed. 'Not Blu! And Pebble!'

But the Tusk guard didn't swing his boat round – he didn't even hear the boy's cry because it was lost in the shrieks of the kittiwakes and the wind. The boat disappeared out of sight and Flint tore across the beach, shouting his sister's name again and again.

Eska didn't wait for her iceberg to grind ashore. She leapt into the shallows, then raced over the snow after her friend.

Flint whirled round. 'Why didn't you warn me?'

He clambered on to the rocks that closed the beach into a bay and, ducking low, peered over the top. Eska grabbed him by the arm and they skidded down into the snow. Then she looked into his eyes and in the silence that followed she willed her friend to understand.

Flint gasped. 'The Ice Queen has stolen your voice ...' And then he struggled against Eska's hold. 'We have to go after them! Blu's in danger!'

Eska tightened her grip; she knew they wouldn't win this way. They had to stay hidden. Because blowing the Frost Horn from the stars was the *only* way to put an end to the Ice Queen and rescue Blu.

Flint brushed his tears away as he listened to the faraway

cry of the eagle. 'Balapan … She'll bring Blu and Pebble back, won't she?'

Eska nodded.

Flint spoke quickly, his thoughts a tangle of panic and pain. 'If Balapan fails, Blu will be made a prisoner, like Ma – so – so the Ice Queen won't harm her immediately. Not until the midnight sun rises tomorrow. We still have time.' The words were spoken as facts, but Flint's voice was wavering. 'If Balapan returns without Blu, she'll be okay until we go for her – with weapons and – and a plan. Right?' He glanced at Eska, then his shoulders slumped. 'But if the Ice Queen already has your voice that means she can use it any time. We're too late …'

Eska looked at her feet.

'I should go after Blu now!' Flint cried, kicking the rocks. 'What better plan are we going to come up with?'

Again Eska held him fast.

'I never should have left her outside on the beach!' Tears sprang into Flint's eyes again, but this time he didn't wipe them away. 'I should have been guarding her, and fighting for her, like Tomkin would have done. Not hiding in that igloo inventing!'

He spat the last word out with disgust, then sat down on a rock, his head in his hands. Eska did nothing for a few minutes. It was hard to work out what to do when there were no words left. Then she sat down, too, and, although she wasn't sure whether warriors turned inventors really approved of hugs, she hugged Flint anyway.

235

They sat beneath the cliffs, but the eagle didn't return and after a while Eska noticed the arm of Flint's fur parka was stained with blood. She tugged at it and frowned.

'Walrus blood, not my own.' He sighed. 'I used my Anything Knife to kill it after it knocked us off the iceberg.' He turned the weapon over in his hand and Eska noticed the turquoise river gem in the hilt was gone. 'We would've drowned if I hadn't remembered, at the very last moment, what that stone contained.' He paused. 'I infused it with a wisp of the South Wind and, when I smashed it open and grabbed hold of a loose piece of ice with Blu, the wind blew us safely back to shore.'

Eska smiled, a smile that was full of pride and respect for her friend.

'But I'm done with inventing now,' Flint muttered. 'It only ever brings trouble.'

There was a squawk from the sky and Balapan glided into the bay and landed, in a tumble of bloodied feathers, by their feet. Eska rushed forward and held the bird tight. Her wounds were not serious – once the eagle preened herself, most of the blood would vanish – but there was no sign of Blu or Pebble.

Flint hung his head. 'My little sister . . . This is all my fault.'

Eska stood up and strode towards the igloo because Flint might be done with inventing, but she knew that his ideas were the only thing powerful enough to take her to the stars.

'It – it won't work,' Flint stammered. 'I was mad to think it would!' He clambered back up on to the rocks and scoured the coast for his sister. But she was long gone. 'We should be going after Blu!'

Eska carried on walking, with Balapan flying alongside her and the long white tusk raised in her hand. It shone like a slither of moonlight – it was impossible not to feel its magic – and at the sight of it Flint gaped.

'You – you found the legendary Frost Horn!' He hurried after Eska. 'But just because you have it doesn't mean my invention will work. It's useless!'

Eska ignored him and broke into a run, then Flint was running, too, back towards the igloo. Eska disappeared inside, her heart thumping at what Flint might have made, but what she saw was not what she had been expecting.

Arrows fletched with snow-goose feathers to replace the quiverful she'd lost in the walrus attack. Eska tried to smile. She was grateful, of course, but how were these arrows going to take her and Flint to the stars?

'I was just using the leftover snow-goose feathers to make you some more arrows.' Flint looked at his feet. 'The invention is *behind* the igloo. It's too big to fit inside.'

Eska hurried outside where Balapan was waiting for her and there, tucked behind the snow house, looking more glorious than she could ever have imagined, was Flint's latest invention.

A vehicle carved entirely out of driftwood, it balanced on three wheels – one at the front, two behind – and in the hollow scoop of the body there were two seats and a small lever in front. But most splendid of all were the wings mounted on wooden rods above the vehicle. Giant white wings made from the hundreds of snow-goose feathers Flint had gathered in the Lost Chambers.

Eska blinked. How could Flint have done all this since the walrus attack that morning?

As if he could sense her thoughts, Flint said, 'I worked through the night to get it done.'

Eska's baffled heart shone because here was a friend who, like Balapan, would never let her down. And as she looked upon Flint's marvellous creation she felt a stream of memories flood back, of someone else whose loyalty and love blazed just as brightly as this. Her pa, Wolftooth, a large man with blue eyes and a gentle face, carrying her on his shoulders when she was very little, wrapping her in an eider-duck throw before a campfire, lifting her across the river's fastest currents. Eska let the memories eddy around her, then Flint reached into his pocket and drew out a handful of little green gems.

'Solidified glow-worm light,' he said quietly. 'Bottled at midnight during our stay in the Lost Chambers – Jay helped me when you and Blu were sleeping. Should shine bright when the night closes in.' He glanced at the engine, a wooden cylinder stoppered by a stone. 'Contains the loudest wolf growl ever heard in Deeproots and a bolt of lightning from the bottle we used on the Grey Man yesterday. But, even so, there's no guarantee it'll keep us going to the stars.'

Eska spun round and hugged Flint tighter than ever and Balapan ruffled her wings in delight.

Flint blushed. 'I call it Woodbird. But I don't know if it'll fly . . .'

Eska grinned. Flint had lost his sister and his beloved fox pup. She had lost her voice. But here lay a way to reach the stars.

Chapter Thirty-Two
The Ice Queen

The Ice Queen blinked two frost-crusted eyelashes at the statue in front of her. The glass was completely black now and swirling inside the neck, behind the key Slither held in place, was a shimmering gold liquid.

Eska's voice.

'Remove the key,' the Ice Queen purred.

Slither took it out and the Ice Queen unscrewed the orb from her staff and slipped it beneath the throat of the statue, forcing the gold liquid to seep out into it. Then, when the last of the gold had dripped inside the orb, the Ice Queen waved her hand over it and the black ice closed round Eska's voice. Placing the orb in the pocket of her gown, the queen turned towards Slither.

'Tonight, I shall play my organ one last time. I shall swallow the remaining voices in my choir, of course, but when that is done I shall feed on Eska's voice before using it to call the outlawed children into my command and tear down the Sky Gods.' She smiled. 'Then, with immortality achieved and the kingdom and the skies under our control,

I will destroy the Fur and Feather Tribes and our rule will begin in earnest.'

There was a scuffle of feet, then a Tusk guard appeared in the doorway of the turret. He shoved a small girl dressed in furs forward. In her hands she held a whimpering fox pup.

The Ice Queen towered above Blu. 'A Fur child,' she hissed. 'Already the tribes are surrendering then?'

'Found her out by the Groaning Splinters,' the guard muttered.

The Ice Queen stalked in a circle around Blu. 'Who are you?'

Blu sobbed into Pebble's fur. 'I scared. Want brother.'

The Ice Queen looked disgusted. 'Pathetic!' She glanced at the guard. 'Feed her to the wolverines; she has no place in my kingdom . . .'

The Tusk guard grabbed the scruff of Blu's neck and her sobs grew louder. 'Want brother, Flint! And Eska. I scared.'

The Ice Queen flinched at Eska's name and – supposing Flint to be the boy who had helped Eska escape from Winterfang – she motioned for the guard to stay where he was. She was silent for a few moments, then she slid her pale face in front of Blu's.

'Perhaps I won't throw you to the wolverines just yet,' she whispered. 'Perhaps I will keep you . . . as bait.' She raked a sharp nail down Blu's cheek. 'I want you to be the first thing Eska and that wretched boy see when I call the tribes in. The sight of your snivelling face will show them who has won.'

The Ice Queen smiled. 'You will *never* survive in my Erkenwald, but tonight you will play your part.'

Chapter Thirty-Three
Flint

'Faster!' Flint cried. 'We need more speed to get this thing off the ground!'

Gripping the side of Woodbird tighter, Eska dug her heels into the snow and ran on.

The vehicle careered forward, bumping over pebbles and juddering across patches of ice, and Flint swallowed as he glimpsed the rocks at the far side of the bay looming through the darkness. They needed to be airborne in the next few seconds.

He pumped his legs harder and Balapan yapped from above, then, just metres before they smashed into the rocks, he yelled, 'Now!'

Eska leapt into the vehicle's back seat while Flint jumped into the front then Flint snatched the lever before him and Woodbird was yanked upwards, her wheels grazing the rocks below. Hardly daring to breathe, Flint hugged the lever to him. The engine spluttered and clanked and for a second Woodbird seemed to hang in the sky, then there was a deep rumble from the back of the vehicle.

'Yes,' Flint breathed. 'Come on. *Come on.*'

The wolf growl grew louder and louder and the spluttering stopped—

'Hold on to your stomach!' Flint cried.

—and Woodbird soared up into the sky, leaving the rocks and the bay far behind.

Wide-eyed, Flint clutched the lever and behind him Eska sat, open-mouthed, with the Frost Horn across her lap. They were racing through the night, side by side with a golden eagle, as the bolt of lightning inside the engine propelled them closer and closer to the stars. The glow-worm light flickered from the wheels and the snow-goose feathers spread out in a white arc above them. They were flying! His invention had actually worked! And the speed and the height and the wonder of it all made Flint's face glow.

Eska reached forward and shook Flint's shoulders.

He glanced round, remembering how he'd envied Balapan before the Groaning Splinters. 'Wings,' he cried above the engine noise, 'make *all* the difference ...'

And they laughed then – despite everything – because they were climbing through the sky and the icebergs were like drops of milk on the silver-black ocean below.

Flint glanced inland, at the peaks of the Never Cliffs and the miles of frozen tundra around them. The night was clear, save for a few stray wisps of cloud, but Woodbird burst through those in a second, on and on towards the flickering stars.

Balapan soared beside them, a rippling silhouette, and

when Flint dipped his head at her she shrieked with delight. The sky was her playground and those she loved had found a way into it.

'Home to the eagles and the Sky Gods,' Flint whispered to himself. 'Now *this* is surely the biggest detour yet.'

He gazed at the crescent moon in the distance – the last one before the midnight sun took over the next day – and moved the lever to the right so that Woodbird veered inland. Towards Winterfang. And Blu and Pebble. The Driftlands below were empty and dark – no lights shone from the Tusk igloos and no shadows moved between them.

'The Tusk Tribe are gone!' Flint cried.

Eska shifted behind him. It seemed she knew as well as he did that they wouldn't be gone for good. They would be waiting somewhere – for both of them ... And, as they rose higher and higher into the sky and eventually the Ice Queen's palace came into view, Flint and Eska saw the dark shapes of an army massed at the foot of the bridge. The Tusks had been called to Winterfang. The Ice Queen was readying for a fight.

Flint's fingers tightened round the lever and Woodbird climbed through the night – up, up, up towards the stars. He lost track of time completely, but he knew they had arrived because of the silence. A quietness that could only exist in a place far removed from people. Here, the stars were no longer small lights above him. They were a sea of dazzling diamonds shimmering every which way he and Eska looked.

'The Sky Gods,' Flint breathed. 'We're floating among the Gods!'

And he turned off Woodbird's engine so that they could glide, in silence, between the sparkling lights. Flint twisted round in his seat.

'Now, Eska. Blow the Frost Horn – before the Ice Queen uses your voice – then, when the Sky Song stops, sing its tune.' He paused. 'With the power of the Gods on our side, we might be in with a chance of saving our kingdom.'

Eska held the narwhal tusk to her lips doubtfully.

'You can do it,' Flint whispered. 'I believe in you. Just like you believed in me with Woodbird.'

Eska threw a worried look over at Balapan and Flint could tell that her courage was waning.

'Think of where we started all this,' he said. 'You trapped in a music box and me thinking tribes were fixed things and letting others in was dangerous.' He glanced around at the stars. 'Well, look at us now, Eska! Look at where we've come! You've silenced the tribes; you've commanded animals! It's time to shake the skies!'

And those, Flint realised, were the words Eska needed. She pressed the Frost Horn to her mouth and breathed in, a great heaving breath that seemed to start right down in her toes – and blew.

The sound was quiet at first – and Flint wondered how on earth such a small noise could make a difference – then the sound grew, louder and louder, until it filled the sky around them, wobbling the moon, and, just as Whitefur had said it would, shaking the stars.

It was a strong, clear note, and low, like an owl's hoot,

then it rose slowly to become a rippling melody which made Flint think of the very first droplets of magic falling on to Erkenwald and bringing it to life. The melody became fuller, bolder, as if it was rising with the strength of mountains and ancient forests, then the tune changed again – softer once more, but filled with such longing and heart that Flint felt that if hope was a song it would sound just like this.

Flint listened on. He had heard trees crash down in Deeproots, he had heard the battle cries of warriors and the mighty roar of a grizzly bear, but those sounds were nothing compared to this. The Sky Song was the call of Eska's tribe, built of wild, unexpected things – Erkenbears, eagles, giants, inventors, little lost girls and the Sky Gods themselves – and it was the fiercest sound of all.

Flint looked at Eska when, eventually, her breath ran out and the sound of the horn died away. She raised a hand to her throat and Flint hoped with everything inside him that the Sky Song had brought her voice back, but, when Eska opened her mouth to speak, nothing came out.

Woodbird floated on through the night beside Balapan. 'The Sky Gods,' Flint whispered. 'They must have heard the song – maybe they'll come to our aid?'

And at that moment, after almost a year without even the faintest flicker of the northern lights, the sky filled with colour. Green spirals rippled through the night, bulging and swelling, before fading away to let ribbons of lilac twirl through. Red arcs curved above them, then beams of blue flooded down. Flint and Eska smiled and Balapan rolled a somersault in joy.

'The Sky Gods are dancing again!' Flint whispered. 'They're acknowledging that *you* are the rightful owner of the Sky Song! Maybe that means—'

The lights dimmed suddenly, out of nowhere the Ice Queen's anthem crawled into the night and then – without warning – Woodbird fell from the sky. Down through the glitter of stars, down through the night, as if the Sky Gods themselves had spat the children out of their secret world. Flint screamed, Eska flung her arms round his waist and Balapan plummeted with them, her wings tucked in tight.

Eyes streaming, Flint grappled for the lever and switched the engine back on. They were going too fast to heave Woodbird up now, but he could still steer – he could land this, if he needed to. He gathered the vehicle back into his control, then he and Eska gasped. Winterfang was directly below them, a sprawl of ice towers and domes.

Flint winced. He could hear the Ice Queen's anthem more clearly now – a dim drone compared to the blast of the Frost Horn – but it was there all the same and it filled him with terror. Because, any moment now, the Ice Queen would sing with Eska's voice.

Flint swerved to miss the ice towers and circled round to the front of the palace. But the rumble of Woodbird's engine was enough to rouse those in the fortress. The anthem cut to silence – there was a dreadful hush – then Flint's heart lurched as he looked down. Standing in an ice arch fronting the hall he'd trespassed into only two weeks before was the Ice Queen, a wolverine on one side and – on the other – his little sister clutching Pebble.

'See?' the Ice Queen screeched, winding a hand round Blu's neck. 'I get everything I want in the end! *Everyone* will bow down to me.' She drew the black orb out from her gown and caressed it. 'The northern lights you saw just moments ago were the Sky Gods recognising *my* claim on Eska's voice!'

Flint shook his head in disbelief. *Eska* had stirred the Sky Gods with the Frost Horn. *She* had journeyed to the Groaning Splinters and then on into the stars. Not the Ice Queen. And yet, as Flint looked at the queen now, and the men, women and children from the Tusk Tribe cheering before the palace, he wondered whether he and Eska had, in fact, been too late. Had the power of the Sky Song belonged to the Ice Queen from the moment Eska's voice vanished?

'My brother!' Blu cried from the arch. 'My brother!'

Flint could barely see through the rage and the pain of what was unfolding below. He and Eska weren't enough, he realised now, not in the face of an Ice Queen and a Tusk Tribe baying for their lives. He circled helplessly above the jeering army, then Balapan cried out beside them and Eska stood up. Red hair streaming in the wind, she raised the Frost Horn to her lips again, and blew. The sound was different from before – instead of the Sky Song, there came a summoning blast, full of spirit and fight – and, at the sound, Balapan's circles widened and the eagle sent her call out into the wild.

The Ice Queen threw back her head and laughed and her army did the same. But, out of the corner of his eye, Flint could see other things happening: children dressed in wolf furs and feathered shoulder plates marching along the cliff tops towards the palace, their arms taut against their bows.

'The Feather Tribe!' Flint gasped, wheeling Woodbird above them. 'They – they came at your call, Eska!'

Eska blinked. Jay and his tribe had kept their promise.

The Tusk Tribe shifted and one or two reached for their spears, but the Ice Queen only cackled.

'And here come the Feather Tribe at last!' she called. 'Sensing the power I now hold with Eska's voice, they have surrendered just hours before the midnight sun rises!'

Flint frowned. Had the Ice Queen drawn Jay's tribe here? Had they come to surrender rather than fight? Then he noticed the Erkenbears flanking the children on either side and the direction the tribe's arrows were pointing – straight at the Ice Queen's heart. He breathed again. This was not a tribe coming in to surrender . . .

Then Flint saw something else. Hurtling across the snow from the south came dozens of sleds pulled by huskies. Flint blinked once, twice and then a third time. The Fur Tribe – *his tribe* – had come, despite the detours and the inventions. *Despite everything.*

Eska pointed to the stone giant charging forward in the midst of the Fur Tribe and Flint's jaw dropped.

'The Grey Man . . .' Flint murmured. 'When he left us, he said he had someone he wanted to talk to. He must've raced to Deeproots to summon the Fur Tribe while we went on to the Groaning Splinters!'

But there was another person Flint was even gladder to see, and as he took in the warrior boy steering the front sled, leading his tribe on towards the palace, his heart burst with pride.

'Tomkin!' he roared.

The Ice Queen shot Woodbird and its passengers a furious look because she realised now who the tribes had come for and that, although she held Eska's voice inside her orb, it was not hers for the keeping quite yet.

'I will tear you down, Eska!' the Ice Queen screamed. 'And your pathetic little friend up there with you! *I* own your voice now!'

The Fur Tribe drew closer and Tomkin leapt off his sled and shouted up to the arch where the Ice Queen stood. 'Oi!' he yelled. 'That's my brother – and *no one* talks to him like that!'

Flint's heart soared at Tomkin's words, then he steered Woodbird between the ice towers and down towards the bridge, where it was flat enough to land.

Flint turned to Eska. '*You* own the Sky Song, Eska, and here is your tribe.' He pointed to the outlawed children, the giant and the Erkenbears below. 'Everyone here has come because of *you.*'

And, at his words, Jay's army released their arrows, a flurry of wood and feathers, into the middle of the Tusk Tribe.

Chapter Thirty-Four
Eska

The battle raged before the palace. Tusk guards smashed at arrows with their ice spears and shadow-shields while the Fur Tribe leapt off their sleds and swung javelins. Wolverines and Erkenbears clashed, Balapan dived towards a rearing wolf and, nestled inside Woodbird, Eska realised there was something strange about the weapons the outlaws were wielding.

The Feather Tribe's arrows were tipped with fist-sized silver balls which burst upon impact and turned the Tusk guards into statues of ice. And the wooden javelins the Fur Tribe launched seemed to unravel as they struck, casting a web of inescapable vines around their enemy.

Flint gasped. 'Blizzard balls . . . Willow-snatching javelins . . .'

And Eska knew what that meant: the tribes – *both of them* – were using magic to fight the Ice Queen.

Flint landed Woodbird on the bridge with a jolt. Down on the Driftlands, Tomkin and Jay were wielding weapons so fast the unravelling vines and ice explosions were just a blur in the moonlight.

Tomkin looked up at the bridge as Flint pulled Woodbird to a halt, then Jay tossed him a quiver and he raced towards his younger brother before thrusting the javelin into Flint's hand and the quiver, filled with blizzard balls, at Eska.

'Get Blu!' he roared, turning back to the fight. 'We'll hold the guards!'

Leaving Balapan in the throes of the battle, Eska and Flint leapt out of Woodbird on to the bridge. They looked up at the arches leading into the palace hall.

'We're going to need a run-up for this . . .' Flint muttered.

They rushed forward together, launching off the bridge and flinging themselves on to the sill of an arch. Eska's pulse quickened at the scene before her. It was as if she had never left. Just metres away lay the empty music box and beyond that the organ shrouded in icicles and the cluster of silver trees strung with baubles. A familiar fear rippled through her.

The Ice Queen stood before the trees, one hand curled round a black orb – her lips parted just before it – and her other hand wrapped round Blu's neck. Beside them, Slither smirked, now and again taunting the fox pup that whimpered in Blu's arms.

The Ice Queen lowered the orb and her expression soured. 'So many interruptions.' She slipped the orb into the pocket of her gown, then opened a welcoming arm. 'Eska, darling. Back so soon?' She paused. 'But with no voice, no plan, no way to set all this right?' She sniggered. 'And with two tribes of children fighting a battle they're sure to lose?'

Blotting out the Ice Queen's words, Eska slotted the Frost

Horn into her quiver, then pushed a blizzard ball on to the tip of an arrow, nocked it to her bow and pointed it at the Ice Queen. The candles in the chandelier hissed and the Ice Queen tightened her grasp on Blu's neck.

'Not so hasty,' she laughed. 'You wouldn't want me to squeeze too tight, would you?' Blu began to cry, but the Ice Queen's gaze slid to Flint. 'And who *exactly* is your ridiculous little friend?'

Flint squared his shoulders. 'Flint, brother of the Chief of the Fur Tribe – and famous inventor.' He readied Tomkin's javelin in front of him. 'I've come for my little sister and my ma.'

Eska and Flint leapt from the ice sill, but they hadn't taken more than a few strides across the hall when a dozen Tusk guards stepped out from the shadows.

Eska gritted her teeth.

'They want a fight,' Flint spat. 'So let's give it to them.'

And Eska, filled with fresh rage as she thought of all that the Ice Queen had taken from her – her parents, her memories, her voice – narrowed her eyes and pulled back on her bow. The guards took another step closer. Then Eska fired. Her first blizzard ball hit true, sending one guard crashing to his knees before hardening into ice, but then another guard released a spear and only in the nick of time did Flint hurl himself forward, slashing the weapon in two with his Anything Knife before sending the willow vines coiling round the guard's legs. Eska whipped another arrow to her bow, her muscles taut with fury, and back to back she and her friend gave the Tusk guards everything they had – for Blu, for Flint's ma and Eska's own pa and for a whole kingdom on the brink of the Ice Queen's rule.

Eska's face flared with sweat and Flint's cheek was bleeding from where an ice spear had grazed his skin, but there were only two guards left now and, while Flint and Eska drew them closer, edging back towards the palace wall, Eska ducked beneath one's legs at the very last moment, giving her and Flint the chance they needed to finish the guards off.

Panting, Eska looked up at the Ice Queen, but she simply thrust Blu towards Slither and reached for her crystal staff. Blu tried to wrench free from the shaman's grasp, but he held her and Pebble fast.

'Don't like it,' Blu sobbed. 'Want go home.'

Eska's heart surged with pity for her friend.

'You call this lump of uselessness a sister?' the Ice Queen sneered. 'What good is she to anybody?'

Eska started forward with Flint, her jaw clenched, but she wasn't quick enough to stop what came next. The Ice Queen held her staff over Blu's body and, though Eska and Flint were now tearing across the hall, they could see the black sparks shooting out of the staff and showering over Blu. The little girl's body stiffened and drained of colour then, a moment later, she was nothing more than a statue carved from ice clutching a frozen fox pup.

'No,' Flint gasped. 'No!'

The Ice Queen smiled. 'Oh, I'm not done yet.'

And, in one deft movement, she smashed her staff into the

statue and the ice shattered upon impact, falling as a shower of glinting crystals. Flint rushed close, but the broken pieces of his sister and his fox pup lay in a heap before him. Eska's blood screamed as she knelt beside Flint and, in that moment of grief, both she and Flint let their guard down.

The Ice Queen seized Eska by the shoulders and Slither grabbed Flint, but the Ice Queen's grip was stronger than her shaman's – two pincers of ice digging into Eska's bones – and she couldn't wrestle free like Flint.

He staggered backwards, his eyes filled with tears, and Eska's heart swelled with hope at the thought that Flint might be able to fix things. But Flint didn't fight for her or call out to Tomkin in the battle outside. His eyes met hers – they were utterly defeated – then he turned and ran from the hall, and Eska could only blink after his fading footsteps.

Slither hastened across the room, but the Ice Queen shook her head. 'Let him go – to his mute ma in the ice tower or just to weep at the loss of his silly sister. He's a coward,' the Ice Queen muttered, 'and we've got more important things to deal with.'

Eska stared at the empty space where Flint had been, hardly able to breathe. How could he have deserted her when she needed him most? Shock and hurt coursed through her. She tried to wriggle free, but the Ice Queen dug her nails in harder, her grasp locking the muscles Eska needed to escape, and as she was dragged across the hall, past the silver trees and the organ, she realised where the Ice Queen was taking her. The music box. The prison she'd fought so hard to get away from. She shot a panicked glance towards the arches, but Balapan was nowhere to be seen.

The Ice Queen breathed on the glass dome and it vanished from sight, then she hurled Eska on to the pedestal. 'The key, Slither!'

Slither fumbled in his pocket, then he drew it out and slotted it into the music box. The Ice Queen smiled as she uttered her spell and Slither turned the key:

> *'Three turns to the left then half a turn right*
> *With a key cut black as the deepest night.*
> *The magic awakes, then limbs unfold*
> *As the stolen child comes under my hold.'*

The music began – soft and chiming – and, as the Ice Queen released her hold, Eska felt her body succumb to the music-box spell once more. The pedestal turned, Eska danced and her eyes blurred with tears. This wasn't how things were meant to end. Blu was gone. Flint had abandoned her. Balapan wasn't there to help. And somewhere in this palace her pa remained trapped.

The Ice Queen turned away with Slither until all that Eska could see was the dark stamp of the tattooed eye on the back of his skull. Confident that she was no longer being watched, Eska tried to swivel her own eyes round to her quiver. Was the Frost Horn still there? If she could just reach it, perhaps it could help her?

There was a low laugh and Slither spun round. 'I have eyes

in the back of my head, child, and I knew that if you thought we weren't looking you'd give away your only escape route.' He marched over to the music box and tore the Frost Horn from her quiver. 'I'll be having that . . .'

Eska danced on, the despair swelling inside her, then Slither drew back his arm and hurled the horn through one of the arches. Eska didn't hear it crash to the ground – the din of the battle drowned the sound – but she knew that she was completely alone now. Without Flint. Without the Frost Horn. Without Balapan by her side. And without any plans to stop the Ice Queen from using her voice.

The Ice Queen breathed on the glass dome over the music box, then she sat before her organ and played. The notes sounded louder than ever before, then her anthem rang out – comprised of just one gloomy voice. A single bauble glowed from the trees and as the gold drifted from it towards the organ, the battle cries of the Fur and Feather Tribes dimmed. Then the Ice Queen swallowed the last of her stolen voices.

Eska's heart sank and as she turned helplessly on her pedestal she watched the Ice Queen lift the black orb from her pocket. She breathed over the orb and a little hole in the top melted to show a golden liquid shimmering inside. Eska could feel the pull of all the words she had ever spoken coming from that glow and she knew then that *this* was her voice.

The Ice Queen drained the golden liquid in one terrible gulp and screwed the empty orb back on to her staff.

Eska hardly dared breathe. The Fur and Feather Tribes would surrender any moment now. The Ice Queen would capture them and swallow their voices to gain her immortality. Then she would wipe out the tribes and use Eska's Sky Song to tear the Gods down. *This* was the start of the Ice Queen's rule.

But it was not the sound of surrender that Eska heard next.

It was an eagle's cry, sharp and high. Balapan swooped through an arch and as Eska saw her she realised why she had not heard the Frost Horn clattering on to the ice. The bird had caught it mid-flight and it was clutched in her talons now.

You came! Eska's heart beat. *You came when everyone else deserted me!*

Balapan soared towards the music box and used the Frost Horn to smash the glass away. But neither the Ice Queen nor her shaman flinched.

'Eska's body is under my spell!' the Ice Queen cried. 'No beast can help her now!'

But the Ice Queen underestimated the eagle and the bond between it and the girl. Theirs was a connection that went beyond music-box spells, ice staffs and cursed statues. And, as Balapan hurled the Frost Horn towards Eska, she felt her body rage against the Ice Queen's enchantment.

Out shot her hand, into it fell the Frost Horn, and as she closed her fingers around the tusk Eska leapt down from the pedestal and glared at the Ice Queen.

Chapter Thirty-Five
Eska

The Ice Queen stood up from the organ. 'Not possible,' she murmured.

Balapan dived low and landed on Eska's shoulder and, with the strength of the eagle willing her on, Eska advanced through the hall.

The Ice Queen turned to Slither. 'Find the boy, just in case he's lurking – and kill him – while I destroy the eagle.'

The Fur and Feather battle cries clamoured again and Eska, holding the Frost Horn in front of her like a shield, strode on towards the Ice Queen. She had no voice, but she had an eagle on her shoulder and a heart full of courage so she kept walking, veering round the organ to the heap of shattered ice where Blu and Pebble had once been.

'Soon the ice will melt!' the queen cried. 'You've lost your friends for ever!'

But Eska wasn't listening. She raised the Frost Horn to her lips and thought of Blu and Pebble – of the little girl who had left her home to follow her brother through every possible danger and the fox pup who had tried his hardest to protect her in the bay. She blew gently this time and the horn sung a different note again – not the Sky Song or the battle summoning – instead the sound was like clouds rippling, and it stirred the crystals on the floor, whisking them up into the air until they swirled and glimmered.

The Ice Queen rushed forward, but a shape was already emerging within the crystals. Only it wasn't a statue any more. In its place stood a girl with ruddy cheeks and a bundle of fur wriggling in her arms.

The Ice Queen raised her staff and shrieked. 'You will not undo my power, Eska!'

Black sparks shot out from her staff, but Eska stood in front of Blu and as she held the Frost Horn in front of her the sparks bounced off and fizzled out on the floor.

'We Eska's tribe!' Blu shouted, no longer scared now that Eska was there to guard her. She stroked Pebble's head. 'We her friends and we never give up!'

Balapan cried out from Eska's shoulder and the Ice Queen stalked closer. 'Except Flint,' she said quietly. 'He seemed very happy to run away earlier.'

Blu shook her head. 'Flint fight for Eska. Always looking for her. Always fighting for her. Never leave.'

The Ice Queen sighed. 'Blind as well as stupid . . .'

There was a scuffle of footsteps from the door.

'Come, Slither!' the Ice Queen called.

But it was not the shaman who emerged from the passageway.

It was Flint.

The Ice Queen snorted. 'If you tied Slither up with willow-snatch, he'll break its curse in an instant.'

Flint raised an eyebrow. 'Not if the willow-snatch is drenched in water gathered from a whirlpool. That'll bind him for months on end.' He paused. 'You didn't think I'd enter your palace without a few inventions up my sleeve, did you?'

Eyes wild, the Ice Queen raised her staff towards Flint, but at that moment Blu rushed forward and kicked the queen in the back of the legs.

Flint's jaw dropped. *His sister. Alive and full of fight!*

Black sparks ricocheted off the walls as the Ice Queen stumbled to her knees, but it gave Flint the chance he needed and he darted towards the trees, grabbing Blu by the hand as he raced past. He thrust a small wooden box at Eska and from her shoulder Balapan croaked.

'Your memories,' Flint panted as Pebble nuzzled round his legs. 'I searched the whole palace until I found this in the throne turret.'

Eska could scarcely believe what she was hearing. Flint hadn't abandoned her. He'd gone to find her past.

'When I saw the Ice Queen's power over Blu,' Flint cried, 'I realised we needed all the help we could get to beat her! You need to remember who you are, Eska, if you're going to take back your voice.'

The Ice Queen was on her feet again, her staff aimed at Eska. 'You won't be able to open it!' she shrieked. 'There is no key! I hurled it to the bottom of the ocean the day I captured you!'

Eska's skin trembled, but Flint held up his Anything Knife to the keyhole and twisted it this way and that.

The Ice Queen strode forward and, though the power of the Frost Horn was enough to keep the black sparks of her magic away from the group, a trail of sweat inched down Eska's back as Flint worked his knife in the lock.

'Come on, brother,' Blu urged. 'Quick!'

Flint fumbled with the knife, but the Ice Queen was upon them now, brandishing her staff, and then, just as she brought it down, a shadow fell across her. Eska glanced up to see a large shape had filled one of the palace arches and she realised she recognised those broad shoulders and wide-set legs.

Whitefur.

The Erkenbear leapt into the room and bounded across the floor towards the Ice Queen. She took a few steps backwards and then remembered herself and aimed her staff at the raging bear. A burst of sparks shot out and the Erkenbear tumbled backwards, but it was up again in seconds. Flint worked harder with his knife until there was a click and, as Whitefur launched himself at the Ice Queen, Eska pushed the wooden lid open.

A swirl of colours twisted towards her and as they fell about her face it felt, to Eska, as if she was looking at a rainbow through the mist. But then the mist seemed to fade and the colours became stronger and, finally, Eska saw her past clearly. She was sledging in the Never Cliffs with her ma, then she was hunting caribou on the Driftlands with her pa. Next she was making necklaces from river quartz with her parents, then she was running, hand in hand with them, across the foothills to catch a glimpse of a golden eagle.

This was her past. A lifetime out in the wild with two people who loved her more than she could have hoped for. And suddenly knowing her place, knowing her beginnings and all that had come after that, made her grip the Frost Horn harder.

Whitefur wrestled with the Ice Queen, a whirl of claws and nails and fizzing black sparks, and as Eska saw them like that a more painful memory surfaced: the last moments with her parents on the Driftlands. Her ma crying out for her as the wolverines closed in, the Erkenbear trying to set things right and then a Tusk warrior dragging her and her pa to Winterfang.

Whitefur hadn't managed to hold the Ice Queen back then, but now he fought with a vengeance and, as he thumped an enormous paw across the queen's chest, pinning her to the ground, he growled at Eska. And Eska could hear the words in that growl because it was the language of those who wandered the wild.

Take what it rightfully yours, it said. *Take back your voice.*

Eska stormed towards the Ice Queen while Flint shoved Blu behind him and took on the stream of Tusk guards pouring through the arches. Whitefur winced as the Ice Queen struggled beneath him and sent a fresh flurry of sparks into his side, but Eska was running now and she swung the Frost Horn at the Ice Queen's staff. The sceptre broke apart upon impact, shattering into fragments of black ice.

The queen gasped as the ice melted before her eyes and a gold mist seeped from her lips. It drifted into the hall and settled inside the baubles on the trees until all of them shone gold once again. The Ice Queen raised a hand to her mouth, but an even brighter mist was slipping through her fingers now – a mist that burned as gold as Balapan's eyes. It swirled into the hall and Eska stood, completely still, as she breathed her voice back inside her.

Leaving Flint to fight the last of the Tusk guards, Eska sped across the room and leapt up into an open arch. Balapan glided to her shoulder and they looked at the fight below, a frenzy of blizzard balls, ice spears and willow-snatching javelins. Then Eska held the Frost Horn high and, desperately hoping she could remember its song, she threw her newfound voice out into the night.

At first she sang the low, clear note – the one that had sounded like an owl's hoot – then she launched into the rippling melody and her song rose like bubbles from the depths of the sea.

A few of the Tusk guards looked up at her, their weapons suddenly limp in their hands, and Eska noticed then that their expressions had changed. They were no longer blank and ice-eyed; their faces were filled with shock and shame and something like hope and, though Eska didn't dare stop singing, she wondered whether the Ice Queen's hold over her Tusk army was gradually weakening.

Eska let the melody grow louder, stronger, and, as the Sky Song burst out, she could feel the power of the mountains and the forests and the glaciers stirring inside her.

More Tusk guards stopped fighting, the wolverines and the Erkenbears broke apart, and Eska saw Rook, her face brighter and kinder than it had been in the Lost Chambers, push her way through the crowds towards the palace until she was standing alongside Jay and Tomkin. Eska blinked. Even the Tusk guards frozen by blizzard balls and imprisoned by willow-snatch were breaking free from the magic that had bound them and looking up to her with eager faces. *All* the tribes were listening now. Because the Ice Queen's curses had worn off.

Eska raised her eyes to the stars, to the mighty Sky Gods glistening from above, and as she sang the last part of the Sky Song – the melody filled with longing and heart and infinite wonder – the sound of her voice swirled up into the night and the northern lights began to dance.

Balapan leapt from her shoulder, wheeling into the colours that spilled into rings and halos across the dark, and Eska knew then that no one in Erkenwald could doubt the presence of magic. The Sky Gods were up there and they were dancing for every tribe to see.

Eska cleared her throat. 'A few weeks ago, I was nothing more than a prisoner here at Winterfang!' she cried. 'The Ice Queen locked me in a music box and told me I was cursed!

265

She stole my parents, she stole my memories and then she stole my voice.' Eska took a deep breath. 'But, together with the bravest inventor I know, I escaped and formed a tribe. And, though it wasn't made up of warriors or people who dressed and thought the same way, it was enough. Because we were brave and we kept hoping, and though the Ice Queen threw everything she had at us – Tusk guards, cursed wolves, mountain ghouls and thunderghosts – we threw more back.'

Balapan settled on her shoulder and ruffled her feathers. 'We kept going when everything fell apart! We trusted strangers even when we didn't have a plan!' She paused. 'And when the Ice Queen tried to silence us we shouted louder!' She raised the Frost Horn high. 'For almost a year, we've lived in a kingdom shrunk to whispers, in a place where the tribes hide from one another in fear, but that is not our Erkenwald! It's time to reclaim our kingdom!'

There was a deafening roar from below as all three tribes cheered Eska on. She spun round to see the last of the Tusk guards sitting on the floor, shaking his head as if waking from a terrible dream, and she knew that the Ice Queen's curse had been broken once and for all.

She watched as Flint raked his Anything Knife through the baubles that hung from the trees. They crashed to the ground, finally free from the Ice Queen's enchantment, and as Blu stamped them into tiny pieces, the golden glow of the imprisoned voices drifted through the palace towards the ice towers.

Whitefur was slumped over the Ice Queen and his weight

held her still, but, as Eska approached, clasping the Frost Horn tight, the Ice Queen's voice trickled out.

'You and I could work together, Eska. Two great voices with the power to—'

Eska didn't wait for any more. The Ice Queen was as weak as a rag doll now her power had been drained and Eska dragged her to her feet before shoving her towards the music box. She forced the Ice Queen on to the pedestal, then, with Flint's help, she hauled the glass dome over the top and turned the small black key again and again, faster and faster, until her whole arm ached.

Music began, a clash of discordant notes this time, and, very slowly, the Ice Queen's body began to break apart into tiny shards of ice.

Moments later, all that was left of her was a gown of frozen tears.

Eska rushed back to Whitefur and bent down beside him. 'Thank you!' she whispered. 'You held the Ice Queen back so that I could call the tribes together!' The Erkenbear didn't reply and Eska's hand stilled over his fur. 'Whitefur?'

She leaned over so that she could see his other side. It was red beyond repair and only then did Eska realise what had happened. While she had been uniting the tribes, Whitefur had been dying.

Flint and Blu gathered close.

'I thought Erkenbears couldn't die,' Eska said in a small voice. 'I thought Whitefur was beyond the Ice Queen's dark magic.'

She let her head rest against the bear's as the tears began to fall and Flint and Blu did the same.

'He fought for you out on the Driftlands last year.' Flint's voice was choked. 'And he fought inside the palace tonight. He would have fought again, Eska, because his heart was good and true and brave.'

'Erkenbears,' Eska said through the tears. 'I remember my pa's stories about them now. Wanderers call them the Ever-Wandering Ones; they believe that even after they die their souls speak to us when fresh snow falls.'

And, though the thought of being able to speak to Whitefur again sent a glimmer of hope through Eska, it didn't ease the pain and she cried on, for the life of her old friend.

They lay with their arms round the Erkenbear for a while longer, then the sound of pummelling footsteps filled the palace.

'The prisoners in the ice towers – they've been freed!' Flint breathed, forcing himself to his feet. 'Ma!'

He rushed from the hall, hand in hand with Blu, and Eska would have followed had her ears not snagged on another sound.

'Eska!'

Eska's legs felt suddenly weak beneath her and her breath scudded through her throat. Because she recognised that voice . . .

'Pa,' she whispered, and then louder, as she rushed towards the arches where the call had come from, 'Pa!'

Grabbing an abandoned knife from the ground, Eska leapt

out on to the palace wall. She dug the knife into the ice there and used it to clamber up on to the top of the highest dome. Then she stood up tall.

'Pa!'

Tomkin and Blade had scaled the ice towers and hacked open the door that blocked the prisoners in and now men, women, uncles, aunts and grandparents were pouring across the bridges that connected the towers to the palace and rushing into the arms of their children. Eska's eyes flitted between the crowds, then they fixed on a tall man with broad shoulders who wore the furs of a silver wolf.

He was faster than the others over the bridges, but he didn't rush into the palace. He grabbed a spear from the ground, snapped it in two, then he dug the spikes into the ice dome and began to climb towards his daughter.

Eska felt her heart shake. 'Pa!'

Wolftooth hauled himself up on to the top of the dome, but he didn't stop to gather his breath. He rushed towards Eska and scooped her up in his arms.

'My little girl!' he sobbed. 'My precious little girl!'

And, as Balapan called out from the velvet sky above, Eska held on to her pa.

Epilogue

And so it was that the Ice Queen's rule crumbled. The sun rose just hours after the battle ended and because this was the midnight sun – the one that would shine all through the Spring and Summer without ever setting – the enchanted iceberg melted as quickly as it had been conjured. Spires fell, walls slumped and the ice oozed out into the sea. Nothing remained afterwards, not even the music box or the silver trees.

The tribes boarded their sleds and, at the invitation of the Feather Chief and Chieftainess, raced across the ice towards the Never Cliffs. There was a time for hiding and a time for fighting, but this, everyone knew, was the time for a feast.

Long into the next day the tribes talked, ate and drank goblets of cloudberry juice inside the Lost Chambers. And as so often happens after adventures end, the stories began. Tales of blizzard balls and wolverines, of willow-snatch and cursed musk oxen. But no story was as bold and as magical as the one Eska, Flint and Blu had to tell.

There were interruptions, of course, for stories in their first telling are rarely neat or simple, but despite Blu's dramatic gurgling sounds when recounting the episode with the thunderghosts, despite Pebble's yapping at the ice spider incident and despite Tomkin's apologies to Flint for ever doubting his inventions or the power of Erkenwald's magic, the trio did, eventually, get to the end of their tale.

And all the while, the golden eagle perched on Eska's shoulder. The girl wondered whether the bird would leave her now that their quest was over. But then a new story was told by Wolftooth – one from a father to his daughter about a woman who had befriended an orca while caught out at sea. The whale was never tamed – for that would be like trying to tame the waves – but the animal shared a bond with the woman right through to the end and Eska began to understand then that even though this adventure might be over, something that would not, and could not, be broken had been left in its wake. Friendship. Between a Wanderer and a golden eagle, but also between them and a fox pup, an inventor boy and a little girl with a very large heart.

There was singing and dancing in the hours that followed. The Feather Tribe sang of ancient giants, much to the Grey Man's delight, but he made a point of not showing it by complaining extra loudly about the cricked back he had acquired when crawling through the entrance to the Lost Chambers (because giants like nothing better than a good dose of sympathy). The Fur Tribe danced, a re-enactment of a legendary hunt which involved a lot of stamping and quite a few drums and the Tusks retold their ancestors' stories through soapstone carvings.

As midnight drew near, everyone gathered outside the Lost Chambers. The sky was still a dazzling blue but, despite the sunlight, six stars glinted like faraway diamonds. The Sky Gods' magic was there for all to see and even though the tail of the Little Bear had lost one of its lights, the constellation seemed to burn brighter than it had done before. And to Eska, Flint and Blu the stars felt like a reminder – of the dear friend they had buried in the Never Cliffs a few hours before and of what the smallest and most unlikely of tribes could do with a pocketful of courage.

Eventually the tribes dispersed, tired from a night of celebration and full of promise for an awakened and harmonious Erkenwald. A plan was formed by Wolftooth and Wild-Paw for the following weeks (because when grown-ups get involved that lamentably happens) but this was a plan built of Wanderer rules and Fur tribe invitations. The hideaway behind the Giant's Beard was to be Wolftooth and Eska's home for a while until the seasons changed and they felt like moving on.

First though, Flint had a detour he wanted to share with Eska. One that involved cloud cushions, weather clocks and moonlight hammocks.

But just as Wild-Paw and Wolftooth were readying their sleds, there was a roar that shook the core of the highest mountain. Two enormous Erkenbears bounded through the snow and stopped before the gathering.

Eska dipped her head at the bears then she climbed up on to one while Flint, Blu and Pebble mounted the other. The children didn't need to tell the bears where they wanted to be taken. The Erkenbears already knew. This was a journey home.

They charged through the cliffs and as her golden eagle cried out in the sky above, Eska leant close to the Erkenbear. Her words were hushed and almost lost to the sound of thundering paws. But the wind heard and it carried her voice up and up – past the eagle's wings and beyond the peaks of the Never Cliffs – until it reached the constellation glittering over the kingdom.

'This is the wild,' Eska whispered to the Sky Gods. 'And the wild doesn't play by ordinary rules.'

Acknowledgements

I started writing *Sky Song* at the same time as my husband and I started talking about having our first baby. The planning for this book took place during the time I lost my first three pregnancies, the writing took place when I mourned them and the edits took place while I spent three months in hospital with complications regarding my fourth pregnancy. Put like that, you might assume *Sky Song* to be a story filled with pain and loss. There is pain and there is loss – how can there not be when life itself is filled with troubles just as worrying and upsetting as snargoyles, thunderghosts and villainous Ice Queens? – but overwhelmingly this is a story about hope. And courage. Because I've learnt a great deal about both over the last two years. About how, even in the darkest of times you can scrabble around to muster up a handful of faith and that, combined with a pocketful of bravery, as Eska discovers in *Sky Song*, can make all the difference. I also learnt much about the kindness of other people in the run up to having my little boy and writing this book, and I want to thank those who supported me and bolstered my spirit so that I felt strong enough to tell Eska and Flint's story.

My first thank you goes to the NHS, to the outstanding Lewis Suite midwives at Queen Charlotte's Hospital (Ruth, Usha, Joyce, Vida, Ann, Marcia, Hayley, Jayne, Ghazala, Elizabeta and Elsie), as well as the healthcare assistants (Danielle, Jumoki, Yulia, Sandra and Ratchna) and the doctors (Samantha, Maya, and Miss Danjal) whose care, encouragement and expertise meant that I could keep writing in the ward despite the daily uncertainties. Thank you also to my incredible friends and book-world buddies who brought stories, pork gyozas, smiles and even mobile nail salons to the hospital to keep me going.

An enormous thank you goes to my publishers, Simon & Schuster, for making every possible effort to support me through writing this book: to my publicist, Hannah Cooper, and marketing gurus, Jade Westwood and Elisa Offord, for re-arranging signings and tour dates; to sales director extraordinaire, Laura Hough, for holding meetings at my house when I couldn't travel further than five minutes from the hospital; to my editor, Jane Griffiths, for turning edits around so quickly, for understanding how to bring out the wild magic in *Sky Song* and for nudging me towards fairytale prologues and epilogues; to designer Jenny Richards and illustrator Daniela Terrazzini for the most beautiful cover I could have dared to hope for. And I also owe a big thank you to my agent, Hannah Sheppard, for checking up on me in hospital and for offering both wisdom and reassurance regarding my writing.

Thank you to the wonderful kids who have read my books, sent me letters (and get well cards) and even quotes to feature in *Sky Song*. Special thanks goes to Toby Crapper from Eagles Class at Whitchurch C of E Primary School for naming Bala, to my epic Canadian cousins, Abigaile, Catelin, Rachel and Meghan, for brainstorming the Fur, Feather and Tusk tribes in Devon and to Sam Prince from Ashley C of E Primary School who helped inspire inventor boy Flint. And a big well done also goes to the winners and runners up of the various competitions I hosted last year: Naomi Betts, Seren James, Louis James Sanders, Lydia Cubley, Sughra Shah, Coleen Junkaluhad-Ives, Harry Dabb, Brendan Culshaw and Sebastiano Alden.

Thank you, as ever, to my incredible family. To Dad for your prayers and thoughts, to Will and Tom for your hospital visits and potato comments, to Charis for the delicious food and care packages and to Mum for giving up so much of your time to rush me to hospital, sit by my bedside and cook me countless meals. I could never have written this book without your constant love and support. And thank you also to my wonderful sister-in-law, Steph. You inspired Blu in *Sky Song* and I hope I have managed to capture a little of your joy, kindness and courage in her. My life is infinitely better because you are in it; thank you for all that you have taught me.

My last thank you goes to my husband, Edo. You adventured alongside me while I researched this book (living with Kazakh Eagle Hunters in Mongolia and dog-sledding across the Arctic) then you carried me through the writing stage when things got complicated (sleeping on hospital floors, driving faster than ambulances to get me the quickest care, bringing endless meals into the ward and purchasing Game of Thrones Monopoly when I hit three months in hospital). I can think of no one I'd rather have faced my battles alongside. Your patience, positivity and love not only kept me sane; they filled me with hope about what our lives still hold in store for us. Our tribe may not be very big (yet) but with you by my side and Logie strapped to my back I feel like we can brave all the snargoyles, thunderghosts and villainous Ice Queens that happen to come our way. Thank you for everything.

Catapult into
Abi Elphinstone's
magical adventures!

'Abi Elphinstone's books are full of with adventure, with, heart, and, above all, bravery'
Katherine Rundell, author of the bestselling *Rooftoppers*

'Bold, breathless and beautifully told'
Jonathan Stroud, author of the *Lockwood & Co.* series

'Reminded me of the very best of the Harry Potter books'
Piers Torday, author of *The Last Wild*